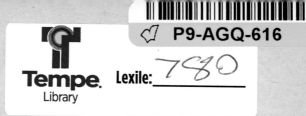
"Wait!" Toklo called after her. "How do you deal with the wolves?"

The she-bear glanced back over her shoulder. "I have my ways," she barked.

But she's alone, Toklo thought. "Are you sure you'll be okay?" he asked, following the she-bear a few paces into the forest. "Those wolves are vicious."

The she-bear turned, fury flaring in her eyes. "Do I look like I need your help?" she hissed. "Leave me alone!" With a snarl, she took a step toward Toklo. "You don't even belong here. I've never seen you before. Just go home!"

Toklo stared after her as she vanished into the trees. "This *is* my home," he whispered.

SEEKERS

RETURN TO THE WILD

MANGA

Also by Erin Hunter

WARRIORS

THE NEW PROPHECY

Book One: *Midnight*

Book Two: *Moonrise*

Book Three: *Dawn*

Book Four: *Starlight*

Book Five: *Twilight*

Book Six: *Sunset*

POWER OF THREE

Book One: *The Sight*

Book Two: *Dark River*

Book Three: *Outcast*

Book Four: *Eclipse*

Book Five: *Long Shadows*

Book Six: *Sunrise*

OMEN OF THE STARS

Book One: *The Fourth Apprentice*

Book Two: *Fading Echoes*

Book Three: *Night Whispers*

Book Four: *Sign of the Moon*

Book Five: *The Forgotten Warrior*

Book Six: *The Last Hope*

DAWN OF THE CLANS

Book One: *The Sun Trail*

Book Two: *Thunder Rising*

Book Three: *The First Battle*

Book Four: *The Blazing Star*

EXPLORE THE
WARRIORS
WORLD

MANGA

SURVIVORS

RETURN TO THE WILD

SEEKERS

FOREST OF WOLVES

ERIN
HUNTER

HARPER

AN IMPRINT OF HARPERCOLLINS*PUBLISHERS*

Special thanks to Cherith Baldry

Forest of Wolves

Copyright © 2014 by Working Partners Limited

Series created by Working Partners Limited

All rights reserved. Printed in the United States of America. No part of
this book may be used or reproduced in any manner whatsoever without
written permission except in the case of brief quotations embodied in
critical articles and reviews. For information address HarperCollins
Children's Books, a division of HarperCollins Publishers,
195 Broadway, New York, NY 10007.
www.harpercollinschildrens.com

Library of Congress Cataloging-in-Publication Data

Hunter, Erin.

  Forest of wolves / Erin Hunter. — First edition.

    pages cm. — (Seekers, return to the wild ; #4)

  Summary: "The four bears have reached the mountains where Toklo
spent his cubhood—but they soon discover that the home Toklo has
returned to is nothing like the one he remembered"— Provided by
publisher.

  ISBN 978-0-06-199645-0 (pbk.)

  [1. Bears—Fiction. 2. Fate and fatalism—Fiction. 3. Fantasy.] I. Title.

PZ7.H916625Fod 2014   2013032157

[Fic]—dc23   CIP

                                                                       AC

Typography by Hilary Zarycky

14 15 16 17 18   OPM   10 9 8 7 6 5 4 3 2 1

❖

First paperback edition, 2015

For Roberta Annabel Baldry, with love

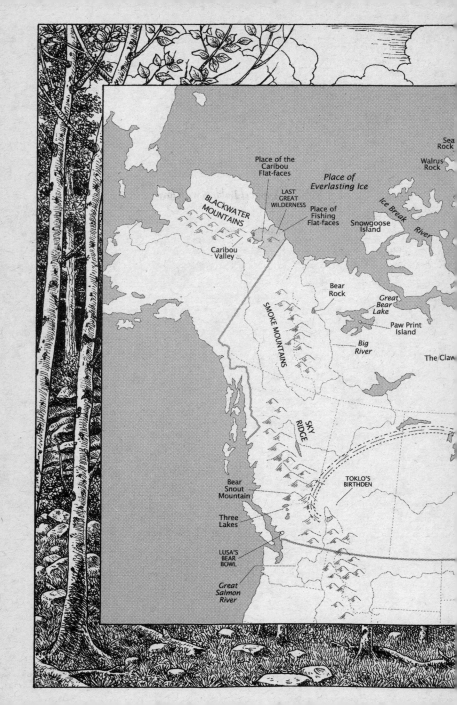

The Bears' Journey: Bear View

Lusa — — — — —
Kallik and Yakone -··-··-··
Toklo --------------------

BAFFIN ISLAND

The Melting Sea

BURN-SKY
GATHERING
PLACE

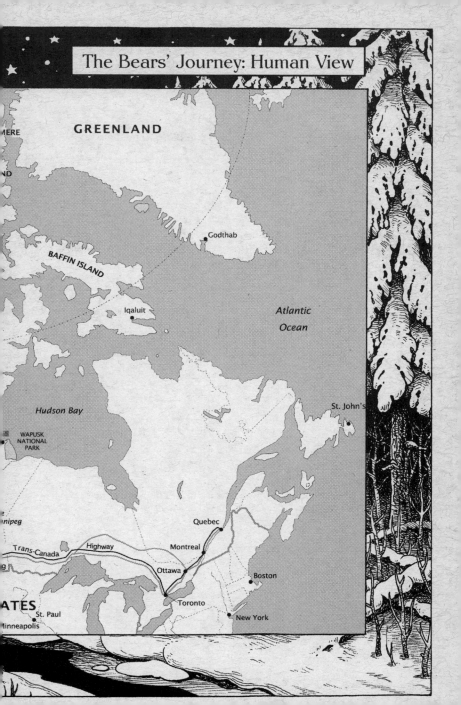

CHAPTER ONE

Lusa

Wind blasted into Lusa's face, flattening her pelt to her sides. Her eyes watered as she stared at the SilverPath forging across the flat, open plain. Shining twin lines stretched ahead as far as she could see, leading the bellowing firesnake toward a smudge of mountains on the horizon. Lusa's body shuddered and her fur quivered as the firesnake rattled over the lines. She still couldn't believe they were doing this! A sharp, fizzing tang flooded her senses, not quite the same as with firebeasts on the BlackPath, but it made her eyes water in the same way, and made her mouth taste sour.

Beside her, Toklo crouched on the rattling floor, his chest still heaving from the battle with the coyote that had tried to follow them onto the back of the firesnake. Lusa squeezed her eyes shut as she remembered the blood of the coyote smearing the SilverPath, and the creature's dying wail of terror.

That could have been Toklo, crushed under the firesnake's paws. Lusa shook herself. *But it wasn't Toklo. He's fine. We're all fine.*

But that wasn't entirely true. Yakone lay on his side, his

injured forepaw stretched out in front of him. He had lost two toes in a trap set by flat-faces, and though the wound had stopped bleeding, the exposed flesh looked red and angry. When Lusa sniffed, she could pick up its nasty, sweetish smell over the reek of the firesnake. Kallik sat close beside Yakone, bending over him with a worried look in her eyes.

Lusa edged closer to the white bears, wincing as the sharp pebbles that covered the floor dug into her pads. *Why is the firesnake carrying these?* she wondered crossly. *Aren't there enough pebbles in the mountains?*

"How do you feel, Yakone?" she barked, raising her voice to make herself heard above the thunder of the firesnake. Looking at him, she felt guilty for her moment's irritation. The brief twinge in her paws was nothing as bad as Yakone's wound; he might never walk properly again.

Yakone looked up at her. There was pain in his eyes, but his voice was resolutely upbeat as he replied, "I'll be fine. It's good to rest, and let the firesnake do the work." Lusa knew he was trying to be cheerful for her. His eyes half closed, but he forced them open again, as if he was struggling to stay conscious.

Lusa gave him a doubtful look. *He's so brave!* Her heart was thudding hard, and she fought the urge to wrap her paws over her eyes and whimper like a scared cub. In all her travels, from the Bear Bowl to the Endless Ice, down to the Melting Sea and then along the River of Lost Bears to the plains, she had never endured anything as terrifying as this journey on the firesnake. The flat segment where they were crouching was open to the sky, with only a narrow metal strip along the sides to keep the pebbles from falling off. They were moving so fast, and so far above the ground, that Lusa felt she might be swept off the firesnake's back at any moment.

Most frightening of all was when she looked ahead, along the silvery side of the firesnake to its head, then back at its long, long tail, made up of segments piled with more pebbles.

It's so huge! And what happens if it realizes we're here? It could flip over and swallow all of us in one mouthful!

Meeting Kallik's gaze, Lusa could see that her friend shared her fears, though the white bear did her best to hide it.

"Do you think we're crazy?" Lusa asked in a low voice, hoping not to disturb Yakone, who had closed his eyes again and seemed to be slipping into a troubled sleep. "When did bears ever belong on the back of a firesnake?"

Kallik shrugged. "We didn't have much choice. It was this, or become prey for coyotes."

"True." Lusa shivered at the memory of the slinking, slavering creatures that had tracked them for days, following the scent of Yakone's blood. "I never want to see another coyote!"

"I just wish I knew where we're going," Kallik went on, the tightness in her voice betraying her worry. "Wherever we end up, we need the right kind of herbs to help Yakone."

Lusa nodded. "Toklo said the firesnake would take us to the mountains. There must be herbs there."

Glancing over at the brown bear, she saw that he had recovered from the shock of the coyote's attack and was gazing intently forward at the line of purple mountains that was just visible on the horizon. Lusa could almost taste his impatience.

Is he so desperate to get home that he's forgotten that Yakone is injured?
A tiny jolt of anxiety stirred in her belly. *I know he's waited a long
time to return to the mountains, but we have to look after our own.*

Kallik and Yakone could have stayed by the Melting Sea,
but they had chosen to go with Toklo and Lusa along the
gigantic river, following the setting sun toward the place
where Toklo had been born. Kallik insisted that until each of
them found a permanent home, their shared journey was not
over. Lusa looked down at Yakone, feverish and in pain, and
wondered if now he wished he had stayed with the other white
bears at the Melting Sea.

The sun sank behind the mountains, streaking the sky
with scarlet, and stars began to appear, but the firesnake never
slowed, roaring on into the night. Kallik and Toklo settled
down to sleep, but Lusa felt as restless as if ants were crawling through her pelt. She sat beside Yakone, listening to his
ragged, raspy breathing. She raised her head and gazed up at
the sky, but her vision was so blurred from the wind that she
couldn't distinguish the patterns of the stars. "Are you there,
Ujurak?" she called softly. "We need you so much!"

But there was no response from the darkness, and Lusa
couldn't feel the presence of their mysterious, shape-changing
friend anywhere around her. Lonely and frightened, she
crouched beside Yakone as the firesnake thundered through
the darkness.

Eventually Lusa drifted into an uneasy sleep. After a while
her friends' voices roused her and she struggled to her paws

again, blinking in bewilderment until she remembered where she was.

"Lusa, the firesnake is slowing down!" Kallik told her excitedly. "We must be getting somewhere."

"But where?" Toklo asked, scanning the land ahead. "That's what I'd like to know."

I thought Toklo knew where we were going! Alarmed, Lusa fought her way back to full wakefulness and looked around. The firesnake was rolling slowly along the SilverPath. The wind had dropped, and she was able to see their surroundings more clearly in the pale, cold light of dawn. The flat plain had given way to ground that sloped upward into rolling foothills. The mountains, which had appeared as purple shadows on the horizon the day before, now loomed up ahead, looking much more solid and real. As the sun rose behind them, casting their shadows forward, Lusa could make out dark forests stretching up the lower slopes of the mountains, and snow still lying thick on the summits.

"Wow!" she exclaimed. "We're getting really close to the mountains!"

The firesnake slowed down even more; Lusa staggered at the uneven motion, then lost her balance entirely as the firesnake shuddered to a halt. Yakone let out a yelp of pain as the pebbles shifted and pattered against his injured paw.

"Get down!" Toklo snapped. "Flat-faces!"

Lusa crouched down and peered around Toklo to see a huddle of flat-face dens several bearlengths away. The firesnake had stopped with its head beside a tall, shiny treelike thing.

"What's *that*?" she whispered.

No one replied. As Lusa watched, a flat-face climbed out of the firesnake's head and detached a long tendril from the silver tree. He stretched it from the tree to the firesnake and somehow inserted the end into the firesnake's head.

"Great spirits! What's he doing?" Toklo muttered.

"I think he must be feeding it," Kallik murmured uncertainly. "A firesnake as big as this must need a *lot* of food."

Yakone let out a snort. "I wish somebody would feed us!"

The white bear's words made Lusa realize how hungry and thirsty she was. She couldn't remember the last time her belly had been full. "Maybe we should get off and look for food," she suggested.

"Yes," Kallik agreed. "We need to hunt, and find water for Yakone. He's so hot he feels like he's burning up."

Yakone opened his jaws to speak, but before he could get a word out, Toklo was already shaking his head. "The mountains are still too far away," he pointed out. "If we get off here, we'll have a long walk in the open."

"I know," Kallik began, "but Yakone—"

"Is better off here where he can rest." Toklo spoke curtly, as if he was in no mood for arguments. "We'll have to put up with hunger and thirst for a while longer, until we're closer to the forest."

Kallik exchanged a glance with Lusa, then sighed. "If you say so. We—"

She broke off at the sound of flat-face voices and the stomp of their paws. Lusa spun around to see two of them walking along the firesnake, coming their way. They seemed to be inspecting its sides.

"They'll see us!" she gasped. "Now we *have* to get off!"

"This way." Toklo gave her a shove toward the side of the firesnake body that was opposite the flat-faces. Lusa half jumped, half tumbled to the ground through an opening in the body and crouched on the dusty earth while Kallik scrambled after her and turned to help Yakone down. Toklo brought up the rear, a low growl of annoyance in his throat.

"Come on," Lusa urged. "Let's get as far away as we can before the flat-faces spot us."

"No," Toklo said stubbornly. "We have to stay close by. The firesnake will start moving again soon, because it's going to the mountains. I'm sure of it." Flattening himself to the ground, he began crawling under the firesnake's belly, beckoning to the others to follow him. "We can hide here until it's finished feeding."

Biting back an irritated reply, Lusa slid underneath the firesnake and poked her nose out on the far side to see what the flat-faces were doing. The two who were examining the firesnake were only a few bearlengths away, while farther up the SilverPath the firesnake was still drinking from the long silver tendril.

Kallik gave Lusa a poke in the shoulder. "Get under here!" she hissed. "They'll see you if you stick your head out like that."

Lusa drew back, hardly daring to breathe as the flat-faces drew closer. All she could see now were their hind legs and their clomping paws. *At least they don't seem to have firesticks,* she thought, feeling slightly relieved. But she knew that if the flat-faces spotted her and her friends, their roars of alarm would alert the firesnake. *And then what would it do to us?*

"There's slimy black stuff down here," Kallik muttered, wrinkling her nose in disgust. "I don't want it on my pelt."

"Hush!" Toklo hissed. "It's better than getting caught by flat-faces!"

Moments slid by in the gloom under the firesnake's belly as the four bears huddled together. The flat-faces had halted nearby; Lusa didn't know what they were doing, but she heard faint tapping sounds as they rapped the side of the firesnake with their naked pink paws. Then her heart thumped with terror as one of them stooped down and peered under the snake's belly. He wasn't looking in their direction, but as soon as he turned his head, he would see them.

The other bears had spotted the flat-face, too. Without a word they all began scrabbling frantically backward until they were clear of the firesnake and could stand up, panting and casting desperate glances around for cover. Lusa felt her belly churning with fear and knew they were all quivering on the edge of panic.

Kallik raised a paw and pointed to a stand of scrubby trees across a narrow stretch of open ground. "We'll have to hide there," she puffed. "If we don't, they'll spot us for sure."

Lusa gazed at the trees. Kallik was right; they were thick enough and far enough away to give them the cover they needed, but she wasn't sure that they should leave the

SilverPath. "What if the firesnake starts to move again?" she asked nervously. "We might not be able to get back to it in time."

"I know," Toklo growled, glancing back over his shoulder at the flat-faces, who were coming closer still. "But we've got no choice. Yakone, can you make it?"

"I'm fine," he rasped.

Yakone set off toward the trees, shambling awkwardly on three paws. Lusa could hear his breath hissing through his gritted teeth, and knew how much pain he must be in, but he kept going. Kallik and Toklo flanked him, supporting him as much as they could. Lusa followed, feeling terribly exposed as she crossed the bare, dusty ground, expecting at any moment to hear shouts from the flat-faces, telling them they had been seen.

But all was quiet as they reached the trees and plunged into the brittle grass. Yakone slumped down with a groan, while Toklo peered around a tree trunk to see what was going on. After a moment he let out a snort. "Look at that!"

Lusa wriggled up beside him. The flat-faces were crawling underneath the firesnake, right in where the bears had been hiding moments before. A shiver ran through her as she imagined what would have happened if they hadn't moved in time.

"What are they doing?" she asked. "Do they think the firesnake is bleeding from its belly? Is that what that black stuff was?"

She felt Kallik's warm breath near her ear as the white bear looked over her shoulder. "I don't know, but if the firesnake moves, they'll be crushed," she murmured.

The air tingled with mounting tension as the bears watched the flat-faces emerge from beneath the firesnake. They straightened up on their hind paws and shouted something to their kin farther up the SilverPath.

"It seems like the firesnake is okay," Kallik commented.

The flat-faces loped alongside the firesnake until they reached its head; then they swung themselves inside it.

"We've got to get back," Toklo growled. "Now!"

As the bears burst out of the clump of trees, the firesnake let out a loud shriek. Before the echoes had died away, it gave a shudder all along its length, then started to drag itself very slowly along the SilverPath.

"Hurry!" Lusa gasped, glancing back to where Yakone was limping, his injured paw held awkwardly off the ground. Kallik was trying to help him, giving him her shoulder to lean on, and they were moving as fast as they could, but the firesnake was already gathering speed, and they were still only halfway there.

Toklo bounded ahead and clambered onto the firesnake's back. "Come on!" he called urgently.

Is he so anxious to reach the mountains that he would leave us here? Lusa wondered, joining Yakone on his other side and trying to give him a boost.

At last they reached the side of the firesnake. The round silver paws began rattling faster and faster over the shining lines. Lusa tried not to think about what would happen if her fur got caught, dragging her down. . . .

"Come on!" Toklo barked again from above her head.

Lusa and Kallik gave Yakone a shove, while Toklo fastened his teeth in the white bear's shoulder and helped him scramble up beside him. Kallik climbed up after Yakone, her forepaws slipping among the pebbles while her hindpaws waved frantically in the air. Toklo grabbed her and hauled her upward.

"Lusa, jump! *Now!*" he snarled.

Lusa ran alongside for a few pawsteps, then hurled herself into the air, scattering the loose pebbles as she landed on the firesnake's back. "We made it!" she gasped, her legs trembling and her chest heaving.

All four bears flopped down among the pebbles, panting from the effort of running. The flat-face dens and the strange silver tree passed in a flash, and within moments the firesnake was thundering along as fast as before. The wooded foothills passed by in a blur, stretching briefly over them before rolling back into the distance.

Lusa sat up and gazed along the length of the firesnake to the looming green mountains. Her belly was so empty it felt like a hollow cave, and her mouth was as dry as sand. There would be prey in those forests, and streams to drink from. But would they get there in time? Lusa knew that before long she would be too weak to hunt, and her friends were no better off.

"I just hope we get there soon," she sighed.

CHAPTER TWO

Toklo

Toklo sat up, his head still spinning from the race back to the firesnake and from the thundering noise of its paws along the SilverPath. Lusa and Kallik seemed to have recovered, but Yakone lay limply on the heaps of pebbles, his eyes half-closed. His struggles to get back onto the firesnake had opened up his wound again; it was bleeding sluggishly and Kallik was hunched over it, giving it an anxious sniff.

After a moment she glanced up at Toklo. "Yakone is getting worse," she said quietly. "There's nothing I can do for him when there's no food or water, and no herbs to treat his wound."

"I know," Toklo began, "but—"

"Maybe we should have looked for something while we were hiding in the trees," Kallik went on, as if Toklo hadn't spoken.

"There wasn't time," Toklo protested. "If we'd tried to hunt, the firesnake would have left without us. I know you're worried," he added softly, "but when we get to the mountains—to

12

the Sky Ridge where I was born—everything will be fine. Trust me."

A spark of anger flashed in Kallik's eyes. "Oh yes, everything will be fine for *you!*" she exclaimed. "But what about me and Yakone? This isn't the right place for us, and you know it!"

Toklo bit back a furious response. He knew Kallik's outburst was just because she was so worried about Yakone. *I'm worried about Yakone, too,* he thought. *And I'm worried that Kallik is regretting staying with me and Lusa until we finish our journeys.*

As the sun rose higher in the sky, the day grew hotter. Toklo could see how uncomfortable Yakone and Kallik were. There wasn't a scrap of shade on the firesnake. At least Yakone's wound gradually stopped bleeding again, and he drifted into sleep.

Toklo crouched beside Lusa, facing forward, almost able to forget his own hunger and thirst as the firesnake drew closer and closer to the mountains. The light on the slopes began to fade as the sun slipped behind the topmost peaks. He drank in the view, feeling long-buried memories stirring in his mind.

I'm home.

The firesnake slowed down to navigate a tight curve in the SilverPath. As he peered through the half-light at the hills on either side, Toklo suddenly recognized where he was. Memories gushed over him like a flood, and he felt like he was staring down a dark tunnel to see a long-gone day lit up in bright sunshine.

This is where I came with Mother and Tobi, and we found the spilled grain!

Toklo remembered how proud he had been some days later when he found his way back to the grain. He pushed away the memory of the huge male bear who had driven them away from their find. *This is home, and that's all that matters.*

Toklo sprang to his paws. "Come on!" he yelped to his friends. "This is the place!"

His voice roused Yakone, who raised his head, grunting in confusion. Kallik heaved her shoulder under him to help him to stand. "Toklo says we're here," she said soothingly. "We have to get off."

While Yakone struggled up, gasping with pain as he put weight on his injured paw, Lusa leaped up and padded to the edge of the firesnake's back. Her berry-bright eyes were gleaming with anticipation. "We're really here?" she whispered.

"Yes," Toklo replied. His fur tingled as he gazed out at the familiar slopes and woodland. For the first time in many, many moons, he had returned to somewhere he had been before. The feeling was overwhelming. "Go on," he barked to Lusa. "Jump!"

The firesnake was still traveling slowly as it rounded the bend. Without hesitation Lusa launched herself through the hole in its side and into the air, and rolled as she hit the grassy slope beside the SilverPath, before bouncing back onto her paws.

"Are you okay?" Toklo called.

"Fine!"

Meanwhile, Kallik prodded Yakone over to the edge of the

firesnake. "Just jump," she said. "I'll be right behind you."

Yakone gritted his teeth. "Okay." He fell rather than leaped off the firesnake, and landed on the ground with a thump. Toklo winced; that must have hurt.

Kallik paused briefly, then scrambled down, her hindpaws barely missing the pounding paws of the firesnake. Regaining her balance, she trotted back to where Yakone was struggling to his paws with Lusa's help.

"Hide!" Toklo called out from his position on the firesnake. "In the bushes over there!"

As he finished speaking, he bunched his muscles and pushed off into a massive leap. He staggered as he hit the ground and yipped with pain as he planted one paw on a low-growing thorn. "Seal rot!" he hissed.

Lusa had already vanished into the thicket that covered the slope not far from the SilverPath. Kallik and Yakone were close behind her. Toklo bounded after them, ignoring the stinging thorn in his pad, and dived into cover. He turned just in time to see the last segments of the firesnake vanishing around the bend. Its thunderous roar soon died away into the distance and the acrid smell faded, leaving the fresh green scents of the forest all around them.

Lusa took a deep breath and stood up, pushing her way through the branches into the open. "We made it," she said.

Toklo and the white bears followed her out of the thicket. Yakone was still limping badly, and his injured paw was oozing blood. His head was drooping, and his shoulders sagged with exhaustion.

"Why don't you rest?" Lusa suggested to him. "I'll look for some herbs to help your paw."

Yakone gave her a glance of gratitude and slumped to the ground again, but Toklo's pelt prickled with unease. "We shouldn't hang around for too long," he said, thinking of the aggressive male who had chased him and his family away from the grain. "There could be more brown bears here."

"Do you think they'd give us trouble?" Kallik asked.

"They might, if they thought we were trespassing on their territory," Toklo replied. "The best thing we can do is to be on our way quickly and find some forest that hasn't been claimed yet."

"Just a short rest, then," Lusa said, glancing over her shoulder at Toklo. "We'll move more quickly if Yakone isn't so tired." She was already sniffing around the bushes for the herbs she needed to help her injured friend.

Toklo grunted agreement, and kept watch while Lusa searched for herbs and Kallik tended to Yakone. Raising his snout to sniff the air, he picked up the lingering tang of the firesnake and the fresh scent of growing vegetation, but no scent of other bears. *For now,* he thought, his muscles tight and tense under his fur.

Lusa returned after a few moments with a mouthful of leaves. Toklo didn't recognize them; they certainly weren't the hornwort Lusa had used before.

"What are those?" he asked.

"I'm not sure," Lusa mumbled as she began chewing up the leaves. "But they smell good. They should help."

Toklo guessed she wasn't as confident as she sounded. *But there's no time to look for anything else,* he thought, working his claws impatiently in the grass. *We have to move. And those leaves can't do Yakone any harm. . . .*

Once Lusa had trickled the leaf juice into Yakone's wound, with Kallik watching worriedly, Toklo led the way up the slope, heading into denser woodland. The uneven ground dislodged the thorn in his paw, and though his pad still throbbed with pain, Toklo was relieved to be rid of it.

As they passed beneath the branches of the outlying trees, Lusa brightened up, gazing around with eager curiosity, but Yakone still seemed exhausted. It looked like it was taking all his strength just to put one paw in front of another. Kallik stayed close by his side, her anxiety wrapping around her like a dark cloud.

Every pawstep Toklo took deeper into the trees brought back more memories for him. The sensation of being pulled back into his old life was so strong that it almost overwhelmed him, and yet there were unexpected differences, too.

That lightning-blasted tree . . . he thought as they padded past the pale trunk and spiky, leafless branches. *Wasn't it by the river? Or was that a different tree?*

"I like it here." Lusa interrupted his thoughts with a happy sigh. "The forest feels safe, somehow, like it's going to look after us."

Toklo just grunted in reply. His memories weren't all good ones, but he didn't want to say this to the others. And now that he was here, in the place that was so familiar to him, he felt the weight of responsibility for his friends even more. *It's my duty to help them, because this is my home.*

Thinking of his friends reminded him of the long path they had traveled together. The cub he had been, playing here in these woods with Tobi, would never have imagined that he would see and do so much in his lifetime. Toklo suddenly realized that he had never really believed he would make it home until now, when he walked beneath the trees that were familiar and at the same time unsettlingly strange.

"Toklo!" Kallik, who had been padding along beside Yakone, put on a spurt to catch up. "Do you really think we'll meet more brown bears in these woods?"

Toklo nodded. "There don't seem to be any others around right now, but sooner or later we will."

Lusa shivered. "I'm not sure I want to. Brown bears guard their territory even more fiercely than black or white bears."

Kallik glanced around uneasily. "I don't know how you two can possibly be comfortable under trees like this," she muttered. "Out on the ice, you can see for whole skylengths. But here . . . there could be a bear behind every bush, just waiting to leap out on us."

"Hardly. We'd scent them first," Toklo reminded her.

Kallik twitched her ears, refusing to be comforted. "And how can you fight in such tight spaces? You'd constantly be banging into trees, or getting tripped up by brambles."

"You just have to make sure the other bear is the one banging into trees, or getting tripped," Lusa told her, giving Kallik a friendly nudge.

Kallik let out a snort, resolutely unamused, and dropped back to walk beside Yakone again. Her nervousness made Toklo even more careful to keep checking for signs of other bears as they plodded on through the forest. But he saw less evidence of them than he had expected: no scent, no scraps of discarded prey, no scratches on trees to mark the boundaries of territory.

That's good, he thought hopefully. Though he had spoken with optimism about finding part of the forest that no bear had claimed, he had never seriously believed that he would be able to establish a territory without fighting for it. Now he began to wonder if it might be possible after all.

But why *are there no other brown bears?* he asked himself after a while. *Did they all leave to find new territories, like I did? And if so, does that mean there's plenty of prey here? Or did they leave because there's a shortage of prey?*

"What about food?" Kallik called out to Toklo as if she knew what he was thinking. "Aren't we ever going to stop to hunt?"

"We need to find water first," Toklo replied.

While keeping a lookout for other bears, Toklo had also been searching for the glint of water in the undergrowth, and listening for the sound of running streams, but so far he hadn't found either. Now he remembered how his mother, Oka, had taught him to look for thick growths of fern, telling him that they always grew best in the wettest parts of the forest.

Trudging to the top of a rise, Toklo paused to look down into the valley beyond. The trees were thinner here, the forest floor covered with grass interspersed with bramble thickets. At the very bottom he spotted the lush ferns he'd been looking for.

"Down there—a stream," he croaked, his mouth feeling drier than ever at the thought of the cool water just waiting for them. *I hope I'm right.*

Lusa ran ahead of him down the slope, stumbling and skidding in her haste to quench her thirst. By the time Toklo reached the valley she was grubbing happily among the ferns, her muzzle slick with water.

"Fern roots!" she exclaimed, clawing one up and crunching it in her jaws. "Delicious!"

Toklo waited until Kallik and Yakone had made it down the slope before dipping his snout into the tiny stream that slipped through the ferns. The cold, clear water seemed like the most wonderful thing he had tasted for moons. When he finally stopped drinking and raised his head, he could feel energy soaking back into his body. Kallik was looking better, too, and even Yakone had perked up a little.

"Now we need to hunt," Toklo announced.

Yakone, who had crouched beside the stream to drink, immediately started to get to his paws.

"No, you stay where you are," Kallik ordered. "Toklo and I will hunt. Lusa, are you okay keeping an eye on Yakone while we're gone?"

Lusa looked up from where she was still digging for fern roots. "Sure," she mumbled around a mouthful. "Or you can just share these if you'd like." She held out a root to Kallik.

The white bear grabbed the root between her jaws and chewed it thoughtfully. Toklo stifled a snort of amusement at the look of distaste on her face.

"No, I guess we'll hunt," she said at last. "Thanks anyway."

Leaving Lusa and Yakone beside the stream, Toklo and Kallik headed up the opposite slope to where the trees grew more thickly. At the top they separated; Kallik followed a narrow path between two bramble thickets, while Toklo paused briefly to taste the air.

Rabbits!

Toklo's jaws watered at the thought of biting into warm, juicy prey. He followed the scent trail, and as the odor grew stronger, he realized he must be close to the burrow. But when he rounded the trunk of a birch tree, he found himself facing a mossy bank where the earth had been torn away and scattered everywhere. It had been dug up so violently that some of the rabbits' underground tunnels had been ripped open, exposing nests of dried grass and tiny piles of droppings. The air was thick with the reek of rabbit and fear, but there was no trace of prey.

Toklo halted in dismay. *Did other brown bears do this?* he wondered. Padding closer to the destroyed warren, he picked up another scent: one that he *thought* he should recognize, but could not remember where he'd smelled it before. There were small pawprints, too, that were definitely not the prints of bears.

Weird...

But it wasn't important to work out what animals had done

this right now. All that mattered was to find food. Toklo dug down into the tunnels; the earth was already loose, making it easy for him to follow the lingering scent of fear. Soon he came to the end of a burrow where a single rabbit was cowering. Its shriek of terror was cut off almost before it began when Toklo killed it with a swift bite to its throat.

"Thank you, spirits, for this prey," he murmured as he hauled it out of the ground.

Heading back to the others, Toklo met up with Kallik, who was returning empty-pawed. She shook her head as Toklo padded up to her.

"Not a sniff of prey," she reported. "Where have all the animals gone?"

Toklo hadn't realized until then how empty the forest was. On their way from the SilverPath they'd seen very few signs of prey and heard hardly any birdsong from the trees. *Something isn't right here,* he thought, remembering the devastated burrows. But he kept his misgivings to himself.

"At least you got something," Kallik said, giving the rabbit an approving sniff. "Let's get back."

Scarlet light was pouring through the trees as Toklo and Kallik padded down into the valley to where Yakone and Lusa were waiting. A cool breeze had sprung up, rustling the leaves and stirring the bears' fur.

Yakone was asleep when Toklo and Kallik reached the stream, though he roused quickly at the smell of prey. "Great catch!" he told Toklo, swiping his tongue around his jaws.

"You three share the rabbit," Lusa said with a contented

sigh. "I'm stuffed full of fern root."

Toklo could have eaten much more than his share of the prey, even with Lusa giving up her portion, but at least it took the edge off his hunger. The last of the light had died away by the time they finished eating. While his friends settled down to sleep, Toklo sat beside the stream, reveling in the faint gurgle of the water and the starlight that turned the trees to silver. His belly churned with excitement, driving sleep away.

I can't wait to explore! I'll find the river, and the cave where I was born . . . and most of all I want to find the place where Tobi is buried.

Toklo was drifting into a doze when he heard the sound of heavy pawsteps approaching through the trees. Kallik and Lusa stirred, too, Lusa leaping to her paws in alarm.

"What's that?" she whispered, her eyes gleaming in the dark.

Toklo stood up, bracing himself to defend his friends. Brown-bear scent flooded over him a moment before the bear himself lumbered out from behind a patch of alder bushes. As Toklo stepped forward, the strange grizzly reared up, huge and shaggy against the night sky, and let out a low growl. Still weak from hunger and the long journey, Toklo knew he was in no shape for a fight.

I'm not looking for trouble, and there's no sense in making enemies when I'm hoping to settle down here.

"Take it easy," he said to the other bear, trying to make his voice quiet and unthreatening. "We're not trying to steal your territory. We're just resting for a while before we move on."

After a pause that seemed to last for more than a moon, the

newcomer dropped to all four paws, huffing with age. Toklo relaxed slightly. *Maybe he's not looking for a fight, either.*

The old bear stood still for a moment, eyeing Toklo with a mixture of caution and hostility. When he peered past Toklo and spotted Lusa, Kallik, and Yakone, he took a pace backward, letting out a snort of astonishment.

"Two white bears and a black bear?" he growled. "Where have they come from? What are they doing here?"

"It's a long story," Toklo responded. Between the old bear's astonishment and his realization that there were other bears on Toklo's side, Toklo sensed that the danger was over. "My name is Toklo," he went on. "This is the place where I was born. Who are you?"

"My name's Maniitok," the old bear told him. "And this isn't my territory. I live over there." He jerked his head toward the area farther upstream. "But I'll warn you—it isn't safe to stay anywhere too long."

"Why not?" Toklo asked.

Maniitok flopped down into the ferns at the edge of the stream. "A pack of wolves have been prowling the forest," he said. "They've come down from the top of the ridge, looking for food."

"Wolves!" Lusa exclaimed, while Kallik let out a disgusted snort.

"They're here to hunt, but they've been known to attack brown bears that get in their way," Maniitok went on. "Some cubs have even been killed. Most of us have moved away . . . it's that or fight to the death over prey."

"Wait—wolves can kill brown bears?" Lusa asked. "Aren't you guys too big for that?"

Maniitok gave her a long look before replying. "A whole pack of wolves can kill a bear if they're determined enough. And these wolves *are* determined, believe me. You shouldn't plan on staying here."

Toklo remembered the pawprints and unusual scent around the rabbit burrow and realized that it must have been wolves that dug it up. "They don't seem to bother you, though," he commented.

Maniitok huffed with amusement. "No, they don't. I'm too old to be a threat, and I don't take much prey anyway." Letting out a long sigh, he hauled himself to his paws and dipped his muzzle in the stream for a drink. Then he swung around, scattering water droplets from his snout.

"There's also one brown bear you need to watch out for," he warned Toklo as he headed for his own territory. "I don't know his name, but some of us call him Old Grizzly. He's been fighting back against the wolves and has become aggressive to all creatures. He won't take kindly to strangers."

"We'll be careful," Toklo responded as Maniitok padded away. "Good luck!" he called after him. "May the spirits be with you!"

When the old bear had disappeared into the shadows, Toklo turned back to his friends. "You'd better get some more sleep," he told them. "I'll take first watch against the wolves."

"But surely wolves wouldn't take on all four of us," Kallik said. "It's the brown bear Maniitok told us about that worries me. He sounds like he could be trouble."

Toklo didn't agree. He'd fought bears before, and won—but he'd never taken on a whole pack of wolves. "Don't worry," he reassured Kallik and the others. "Let's deal with one thing at a time."

Lusa butted him affectionately with her head. "Old Grizzly should be more worried about *you*," she teased.

She curled up among the ferns and wrapped her paws over her nose. Kallik and Yakone settled down together and were soon asleep.

Toklo noticed that Yakone's breathing was still too fast and irregular, even though his eyes had been brighter after food and water. His scent was sharp and rank, and Toklo knew his wound must be infected. He hoped Lusa's herbs would start working soon. The same plants must grow all over, right?

As he sat watching over his friends, Toklo heard a drawn-out howl in the distance. A chorus of howls answered, slicing through the still night air and echoing around the hills. He stiffened.

Wolves!

Toklo thought about how far he had traveled, how long it had taken him to find his home again. Now that he was here, he wasn't going to give it up to creatures that didn't even belong.

"This forest is territory for brown bears, not wolves," he muttered.

CHAPTER THREE

Kallik

Kallik sat watching the sky grow lighter, the boughs above her head taking shape against the clouds. Beside her the other bears still slept. Lusa was curled into a ball, her ears twitching as she dreamed. Toklo sprawled among the ferns, snoring gently. Closest to Kallik, Yakone was deeply unconscious, his breath rasping.

Lusa had taken the watch after Toklo, waking Kallik toward the end of the night. As dawn broke the air was cool and damp, with white tendrils of mist coiling around the trees. The forest was utterly silent, except for the faint creak of branches and the babbling of the stream. Kallik was grateful for the coolness, but she still felt smothered underneath the trees. *I can't even see the sunrise,* she grumbled to herself. Traveling beside the Big River had been easier, because the wide stretch of water had given her the sense of space and escape she craved, but now she felt penned in on all sides. She longed for the open spaces of the ice, with the horizon a skylength away on all sides.

Kallik leaned closer to Yakone and winced when she felt how hot he was. Her heart ached as she remembered when she had first seen him on Star Island, standing on a rock and watching the strange bears. He had been so strong then, brave and curious and willing to leave everything he had ever known to travel with them. He had no idea of the price he would pay, Kallik thought. *He can be strong like that again,* she told herself, but it was hard to believe it when she looked at the thin, weak bear lying beside her, his wounded paw stinking of infection.

"Oh, Yakone," she sighed. "This is all my fault. You should have stayed safe with your family on Star Island!"

The beating of wings in the undergrowth roused Kallik from her thoughts. Instantly alert, she sprang to her paws and followed the direction of the noise. Sliding through the ferns, she spotted a grouse foraging among the roots of a nearby tree. Her belly rumbled at the thought of prey.

Kallik crept toward the grouse, acutely conscious of the damp ground beneath her paws and the lush moistness of the air. She could never get used to this way of hunting. A pang of homesickness shook her; she wanted to be out on the ice, with the endless white all around her, crouching beside a seal hole as she waited for the turbulence in the water that signaled the approach of prey.

But you're stuck here for now, she told herself, *and you have to make the best of it. Stay there, little grouse!*

But although Kallik wasn't aware that she had made a sound, something spooked the grouse before she was close enough to pounce. It let out a harsh call and took off, half running, half flying just above the ground. Kallik galloped after it, weaving her way through the trees. The bird tried to flutter up to a low branch, but before it could gain height, Kallik pushed off from the ground in a gigantic leap, her forepaws outstretched. As her claws sank into the plump body, she slammed into the tree just beyond. Falling to the ground half-stunned, she barely managed to keep her grip on her struggling prey.

"Kallik!" Toklo's voice sounded through the trees.

Staggering to her paws, Kallik gave the grouse a killing blow and stumbled back toward the stream where she had left her friends, the bird dangling from her jaws. "Stupid tree!" she muttered. "Why did it have to get in my way?"

Toklo came to meet her. "Where have you been?" he snapped. "You're supposed to be on watch."

Kallik knew that Toklo was only annoyed because he was worried about what might have happened to her, but she felt too battered to be tactful. "Don't you want to eat?" she retorted.

Toklo sighed. "Okay, okay, I'm sorry. It's great that you caught some food, but you know it's not safe to go off on your own. Not with wolves around—and that brown bear Mani-itok told us about."

"I didn't go far," Kallik told him, still annoyed. *After all we've been through, doesn't he think I can take care of myself?* Then she forced herself to take a deep breath. She knew she was just on edge from her worry about Yakone, and the stress of being here in this stifling, eerie forest, so very, very far from her beloved oceans of ice and snow.

Back by the stream the group enjoyed the grouse, though Kallik noticed that Yakone didn't eat much.

"Time to get moving," Toklo announced once the bears were through.

Kallik rose reluctantly to her paws. She knew that Toklo was right; it was too dangerous to stay in one place. But Yakone was so ill that she was afraid that traveling would take more strength than he had left. *I'll have to help him, and hope he can stay on his paws.*

As soon as they set out, Kallik realized how much more nervous Toklo was today than the day before. His glance was never still, flicking here and there as if he expected an enemy behind every bush. *Just like I told him yesterday,* Kallik thought. *You can't see what's creeping up on you among all these trees.*

Toklo kept on darting from the front of the group to the back, as if he couldn't decide whether he wanted to lead or bring up the rear to watch for danger from behind.

"Toklo, *stop* it!" Lusa exclaimed after a while. "You're making me tired! You know where we're going, so you should lead us. I'll keep a lookout behind."

Toklo replied with no more than a grunt, but to Kallik's relief he stopped skittering about and forged on steadily up the hill.

Kallik trudged along beside Yakone, who was weaker than ever, his pawsteps unsteady. She had to guide him around roots and low branches, and took almost his entire weight against her shoulders when they had to cross a stream. Yakone blundered on as if he didn't know where he was anymore.

"We need to hunt," he murmured. "Kallik, can you find a seal hole?"

Toklo glanced back, alarm in his eyes. "Yakone, we're not on the ice," he said. "There are no seals—"

"Shh," Kallik interrupted, her heart twisting with pain at Yakone's weakness and confusion. "Don't tell him that," she whispered to Toklo. "Let him think he's somewhere safe."

Toklo looked as if he was going to argue, then let out a sigh. "Okay, Kallik. Whatever you think is best."

I just wish Yakone was right, Kallik thought as they trudged on. *He wouldn't be sick if we'd stayed on the ice. There are no flat-face traps there.*

By sunhigh Kallik was starting to stagger, too. Even the shade from the trees wasn't enough to protect her and Yakone from the stifling heat. The moist scents of earth and leaves made her feel as if she couldn't get her breath. Grass and brambles twined around her paws as if they were deliberately trying to trip her. Yakone stumbled and let out a groan of pain as he stubbed his injured paw against a root.

Kallik halted. "I'm sorry," she said to the others, "but Yakone and I have to rest. We can't keep going when it's so warm."

"But it's not really hot at all," Toklo began to object. "We need to—"

"I could do with a rest, too." Lusa padded up and stood beside Kallik. There was a stubborn gleam in her dark eyes.

"Okay, fine." Toklo's shoulders sagged, and he cast a worried look at Yakone.

Kallik could read his thoughts. Toklo was afraid that Yakone would hold them back and put them all in danger if the wolves or the dangerous bear they'd been warned about attacked. He wanted to get clear of this part of the forest before any hostile bears or wolves found them. But she knew they wouldn't make it much farther without letting Yakone rest.

"Just for a little while," she said.

Yakone had already sunk down beneath a tree, his breath fast and shallow, his eyes closed. Kallik settled down beside him, waving one paw through the air to give him a bit of cooling breeze and keep the flies away from his wound.

Toklo paced restlessly, trying to keep an eye on all directions at once. Lusa sat nearby but soon started to fidget; Kallik could tell that she had only asked for a rest because she could see how badly Yakone needed one.

After a few moments, Lusa rose to her paws again. "I'm going to look for herbs," she announced. "There should be something around here that will be good for Yakone."

"No, you're not wandering off by yourself," Toklo said instantly.

"But—" Lusa began to argue, then broke off as Kallik got up, too.

"I'll go with her," Kallik told Toklo, determined not to let the brown bear order them all around. "If you'll keep an eye on Yakone," she added.

Toklo glanced at the sick white bear lying motionless beneath the tree, then back at Lusa. "Okay, but don't go too far," he warned.

Lusa immediately bounded off, checking back and forth across the hillside as she sniffed at likely-looking clumps of vegetation. Kallik followed her to a shallow dip in the ground with a small pool of water at the bottom. The ground around the water was covered by a luxuriant growth of plants.

"This looks promising," Lusa murmured, half to herself.

She led the way down toward the water, smelling the plants and occasionally tasting a leaf as she went. But before she reached the pool, she halted and looked back toward Kallik, frustration and worry in her eyes.

"I feel so stupid!" she blurted out. "I can't remember all the things Ujurak taught me. I should have paid more attention, but I thought he would always be with us."

"I know. We all thought that." Kallik tried to be reassuring, in spite of her own anxiety. "It's not your fault."

"But it is, if I can't find something to heal Yakone!"

Kallik tried to push away the dreadful thought that *nothing* was going to heal Yakone. "There must be something here," she said. "We've hardly started to look yet. Come on, let's get a drink from the pool and then see what we can find down there."

Still looking dispirited, Lusa agreed. Padding down to the poolside, Kallik drank her fill. As she raised her head from the water, she spotted a moss-covered stone jutting out over the pool. "We can take some of this moss," she suggested to Lusa. "It's clean and will be good to pack Yakone's wound, so it doesn't start bleeding again."

"Good idea," Lusa responded, sounding slightly encouraged.

While Kallik peeled moss off the stone, Lusa searched around the edges of the water, thrusting her snout deep into the clumps of plants. Eventually she straightened up with a bundle of leaves in her jaws.

"I think I recognize these. They should ease the pain," she told Kallik hopefully. "And now we'd better get back before Toklo loses his fur."

She bounded back to the top of the dip, and Kallik followed more slowly, carrying the moss. Though she was pleased that Lusa seemed to have recovered her optimism, Kallik couldn't share it. However hard she tried, she couldn't banish her deepest fear.

Yakone is so ill! What difference can a few scraps of greenery make?

When they returned to the place where they had left their friends, they found Yakone still asleep, while Toklo was pacing fretfully up and down.

"I thought you'd gotten lost!" he exclaimed, coming to meet them. "Or that the wolves got you."

"If we'd met any wolves, you would have heard us," Kallik retorted, padding up to Yakone and beginning to lick his wound clean before packing it with the moss. He twitched his ears at her touch but didn't wake.

"While you do that, I'm going to see what's up ahead," Toklo announced. "Lusa, keep watch." He swung around and headed up the hill before any bear could reply.

Lusa shrugged, dropping her leaves beside Yakone. "He always has to be doing something," she said.

It wasn't long before Toklo returned. Kallik had finished

dressing Yakone's wounded paw and was trying to rouse him to eat some of the painkilling leaves. She started as the bushes rustled, half expecting an attack, then relaxed as Toklo emerged into the open.

Lusa, too, had turned alertly toward the noise. "Did you see anything?" she asked Toklo. "Any wolves?"

Toklo shook his head. "No wolves, other bears, or prey," he replied. "But we still need to get moving. I want to reach the top of this hill before nightfall."

Kallik glanced down at Yakone, who was sunk deep in unconsciousness. She wasn't sure how they were going to continue on, yet she knew Toklo was right. *We have to keep going, however difficult it is.*

"There's a hollow just on the other side of the ridge, where we can spend the night," Toklo continued, as Kallik began to wake Yakone. "It's sheltered, and there aren't as many trees, so it'll be harder for anything to sneak up on us."

"Sounds great," Lusa said.

With a huge effort, Kallik managed to get Yakone onto his paws. The white bear mumbled something, but Kallik couldn't make any sense of what he was trying to say. He seemed to have shrunk since they left the firesnake, his pelt hanging loosely on his bones, and his eyes glazed with fever.

When they set out, Yakone could barely walk, and as the slope grew steeper, he kept slipping back, his limp paws unable to get a solid grip on the dry earth. Kallik was taking almost all his weight by now, boosting him along on her shoulder. The top of the hill never seemed to get any closer.

"This is no good," Kallik panted, letting Yakone slump to the ground again. "Toklo, let me see if there's an easier way to get up there."

Toklo's ears twitched impatiently. "Okay, but hurry," he said.

Kallik padded along the side of the hill, scanning the undergrowth. Eventually she spotted a track that wound back and forth with a shallower slope. It was a longer route to the top but would be much easier for Yakone to manage.

"Over here!" she called.

Her friends made their way toward her with Toklo supporting Yakone, while Lusa once more brought up the rear and kept an eye out for danger. But as soon as Toklo reached Kallik and began to examine the track she had found, he stiffened and gave the air a long, careful sniff.

"What's wrong?" Kallik demanded.

Toklo paused before replying. "I can smell another brown bear," he told her, shifting his paws uneasily. "The scent's pretty strong, and that might mean we're trespassing on its territory. It might be Old Grizzly, the bear Maniitok warned us about."

Kallik tasted the air and realized that Toklo was right. She had been so relieved to find the track that she hadn't thought to check for scent. "But if the bear's not here now . . ." she began, reluctant to accept that they couldn't use the route she had found.

"We don't know that," Toklo snapped. "And even if you're

right, he could come back at any time. We'll have to go the other way."

Kallik wondered what was making Toklo so irritable. The night before he had been determined that no bear was going to push them around. But Kallik knew there was no point in arguing when he was in this mood. "Okay," she sighed. "But how are we going to get Yakone up there?"

"We'll do it together," Toklo told her, back to his old supportive self now that the decision had been made.

The struggle up the hill was worse than Kallik could have imagined. Yakone was barely conscious, a dead weight that could only be raised by Kallik pushing from behind while Toklo gripped Yakone's shoulder in his jaws and hauled him upward. Lusa scurried past them to the top of the slope, where she stood with her head raised, scanning the forest for any approaching threat.

But they reached the ridge without seeing any trace of wolves, and although there was bear scent here, too, the bear itself did not appear. The mountains loomed larger on the horizon, so close that Kallik almost felt she could reach out a paw and touch them. Looking down the slope on the far side of the ridge, she could see the hollow Toklo had told them about. It was deep and narrow, overhung by bushes, an easy place to hide while they rested overnight. Best of all, they reached it by an easy scramble down a fern-covered slope.

By the time they were hidden under the sheltering bushes, the sun was going down. Kallik was thankful for the cool of the evening, though it didn't seem to help Yakone much. The white bear lay muttering and twitching, then at last sank into a quieter sleep. His breath was so shallow that Kallik kept checking to make sure his chest was still moving up and down.

As they settled down to sleep, a mournful howling broke out from somewhere above them.

"Wolves!" Lusa stiffened, her black fur standing on end. "They sound closer than last night," she added.

More howls followed the first, breaking out in all directions at once, so that Kallik felt as if they were surrounded.

"Definitely closer," Lusa said.

"We'll be fine," Toklo asserted. "The wolves won't bother us as long as we stay out of their way. Lusa, you take the first watch tonight."

Kallik guessed that the brown bear didn't believe what he was saying; the worry in his eyes, and his precaution in setting a watch, told another story. But there was no point in challenging him. Arguing among themselves wouldn't drive the wolves away.

And I have more to worry about than wolves, she said to herself, peering closely at Yakone. Dread stirred deep inside her; she was afraid that the time would come when Yakone would lie completely unmoving, and nothing she could do would rouse him from the sleep of death.

I'd do anything to help him! But what can we do, if the right kinds of herbs don't grow in this forest? Lusa had tried her best, but she couldn't make healing herbs appear out of thin air. *And we don't get much of a chance to search when we have to keep moving.*

"I'm so sorry, Yakone," Kallik whispered.

After a while, she sank into sleep. She dreamed that she was back at the Melting Sea, with ice stretching all around her, gleaming in the frosty light of a full moon. Yakone lay beside her, deep in sleep.

Kallik bent over him and prodded his shoulder with one paw. "Yakone, wake up! We're home!"

But Yakone never moved, and Kallik realized that he was still hot and feverish. The wound in his paw looked black against the silver ice.

Kallik straightened up and gazed around her as if there might be someone to help in the white wastes. Almost a sky-length away she spotted two white she-bears approaching; as they drew nearer she recognized them.

"Nisa! Nanuk!" she cried.

Joy flooded through Kallik as she bounded forward to meet the she-bears. Memories flashed through her mind of how her mother Nisa had died saving her from the orca. Nanuk had taken care of Kallik in the giant den of lost bears, and calmed her fears when they were trapped inside the no-claws' clattering metal bird. She had died when the metal bird had plummeted from the sky.

These bears are both so dear to me, Kallik thought. *I owe my life to both of them.*

Reaching the two she-bears, Kallik pressed herself up against her mother's chest. "It's so good to see you!" she exclaimed. "And you, Nanuk! I've missed you so much."

"And we have missed you, dear one," Nisa replied, nuzzling

her snout into Kallik's shoulder.

"Are you here to help me?" Kallik asked, remembering Yakone. "I think . . . I think my friend will die if I can't do something to heal him."

Swinging around, she led the way across the ice to where Yakone lay, the faint movement of his chest the only sign that he was still alive. Turning back to her mother and Nanuk, Kallik saw that they were looking down at Yakone, their heads bowed and their eyes full of sorrow.

"Yes, dear one, we can end his suffering," Nisa said.

Relief made Kallik's legs feel shaky, though she didn't understand why her mother and Nanuk were looking so sad. "Great!" she barked. "What do I have to do? There aren't any healing herbs out here, are there?"

"You don't understand. I said we can end his suffering." There were stars in the depths of Nisa's eyes as she faced Kallik. "It is time for him to join the spirits."

For a moment Kallik stood frozen, hardly able to understand what her mother was telling her. Then realization hit her like a blow. "No!" she burst out. "You're not going to take him! I won't let you!"

"You must," her mother said gently. "It's time."

"No!" Kallik bared her teeth. "Yakone is mine. I'll fight you for him if I have to!"

Nanuk took a step toward Kallik, who spun to face her, one paw raised to strike.

"Let him go," Nanuk said. "With us, he'll be free from pain."

Kallik let out a low growl from deep within her chest. "I won't," she replied through gritted teeth. "Yakone belongs with me. Somehow I'll find a way to help him. I'll never give up!"

She faced her mother and Nanuk, bracing herself to fight. Then she saw that their bodies were fading, and she could see stars through their fur. She realized, too, that she couldn't pick up their scent; even at first when she had pressed so close to her mother, she had smelled nothing but the ice and the stars.

They're not real, she thought as the last of their outlines vanished and the she-bears who were so dear to her became nothing more than a wisp of ice crystals blown away on the wind. For a moment, she had never felt so alone.

The wind grew stronger, scouring the ice and flattening Kallik's fur against her side. But the sound it made wasn't the familiar blustering. It was a drawn-out, wailing howl. . . .

Kallik jerked awake. Piercing howls came from the forest around their hiding place. Silver light sliced through the bushes, telling Kallik that the moon had risen. Lusa and Toklo were already on their paws.

"The wolves are getting closer," Toklo growled. "It's better if we wake up and move on, just to be on the safe side."

"Why?" Kallik asked. "The wolves won't attack us. We're too big to be prey. And Yakone shouldn't have to move if it's not necessary."

Toklo let out an irritated snort. "And what are we going to eat, if the wolves take all the prey? No, it's best that we get as far away from them as possible."

Kallik could understand the sense in what he was saying, but she still wondered if Yakone would be able to travel. A pang of apprehension shot through her as she saw how still he was lying, the horror of her dream clinging around her like shreds of mist. Then as she looked more closely and saw that he was breathing steadily, she managed to relax a little.

"Which way?" Lusa whispered.

Toklo raised his head, listening to the howling, which seemed to have grown closer still in the few moments since Kallik woke. "They're coming from over there," he decided, raising one paw to point. "So we'll go the other way. Kallik, get Yakone on his paws."

"I'll try," Kallik muttered.

She prodded Yakone until he blinked awake and looked up at her blearily. "K'lik . . . what's the matter?"

"Wolves," Kallik replied tersely. "We have to move."

It tore her heart to see the effort Yakone was making just to stand. When he was upright, his legs wobbled, and he would have fallen over again if Lusa hadn't darted to his side and thrust her shoulder under him. Kallik supported him on the other side, and they followed Toklo up the side of the hollow. Kallik winced at the sound of their pawsteps; it was impossible to walk silently and still help Yakone.

But the howling of the wolves was louder still. *Maybe they can't hear us when they're making that racket,* Kallik hoped. Their harsh, rotten-meat scent washed over her, making her retch. She couldn't smell anything else now, which meant the wolves must be almost upon them.

"Here!" Toklo was beckoning from the top of the hollow, pointing to a bramble thicket. "In here—hide!"

Lusa and Kallik shoved Yakone into the brambles and plunged in after him, the spiky tendrils tearing at their pelts. Toklo followed them and turned to see what the wolves were doing. Kallik peered over his shoulder in time to see several rangy gray shapes slinking down into the hollow where they had been resting moments before. They snuffled around the bushes, letting out yelps and growls as they padded to and fro.

"They must think we have prey," Toklo whispered. "And now they're picking up our scent."

Kallik's heart sank. *We can be tracked now—and if Yakone's paw starts bleeding again, we'll leave a clear trail for those mangy creatures to follow.* She shivered, remembering how the coyotes had tirelessly tracked them down. *And if they won't leave us alone, we will have to fight them for prey!*

CHAPTER FOUR

Lusa

"Follow me," Toklo whispered. *"This way!"*

Breaking out of the brambles on the other side of the thicket, he led the way uphill once again. Glancing back, Lusa saw that the wolves were still sniffing around their sleeping place. Her heart was pounding, and her head spun with a mixture of weariness and terror. All she could think of was the way the coyotes had chased them onto the firesnake, never giving up the pursuit until the fearsome silver creature had carried them out of reach.

But there aren't any firesnakes here. And why were the wolves even chasing them? They didn't have any prey the wolves would want!

Lusa helped Kallik guide Yakone's wavering steps as they followed Toklo up the hill. But she knew it wouldn't be long before the wolves were on their trail. As they approached the summit, the slope grew steeper, and they had to haul Yakone upward again, leaving his paws to drag in the dust. Lusa winced when she saw smears of blood left behind on the stones.

At the top of the ridge Toklo halted, gazing out across the next stretch of forest to where an exposed cliff reared up in front of them, its surface silver in the moonlight. "I know that place," he said. "Come on—and hurry!"

He veered aside and plunged into a steep ravine that opened up in front of his paws. Loose pebbles covered the ground, and Lusa had to grab Yakone's fur in her teeth and hang on to him to stop him from slipping down the steep slope. Kallik walked in front of him, supporting most of his weight, while Toklo called out a warning if there were rifts and potholes in the track.

Bushes and trees lined the sides of the ravine, cutting off most of the moonlight, and it was even harder for the bears to keep their footing in the dark. Lusa kept her ears pricked for the sounds of howling behind them, though she couldn't hear anything except their own pawsteps and labored breathing. Then gradually she began to hear the sound of water running fast over stones. The ravine opened up slightly, the bushes giving way to bare rock with a few straggling thorns pushing their way through. In the moonlight Lusa saw a stream running along the bottom of the ravine, its surface glinting in the silver light.

"We need to wade along in the water," Toklo said. "It'll hide our scent."

He bounded over the last few bearlengths and lowered himself cautiously into the stream, careful not to make a splash. Kallik and Yakone followed; Kallik supported Yakone as he slid down the bank, making sure that he was steady on his paws before wading after Toklo. Lusa brought up the rear. She gasped with shock as the icy water soaked through her fur, and staggered with the force of the current, strong and fierce with snowmelt from the mountains. The water tugged at her belly and resisted every step that she took. *If I'm not careful, I could be swept off my paws.*

Glancing over her shoulder, she could see no signs of the wolves following them down the ravine. The howling had grown more distant, too. But Lusa had no doubt that sooner or later the wolves would reappear, loping along much faster than the bears could manage, following them for prey. She trudged along miserably against the force of the water and couldn't see any reasonable cover on either side of the stream.

As they struggled on, Lusa heard a low, booming noise that began as a faint rumble in her ear fur and strengthened to a thunderous roar. Before long they followed the stream around a jutting rocky outcrop and found themselves confronted by a waterfall of tumbling, sparkling water. It plunged from a cliff above their heads, crashing down into a pool at the foot of the rock face. It was much smaller than the waterfall in the River of Lost Bears, but still dauntingly high, and it filled the entire gap in the trees without leaving bare rocks on either side.

"Seal rot!" Kallik exclaimed. "We can't climb that."

"Not in the dark," Toklo agreed. "We might be able to find a way in daylight. But we'll have to stay here for the rest of the night."

Weary and discouraged, the bears dragged themselves out of the water. The sides of the ravine sloped steeply down to the edge of the pool and were covered with loose scree; it was hard to keep their balance.

"We can't stay here," Kallik said. "We could slide right back into the stream, and there's nowhere to hide from the wolves."

Lusa gave her pelt a good shake, scattering water drops everywhere. "I'll go and explore," she offered. "Toklo, call out if you see the wolves."

Toklo looked as if he was going to object but said nothing. Yakone was splayed out, exhausted, on the stones, and Kallik was bending anxiously over him; it made sense for Toklo to stay on guard in case the wolves caught up.

Lusa set off toward the waterfall and clambered over the boulders at the foot of the cascade. Spray misted on her pelt, and she kept slipping on the rocks, which were slick with water. There wasn't enough space among the boulders for four bears to hide, but soon she spotted a narrow path leading to a ledge behind the falls. Cautiously she followed it, putting each paw down carefully one in front of another, terrified that the thundering water would catch her and hurl her into the pool.

The track ended in a shallow cave shut off from the ravine by the tumbling water. The roof was low and the floor covered with grit, but as she examined it, Lusa's hopes started to rise. *The wolves will never find us here! The waterfall will drown out any sounds we make, and the rocks are too wet to hold our scent.*

"Come on!" she called as she hurried back to her friends as quickly as she dared. "I've found a place to hide."

Kallik nudged Yakone to his paws, and the other bears followed Lusa along the track. It was harder for the bigger bears to make their way along the narrow ledge; Yakone especially stumbled and wavered, and Lusa's heart pounded with fear that he would lose his footing and slide down into the churning water below.

At last all four bears reached the cave, wedged uncomfortably together in the shallow space.

"Good find, Lusa," Kallik murmured as she settled herself beside Yakone. "We'll be safe here."

Toklo let out a grunt. "I hate this. We're bears. We shouldn't have to hide like prey."

"We all hate it," Kallik pointed out. "But it's better than trying to spend the night in the open."

"Right." Lusa gave Toklo a friendly prod. "Come on, try to get some rest. Then we'll be ready to get out of the ravine at dawn."

Toklo huffed irritably but didn't argue any more. Lusa curled up against the cave wall, but for all her weariness, she couldn't sleep. She was squashed up against Toklo, and the waterfall was like thunder in her ears. She could feel the others shifting uneasily, too. Yakone was clearly in pain, muttering confusedly about hunting on the ice. At last she dropped into a disturbed doze, but she was relieved when dawn light began to filter through the falling water, and she was able to get up and stretch her cramped limbs.

Toklo led the way back along the ledge and cautiously emerged among the boulders at the edge of the pool. He raised his snout and sniffed. "I can't smell the wolves," he reported.

Lusa followed him out, while Kallik and Yakone brought

up the rear. Lusa was glad to see that Yakone seemed to be a little better; at least the icy water of the stream had stopped his wound from bleeding.

At first when they left the cave the ravine was still in shadow, but while they were still checking their surroundings, the sun rose over the top of the rocks, its slanting rays striking the track where they stood.

"That feels good," Lusa murmured, hoping that the warmth would dry her pelt.

"We have to move." Toklo was examining the edge of the cliff where the water cascaded down. In daylight, Lusa could see a narrow gap, just wide enough for a bear, between the water and the trees. "Do you think we can climb up there?" Toklo asked.

Lusa looked upward, assessing the cliff. It was almost sheer, but there were plenty of ledges and cracks in the rock that they could use for pawholds. "I think I could manage it," she said.

"Well, Yakone certainly can't," Kallik retorted. "You must be cloud-brained if you think he could get up there. We'll have to find another way."

"Why don't I climb up and wait for you at the top?" Lusa suggested. "Then you and Toklo can help Yakone, and I can keep a lookout."

Toklo hesitated, then nodded. "Okay. But stay under cover."

Lusa gave him a poke with one paw. "Whatever you say, bossy!"

Without waiting for Toklo to respond, she began scrambling up the cliff. Before she had climbed more than a couple of bearlengths, a stone under her paw gave way, and she lurched into thin air. Lusa clutched at the wet rocks, swaying, then managed to claw herself up to the safety of a ledge, where she paused for a moment, her heart thumping and her legs trembling. *Bee-brain! You should be more careful.* Lusa glanced down to see if her friends had noticed that she'd almost fallen. She was thankful to see that all three of them were picking their way back along the edge of the stream, their backs to her.

Once the quivering in her legs had died away, Lusa started to climb again more slowly. In a shorter time than she expected, she reached the top of the cliff. A grassy slope stretched in front of her, dotted with trees. A lush growth of ferns and bushes grew along the edge of the stream. Thicker forest lay just beyond the grass, and in the distance Lusa could see the exposed cliff that Toklo had recognized in the moonlight the night before. There was no sign of wolves or any other bears.

Lusa took a drink from the stream, then padded along the top of the ravine until she caught sight of her friends, who were toiling up a narrow track that wound back and forth up the slope, furtively scrambling from the shelter of one rock to the next.

Kallik's voice drifted up to her, sounding annoyed. "Toklo, slow down! Yakone can't keep up."

"Okay, okay!" Lusa saw Toklo turn back and grab Yakone by one shoulder, dragging him up.

With Kallik boosting him from behind, Yakone managed to reach the top of the ravine, and immediately flopped down to rest. Kallik joined him, while Toklo, looking harassed, turned to Lusa.

"I thought I told you to stay under cover," he snapped.

Lusa admitted to herself that she'd forgotten, but she wasn't going to take that tone from Toklo. "I took a good look around," she defended herself. "No wolves, no bears. Not even any scent. So what would I be hiding from?"

Toklo gave an ill-tempered grunt. Turning to Kallik, he growled, "Come on, get Yakone on his paws again. We need to move into the shelter of the trees."

Kallik glared at him but didn't argue. Lusa knew she understood, just as they all did, that even though Lusa hadn't seen anything, the sooner they got away from the open ground the better. Toklo took the lead as they headed up the slope and into the woodland. Once there, he seemed to relax and strode on confidently, checking out the terrain ahead and then waiting for the others to catch up.

In spite of Toklo's confidence, Lusa was still worried about meeting the fierce Old Grizzly that Maniitok had told them about. But she couldn't smell any brown-bear scents, or see any scratches on the trees that warned they were entering another bear's territory.

Yakone was growing weaker with every pawstep. Faced with a fallen tree that the others had easily hopped over, he crumpled to the ground. He made one feeble effort to get back on his paws, then collapsed again and lay still beside the smooth gray trunk.

"Toklo!" Kallik called, scrambling back over the tree. "We have to stop and rest."

Toklo, who had drawn some way ahead, turned back. "We can't stop," he replied as he padded up. "We've hardly started. It's not even sunhigh."

"I don't care!" Kallik flashed back at him. "I'm not going to force Yakone to get up again. We're all starving and exhausted, and we need to rest."

Toklo glared at her, his lips drawn back into a snarl. "Don't tell me what we *need*! I know this place, and what we *need* is to move on before we run into trouble. We *know* there are wolves around, and an aggressive brown bear."

Anxiety welled up inside Lusa as she heard the anger in her friends' voices and saw them ready to lash out at each other. "Look, maybe we should—" she began.

Both Kallik and Toklo ignored her.

"Toklo, this isn't about *you* all the time!" Kallik hissed. "Fine, we've arrived at your home, but do you think we want to die here? Soon we won't need wolves or bears to attack us— we'll just collapse all by ourselves if you won't let us rest or eat."

"I'm as hungry and tired as any of you," Toklo retorted. Then he swung around with an angry snort. "Fine. I'll hunt. Does that satisfy you?"

Kallik didn't respond, just turned her head away.

Lusa padded up to Kallik. "Are you okay watching Yakone?"

she asked. "If you are, I'll go and look for herbs now that we've traveled a bit, and see if there's anything that will help him."

Kallik hesitated for a moment, clearly still seething with fury, then let out a long sigh and nodded. "Thanks, Lusa. We'll be fine. You be careful, though."

"Watch out for wolves and bears," Toklo added.

Lusa rolled her eyes. "Yes, Toklo, you've told me that, like, a *thousand* times!" Not waiting for a reply, she headed into the trees.

Once she was on her own, Lusa began to feel more peaceful. She hated it when the others quarreled. It was as though their anger might destroy the deep connections between them. *Please, Arcturus, let them be friends again by the time I get back!*

Without Toklo's relentless urging to move on, Lusa began to realize how tired she was: bone-weary and longing from the depths of her heart for somewhere they could stop and be safe. Her paws felt so sore that she winced as she set them down. She was so exhausted that she couldn't think clearly, and when she started searching for herbs, she couldn't remember what to look for. Even when she dug up one or two plants, she wasn't sure that they had the right scent.

Lusa let herself sink to the ground, black despair sweeping over her like a storm cloud. *It's my job to find a way to make Yakone better. I was the one who used to help Ujurak with his healing herbs. I've found plants so many times before.* But now the vegetation that stretched around her seemed unfamiliar, and of no use. *Nothing seems to help Yakone. He's going to die, and it will be all my fault. . . .*

Gradually Lusa forced herself to be calm. *We've all suffered injuries before. Yakone's is by far the worst, but that doesn't mean I should give up. If herbs don't work, what else can we do?*

Then Lusa remembered the time in the Wilderness when Ujurak, in goose's shape, got a fishhook stuck in his throat. She and the others had made him change into a flat-face, and carried him to a flat-face healer. The flat-faces had whisked him off in a clattering metal bird and taken him to a huge den full of other sick flat-faces. And there in the den they had healed him.

Could the flat-faces do the same for Yakone, even though he's a bear? Lusa wondered. *At least they might have different herbs. It's worth a try!*

Her despair vanishing like mist in the sun, Lusa sprang to her paws. Then she realized a problem. *There are no flat-faces here . . . not that I've seen, anyway. How will I find a flat-face healing den?*

Lusa bounded on up the slope until she came to a very tall fir tree. Sinking her claws into the bark, she climbed it quickly, until the trunk grew narrower and swayed under her weight.

"Bear spirit, please watch over me," she prayed as she climbed even higher, more slowly now, up and up through spindly branches that bent and threatened to send her crashing to the ground. At last she reached the top of the tree and clung there with the wind buffeting her fur and making the trunk lurch with each gust.

A huge view opened up in front of her as she poked her head above the forest canopy. Rolling forested hills stretched in every direction. Rivers wound a course through the trees, flowing into lakes that reflected the blue of the sky and sparkled in the sunlight. Snow-topped mountains reared up on one side, while far away in the opposite direction she could just make out the flat plains that they had crossed on the firesnake.

"It's amazing!" Lusa breathed, almost forgetting her precarious perch at the top of the tree. She remembered this view from the Sky Ridge at the beginning of her journey, but now it felt as if she was seeing it with new eyes, because there was something very particular she was looking for. Her heart beat faster as she caught sight of a huge flat-face denning place in the middle of the forest. BlackPaths cut through the trees toward it, encircling the mass of white dens.

With so many flat-faces, there must be a healing den!

Judging the distance, she thought it would take her about a day to walk to the denning place. *And another day to get back.* Her belly churned at the thought of traveling alone through the forest, but she swallowed her fears. *I've got to try.* There was no way Yakone could walk that far, Kallik wouldn't leave him, and Toklo had to stay to guard them both in case the wolves found them again and grew aggressive over prey.

From her perch, Lusa took one more careful look at the forest below her, searching for landmarks. *I can follow that river nearly all the way . . . and if I head straight for the mountains, I'm bound to reach the riverbank.* Then she scrambled down the tree and raced back to where she had left the others. As she hurried toward them, she saw that Toklo had caught a squirrel, which he and Kallik were sharing; Yakone was still unconscious. To Lusa's relief their quarrel seemed to be over.

Kallik looked up hopefully as Lusa approached, but her

hopeful look died when she saw that Lusa wasn't carrying anything. "You didn't find any herbs?" she asked.

"No. But I've thought of a way to help Yakone!" Lusa burst out.

"What?" Toklo looked up with a mouthful of squirrel in his jaws. His tone was sharp, and there was suspicion in his eyes.

Lusa suddenly realized there was no way her friends would let her go into the flat-face denning place, especially not alone. *They'll say it's too dangerous, and that we don't need flat-face help. But we do! It could be the only way to save Yakone.*

"Er . . ." Lusa began, improvising desperately, "I saw a place at the bottom of a valley where I think the right herbs will grow. It looks like the sort of area I've seen before with Ujurak. But it'll take a day to get there, so I'll be gone for two days."

Toklo stared at her. "No way!" he snapped. "You're not going off by yourself for two *days.* What about the wolves?"

"We haven't scented any wolves since last night," Lusa pointed out. "If I spot any, I'll climb a tree to get away from them. And I can sleep in a tree tonight."

Kallik glanced at Yakone, who still lay inert, his shallow, harsh breaths the only thing that showed he was alive. Then she looked back at Lusa, clearly torn between her fears for her two friends. "It's too dangerous," she said.

"No, it's not," Lusa insisted. "And I promise if I run into trouble I'll turn back."

"You might not get the chance," Toklo grunted. "No, it's a bee-brained idea."

Lusa looked him straight in the eye. "Yakone might die if I don't do this."

There was a murmur of protest from Kallik.

Toklo met Lusa's gaze, then rose to his paws. "Okay, but I'm coming with you."

Lusa hadn't expected that. *I can't let him. If Toklo doesn't want me to go to a valley with herbs, he'll never let me anywhere near the denning place!*

"You can't," she said. "You have to stay here and help Kallik take care of Yakone. She can't do that on her own."

Toklo was silent for a moment, looking frustrated. "I don't like it," he muttered at last.

"I know," Lusa replied, "but it could be Yakone's only chance. Remember all the times you risked your lives to help me?" she continued, glancing from Toklo to Kallik and back again. Her heart grew full at the memories of how they had been willing to sacrifice themselves for her, time after time. "Now it's my turn. You have to trust me."

Toklo turned to Kallik. "What do you think?"

Kallik hesitated, then let out a long sigh. "It's hard . . . but I think Lusa's right. If there's a chance to help Yakone, we have to take it."

Toklo gave Lusa a long look, as if he was sizing her up. Then he nodded curtly. "Okay. But I still think you're bee-brained."

"Great!" Excitement surged up in Lusa again. "I'll start right away."

"Try not to do anything stupid," Toklo said.

Kallik rose to her paws and padded along beside Lusa for a few bearlengths. "Thank you," she whispered. "I pray that Silaluk will watch over you."

Lusa touched her snout to her friend's shoulder. *Kallik didn't say Ujurak,* she thought sadly. *We all feel like we're on our own now. None of us know if Ujurak is still watching over us.*

CHAPTER FIVE

Lusa

Lusa plunged down the slope toward the river that she'd seen from the treetop. *It will take me almost all the way to the flat-face denning place.*

But now that she was on her own, the trees seemed eerily quiet, more close-packed than the part of the forest where she had left her friends. She kept all her senses alert for danger, scanning the ground for the small pawprints that would betray the presence of wolves. A creaking sound scared her, and she spun around, only to realize that it was just an ancient oak tree shifting in the wind. She crouched down in a clump of ferns when an unfamiliar scent tickled her nose, and watched as a fox trotted across her path. As she set off again, her heart was pounding.

Have I taken on too much? It's such a long way . . . but I have to help Yakone! I have to!

Sunhigh came and went, and Lusa trekked on, stopping only to tear off some leaves from a particularly juicy-looking bush. As she munched the succulent greenery, she heard the crunch of large pawsteps. At the same moment the scent of brown bear washed over her; the strong smell of the leaves had masked it until the bear was almost upon her. He was big, old, strong, moving confidently through the bushes. *Could it be Old Grizzly?*

Lusa hurled herself into the bush and peered out from beneath the lowest branches. The huge brown bear lumbered by, his head swinging from side to side as if he was looking for prey. Lusa froze, hoping that the smell of the bush would hide her scent, like it had hidden his from her. *He's massive!*

The brown bear paused, sniffing the air suspiciously, and Lusa squeezed her eyes shut, convinced that her last moments had come. When she dared to look again, the bear had swung around and was plodding away into the undergrowth. Lusa waited until she was sure he had gone before she crawled out of the bush again.

Thank the spirits! He never saw me.

Lusa sniffed and picked up the bear's scent all around her—old scents as well as new. She had walked straight into his territory. *I was so busy looking for wolves that I must have missed his scratch marks on the trees.* Turning, she ran as quietly as she could away from the big grizzly and his territory. Fortunately, he had gone in the opposite direction from where she wanted to go. The strong scent of the leaves still clung to her fur, and she thought that her legs would never stop shaking, but she kept on heading downhill.

Before long Lusa spotted the glint of the river through the trees and emerged onto the bank. Dipping her snout into the water for a drink, she felt her confidence begin to return. She followed the bank through the forest, more cautious now as she kept a lookout for bears and wolves. Her ears pricked, and she picked up the sound of firebeasts long before she came to the Black Path. It ran straight through the trees and crossed the river by a bridge before vanishing into the forest on the other side.

I know how to deal with this, Lusa thought, as she ducked behind a bush and waited while several firebeasts growled past in both directions. Even though the firebeasts didn't seem able to get down onto the riverbank where she was, she didn't want to risk being seen. When everything was quiet, Lusa burst out of her hiding place and ran swiftly under the bridge, not pausing until the Black Path was safely behind her. Even more confident, she marched on.

As the day wore on, the land flattened out, opening up into a wide valley with the river running along the bottom. Lusa began to hear more scuffling in the undergrowth from tiny forest animals, and more birdsong in the trees. *Maybe that means the wolves don't come here.*

The sun went down, casting long shadows across the landscape. In the gathering darkness the river looked eerie, like a long black snake slipping along with glints of starlight on its surface. A fluttering on the ground startled Lusa, and she slammed her paw down to discover that she had caught a bird. It looked so small that it was barely able to fly, and Lusa crunched it down in a couple of mouthfuls. "Thank you, spirits, for this prey," she whispered.

When it was too dark to see where she was putting her paws, Lusa found a hollow place among the roots of a huge tree, then remembered her promise to Toklo and climbed until she came to a fork between the trunk and a large branch, where she could curl up to sleep. At first anxiety kept her awake as she wondered what the others were doing. *Yakone, just hold on. Give me a chance to find something that will help you.*

She felt uneasy, too, about sleeping alone; it was a long time since she had spent a night without at least one of her friends close by. *Not since I left the Bear Bowl . . .* At last, worn out by traveling, she sank into a deep sleep.

Dawn light trickling through the leaves woke Lusa. She slithered down the tree and stomped around for a few moments to work the aches out of her legs. The sky was pale blue, promising a warm day to come, and a breeze blew from across the river, ruffling the surface of the water. A dull roar in the distance blotted out the scuffling of small animals in the undergrowth and the song of birds. It warned Lusa that she wasn't far from a BlackPath. *I hate them,* she thought, suppressing a sigh. *But I knew what I was in for when I decided to go find flat-faces.*

Pausing only to munch some leaves from a nearby bush, Lusa set out along the river once more. The roaring sound grew louder, and soon she was faced with a huge BlackPath slicing through the forest. Heading for the bridge, she was dismayed to see that this time the river vanished under it with no space for her to walk.

I'll have to climb up and cross the BlackPath.

Crushing down her fear at the thought of the thundering firebeasts and their enormous round paws, Lusa scrambled up the embankment. There was no cover except for a few scrubby thorns. Lusa retched as the stench of the firebeasts caught in her throat and blasted against her fur. The noise made her ears ache. Worst of all was the sight of huge firebeasts carrying loads of tree trunks on their backs. It took Lusa straight back to the River of Lost Bears, where so many trees had been hacked down and thrown into the water. She thought her heart would break all over again at the thought of the bear spirits trapped inside these logs, carried away forever from their beloved forest.

"Arcturus, help them!" she whispered.

Lusa crouched beside the BlackPath and waited for the chance to cross. Her paws twitched impatiently. As soon as there was a gap, she hurled herself across the BlackPath, wincing at the feel of the hard surface on her paws. She paused for an instant on the strip of grass that ran down the middle, then raced on again. She was still a couple of bearlengths from the other side when a high-pitched screech sounded almost on top of her. Lusa glanced sideways to see a massive firebeast bearing down on her. The screech seemed to be coming from it. Letting out a yelp of panic, she forced her legs to move even faster. A gust of hot wind washed over her as she reached the far side of the BlackPath and tumbled into the shelter of a thornbush.

That was close!

Panting and terrified, Lusa crouched among the thorns

until her legs stopped shaking. Then she flicked dirt from her pelt and trudged on, forcing her way through dense, prickly undergrowth. The air tasted different now, thicker, smokier, and the trees here were smaller and more spindly. Before long they thinned out and stopped, and Lusa found herself staring at the outskirts of the flat-face denning place. The dens here all looked alike: flat-topped gray buildings separated by narrow BlackPaths. Their unnaturally straight lines made Lusa uneasy, and the blank windows looked as if they were staring at her.

Some huge shiny mesh reared up between Lusa and the dens, forming a barrier that stretched several bearlengths above her head. Sharp stones dug into Lusa's paws as she padded cautiously toward it. Before she reached the barrier, the roar of a firebeast made her dart back into the cover of the nearest trees. Peering out from behind a trunk, she spotted more firebeasts zooming past on the other side of the mesh. They didn't slow down, so Lusa guessed they hadn't seen her. But even if she could climb over the shiny mesh, more firebeasts might come, and there would be no way of hiding out there.

Suddenly Lusa felt very small. *This was such a bee-brained idea! I can't even get into the flat-face place, so how will I ever find the healing den?*

CHAPTER SIX

Toklo

Toklo looked down at Yakone, suppressing a sigh. After Lusa left the day before, he and Kallik had half carried, half pushed the white bear into a hollow screened by bushes and brambles; the makeshift den was the best they could come up with. Yakone was sleeping deeply, but he didn't seem comfortable. His breathing was quick and shallow, and heat was rising from his fur. A foul stink came from his injured paw, in spite of the fresh leaves Kallik had wrapped it in.

He's so sick, Toklo thought despairingly. *Perhaps he would rather be left in peace to slip away.*

But then Toklo felt the tug of friendship between him and Yakone, and remembered all the times the white bear had helped him—had helped all of them on the journey that was never his own.

No. I won't give up trying to save Yakone!

A rustle in the bushes alerted Toklo, and he glanced up to see Kallik pushing her way into the den. A small hare dangled from her jaws.

"I know it's a little thing," she said apologetically as she dropped her catch at Toklo's paws. "But it's all I could find."

Toklo shrugged. "It's because of the wolves that there's hardly any prey around here."

He and Kallik shared the hare in a few mouthfuls. "I hope you didn't leave a scent or a blood trail leading here," Toklo growled to Kallik, knowing how quickly the wolves could pick up the scent of a dead animal.

Kallik glared at him. "What am I, a cub?" she snapped. "I made sure the hare didn't brush against anything on my way here."

Toklo bit back a sharp retort. It was too easy to fight, tense as they were with Yakone's illness and Lusa's absence. Rising to his paws, he scrambled out of the hollow and thrust his way through the bushes into the open. The forest was washed in scarlet light as the sun went down behind the trees, casting long shadows across the ground. *Where's Lusa?* Toklo wondered, with a sudden stab of anxiety. *She said she would be back by tonight. Has she gotten lost, looking for this herb place?* For a moment Toklo felt a stab of frustration with Lusa for coming up with such a bee-brained plan. But cold fear drove his irritation away. *Maybe the wolves got her . . . or that bear called Old Grizzly found her on his territory.* Toklo's pelt bristled.

Padding a few paces forward, he crossed the scent trail Lusa had left when she set out the previous day. Hardly aware of making the decision, he began to follow it. *Maybe I'll meet her on the way back, and I can help her carry the herbs.*

But Lusa's scent was stale and beginning to fade. Toklo struggled to keep track of it, and when he reached a dense bramble thicket woven with aromatic vines, he lost the trail altogether. He sniffed all around the thicket but couldn't pick up the scent on the other side.

For a while Toklo cast about in one direction, then another, trying to find Lusa's trail again. Then he realized how much noise he was making, crashing around in the undergrowth of this silent and empty forest. Toklo froze, listening for the approach of danger, but there was nothing. Once he knew he was still alone, he carried on more slowly, heading upward across the mountain slope. He wasn't sure what he was looking for anymore; he didn't dare call out to Lusa in case he attracted wolves or other bears.

Eventually the trees thinned out, and he emerged in a meadow. It was covered with grass and small scrubby bushes, with flowers dotted here and there. Toklo stared around, haunted by an unexpected familiarity.

Did I know this place when I was a cub? I think this is where I played with Tobi!

An image flashed into his mind of two brown bear cubs, tumbling together in the grass. That had been one of Tobi's good days, when he felt strong enough to play. Toklo had pretended to be a mountain goat, and Tobi had chased him.

"Come on, Tobi!" he had called. "I'm fat and juicy! Don't you want to eat me?"

Tobi scrambled after him. Toklo could easily outpace him,

but after a while he let his brother catch him and leap on top of him, letting out tiny high-pitched roars to announce that he had killed his prey.

But then the memory darkened.

"Come on, Tobi," Toklo urged his brother. "You be the goat now."

"No, I'm tired," Tobi replied, huddling in the grass. "I want to rest now."

Toklo tore at the grass in anger and frustration. "You're no fun!" he snorted, turning to Oka, who was digging up roots a couple of bearlengths away. "Tobi won't play anymore," he protested.

Oka padded over to him and gave him a stinging cuff around the ear. "You should know better than to tire him out," she growled. "He's not as strong as you." She turned to Tobi and licked him comfortingly around the ears.

But we were having fun, Toklo thought, pulling himself out of the memory. He felt troubled and annoyed, as much with himself as with his mother. *I shouldn't have complained about Tobi all the time,* he thought, a pang of regret shaking him. *It wasn't his fault that he was weak.* A sudden longing to see his brother again surged over him, though he knew that wasn't possible. Tobi's spirit had traveled downriver long since. *But now at least I'll be able to find the place where he's buried.*

Movement from the other side of the meadow startled Toklo from his thoughts, and he took a pace forward. "Lusa?" he called softly.

A bear emerged from the undergrowth, paused, then loped

toward Toklo. It wasn't Lusa, but a brown she-bear about the same size as Toklo. She looked strong and fit, and moved confidently as she crossed the meadow and halted in front of him.

"Who are you?" she asked. Her tone was reserved, and there was suspicion in her gaze as it flicked over Toklo.

"My name's Toklo," the brown male replied. "When I was a cub, I—"

"That's my territory, over there," the she-bear interrupted, pointing with one paw toward the other side of the meadow. "Stay out of it, okay?"

Toklo bristled, drawing his lips back in the beginnings of a snarl. *Don't talk to me as if I'm a wandering cub.* "If I stay away, it'll be because I choose to," he retorted. "You don't scare me."

"Well, I should," the she-bear snorted. "I can fight as well as any bear around here." She swung around and headed back across the meadow.

Toklo stared after her. The longer he stayed here in the meadow, the more familiar it looked. He became almost sure that this was the place where he and Tobi had played. *That tree stump over there . . . if I crouch down, it looks just like a fish. There was a stump like that where Tobi and I used to race. Sometimes I'd let him get there first.*

Not far off through the trees, Toklo could hear the sound of a stream. He could remember trying to fish there on his own, though he never caught anything. *If I'm right, Tobi is buried over there, somewhere in those trees. On that she-bear's territory . . .*

The she-bear had almost reached the other side of the meadow. Toklo galloped after her and caught up to her beneath the outlying branches. The she-bear whirled around to face him, her teeth bared in a snarl.

Toklo retreated a pace, ducking his head to show that he wasn't a threat. "Please may I go onto your territory?" he begged. "There's something I want to see."

The she-bear glared at him. "You must think I'm a fool!" she snapped. "You'll steal prey."

"No—I won't, I promise."

To Toklo's dismay, a low growl came from the she-bear's throat. He realized that if he didn't back down, she was ready to fight. *She's brave, I'll give her that,* he thought, reluctantly impressed. Even though he longed to see Tobi's burial mound, he knew he couldn't keep pushing her. Somehow it didn't seem fair to ask her to fight. "Okay, I'll leave," he grunted.

"You'd better," the she-bear muttered, and turned away again, heading into the trees.

"Wait!" Toklo called after her. "How do you deal with the wolves?"

The she-bear glanced back over her shoulder. "I have my ways," she barked.

But she's alone, Toklo thought. "Are you sure you'll be okay?" he asked, following the she-bear a few paces into the forest. "Those wolves are vicious."

The she-bear turned, fury flaring in her eyes. "Do I look like I need your help?" she hissed. "Leave me alone!" With a snarl, she took a step toward Toklo. "You don't even belong here. I've never seen you before. Just go home!"

Toklo stared after her as she vanished into the trees. "This *is* my home," he whispered. *But I barely remember it. The bears are unfriendly, and everywhere has been taken over by wolves. . . . It hardly feels like the same place.*

As if his thoughts had called it up, a distant howl sounded from deep within the trees. Toklo realized that while he'd been talking to the she-bear, the last of the day's sunlight had vanished, and twilight covered the meadow.

Kallik and Yakone—they need me!

Toklo raced back to the den where he had left his friends. As darkness gathered, he became confused among the trees and only found his way by following his own scent trail. At last he discovered the makeshift den among the brambles and slid inside. Kallik was there, huddled against Yakone's unmoving white bulk.

"Where's Lusa?" Toklo demanded.

Kallik shook her head worriedly. "She isn't back. I thought she would be with you."

"I couldn't find her," Toklo admitted, feeling a rush of fear.

"Then she's in danger!"

"We don't know that," Toklo said, though he wasn't sure that he believed his own words.

"I know." Kallik scraped her claws on the earth floor of the den. "But she said she'd be back by now."

A dark pit opened up inside Toklo. "Do you think I should go out to look for her again?"

As he spoke, Yakone stirred and murmured something, too quietly for Toklo to make out what he was saying. Kallik turned to the white male and rested a paw on his shoulder.

As if the touch reassured him, Yakone slid back into quieter sleep.

"Toklo, please don't go," Kallik said. "If wolves attack, I can't defend Yakone on my own. Lusa knows how to survive in a forest." She hesitated, then added, "We need to trust that she'll be okay."

You don't believe that any more than I do, Toklo thought. But at the same time, he realized that Kallik was right. However much their instincts cried out against it, the three of them had to stay together. Split up, they were all vulnerable. "Okay, I'll stay," he said.

To distract them both, Toklo told Kallik about the she-bear he met in the meadow. "She looked really hostile—as if she'd be glad to take a bite out of me," he told her.

"You'd be the same way if you wanted to guard your territory against a bear who just came wandering by," Kallik pointed out.

Toklo shrugged. "I've learned not to be suspicious of every stranger. But then, none of the bears around here seem particularly friendly."

"It's the wolves." Kallik sighed. "They've made every bear jumpy and anxious. And they've stolen prey—that sets all the bears against one another."

Toklo nodded. "You'd better get some sleep. I'll take first watch."

He hauled himself out of the den and crouched on the edge, staring into the dark night. *I hope Lusa's safe,* he thought.

CHAPTER SEVEN

Lusa

As sunhigh approached, Lusa crouched in the shadow of the tree, wondering what she could do next. Then she heard a loud clattering sound from somewhere overhead. Looking up fearfully, she spotted one of the flat-faces' metal birds heading across the shiny barrier toward the dens beyond.

I wish a flat-face bird could carry me over there!

Lusa pricked her ears as she realized that this noisy bird looked very similar to the one that had carried Ujurak to the healing den when he was injured by the fishhook in his throat. It was the same size, and the same red-and-white color.

Maybe all those birds nest in healing dens! I must be close.

Lusa scampered up the tree and tracked the metal bird with her gaze as it swooped over the denning area. It landed on the roof of a tall white den some distance away, but still close to the shiny barrier.

That has to be the healing den!

Fizzing with excitement, Lusa half fell, half scrambled down the tree and headed alongside the barrier in the direction of the white den. There was little cover except for a few scrubby bushes, and as she darted from one to the next, Lusa's pelt crawled at the thought of being spotted by the flat-faces inside the denning place.

I should wait until dark . . . but I can't waste the whole day. That's time Yakone might not have.

After a while, when she seemed to have gone unnoticed, Lusa decided that the flat-faces were too busy roaring about in their firebeasts to pay much attention to one small black bear, and her confidence began to return.

At last she reached the part of the barrier close to the big white den. All her instincts were telling her to scramble over the shiny metal mesh, but now she realized that she *would* have to wait until the sun went down. While she was on the ground, she stood a chance of hiding, but once she began to climb, she would never get past the flat-faces in daylight.

Lusa spent the rest of the day crouching in the bushes a little ways off from the silver mesh. Her belly felt hollow, and she tried munching a few of the leaves, but they were dry and tasted like firebeasts. The sun had never seemed so slow as it crept down the sky.

I said I'd be back by now, Lusa thought as the sun dipped lower. *Kallik and Toklo will be worried.*

As soon as the scarlet light of sunset had faded, Lusa sprang out of her hiding place and raced up to the barrier. It was higher than she first thought, and the holes in the mesh were too small for her paws, which would make it almost impossible to climb. Perhaps she could go under it? Sniffing at the foot of the mesh and testing it with one paw, she discovered that it was fastened to the ground somehow. Slowly she padded alongside the barrier, testing again at every pawstep. It held firm, barely swaying even when she leaned her whole weight against it. Lusa started to worry that she would have to go a long way from the healing den before she found a way in.

I wish I was like Ujurak, she thought, feeling a fresh pang of loss for her friend. *I'd change into a bug and hop through the mesh, then change back into a bear on the other side.*

Every so often a firebeast would roar past Lusa on the other side of the barrier, its glowing eyes dazzling her and momentarily lighting her up for any watching flat-faces. Once a firebeast stopped very close to her, and Lusa's heart started to pound as the flat-face inside it got out. She squeezed her eyes shut and pressed herself to the ground, desperately trying to hide, even though she knew there was no cover on the flat, exposed ground.

Then she heard a bang and looked up to see that the flat-face was back inside the firebeast. A moment later it roared away.

"That was close!" Lusa murmured.

Making her way slowly along the barrier, at last she discovered a spot where the mesh had come away from the ground for about a paw's width. Lusa stuck her paw into the gap and pulled; another section of the barrier tore away, scattering some curved metal thorns that had been sunk into the ground. With a bit more effort, Lusa made a gap that she thought was big enough for her to crawl underneath.

She waited for another firebeast to pass, then flattened herself to the ground and squirmed forward under the gap, feeling the mesh scrape along her back. Something snagged in her pelt, and for a few terrible moments she was stuck.

Tugging determinedly, Lusa managed to free herself and wriggled forward until she was inside the barrier. Quickly she scuttled alongside it until she approached the white den. It lay on the other side of a broad stretch of BlackPath; Lusa checked for firebeasts before racing across. As she drew nearer to the den, her nose tingled with the scents that came from it: blood, and something else, harsh and nauseating.

It wasn't a pleasant smell, but Lusa's spirits rose. *That's the same scent that came from the healing den where they took Ujurak!*

The side of the den that faced Lusa was blank, with no way in except for some small windows high up in the wall. Cautiously she headed for the nearest corner and peered around it. This side of the healing den was shaped in a shallow curve. In the middle of it was a wide doorway made of transparent stuff; yellow light streamed out onto the BlackPath in front of it. As Lusa watched, a firebeast swept up to the door. Several flat-faces leaped out and unloaded another flat-face, who lay on a flat board with stiff metal legs and small round paws. The doors opened by themselves as the flat-faces approached it, and closed after they had all disappeared inside.

Great! Lusa thought, remembering that Ujurak's healing den had had doors exactly like that. *I can get in that way.*

But though Lusa waited for a long time, there was never enough time for her to slip through the doors before more flat-faces appeared, going in or out. Once she even made it far enough that the doors slid open for her, but just then another firebeast growled up behind her, making a harsh braying noise that almost made her jump out of her fur. Lusa had to gallop back into the shadows around the corner, her heart thudding.

"This is no use," she muttered, conscious of how the night was slipping by. "I'd better look for another way in."

Padding alongside the wall of the den in the opposite direction, Lusa turned the corner and was confronted by a row of shiny metal cans with lids on top. Her belly rumbled, reminding her that there had been food in cans like those beside Ujurak's healing den.

"No time," Lusa told herself firmly.

Then she noticed that there were windows in the wall just above the cans. *I might be able to get in that way, just like we got out of Ujurak's healing den.*

The sides of the cans were smooth and slippery, not at all like the rough bark of a tree. Lusa slid back down several times before she managed to scramble to the top, and her pelt tingled every time the can clanged beneath her. Bears in the forest must be able to hear her! But no flat-faces came.

She stood on top of the can and put her forepaws on the ledge below the window. The space in the wall was covered with the same transparent stuff as the big doors; beyond it Lusa could see that the den was dark and silent, with no flat-faces around. Encouraged, Lusa lifted her paws and pushed against the transparent stuff. But it didn't budge. Instead, her hindpaws slid off the top of the can and she fell, paws flailing, until she hit the ground. The can tipped over, the lid fell off, and the still night air shattered with noise. Half-stunned, Lusa looked up, terrified that flat-faces would come running to see what the racket was. Her legs were shaking as she pushed her way between another one of the cans and the wall. Panting in fear, she poked her snout out and waited to see what would happen.

When the noise died away, the night was silent again, except for the distant roar of firebeasts. No flat-faces appeared, but it was a long time before Lusa dared to emerge from cover. Clearly getting in through the window wouldn't work, so she continued her search for a way in, peering cautiously around the next corner. There she spotted another door. This one was shut, so she couldn't see what was beyond it. Several firebeasts were crouching nearby, but after she had watched them for a while from the shelter of the corner, she figured they were all asleep. Casting cautious glances at them, she trotted up to the door, expecting it to open and let her in like the transparent doors on the other side of the healing den.

"Ow!" Lusa let out a yelp of pain as her snout struck the door, which stayed obstinately closed. She raised a paw and rubbed her throbbing nose. "Stupid flat-face thing," she muttered.

When the pain had ebbed, Lusa reared up on her hindpaws and pushed at the door with her forepaws. It didn't budge. She gazed at it in frustration, then slid into the shadows beside one of the sleeping firebeasts so that she could think.

I don't believe this! I'm so close to the healing den, but I can't get inside to find the flat-face herbs that Yakone needs!

Lusa still hadn't decided what to do when she heard the sound of the door opening. Yellow light spilled out onto the ground as a flat-face emerged. He strode out, leaving the door ajar, and got into one of the sleeping firebeasts—fortunately, not the one where Lusa was hiding. The firebeast broke into a roar and opened its glaring yellow eyes. Lusa had to wait for it to move away before she dared race across to where the door was slowly closing. It shut with a mocking click a moment before Lusa reached it. Frustrated, she threw herself against the unyielding surface, then slumped to the ground in front of it.

"Oh, Arcturus! Why is *everything* going wrong?" she wailed out loud.

Lusa retreated to the shelter of the firebeast, but no more flat-faces came out of the door. At last she realized that the sky was growing paler; dawn was breaking. *I can't stay here in daylight,* Lusa thought. *The flat-faces would catch me for sure, and kill me or take me off to bear jail. What am I going to do?*

Already she could hear the sound of more firebeasts, and the voices of flat-faces coming from somewhere nearby. Stiff from crouching for so long behind the firebeast, she rose to her paws and tottered back to the gap under the shiny mesh barrier. Lusa dragged herself underneath the mesh and staggered over to the shelter of the nearest bush, where she flopped down, worn out from the tension and frustrated that her wonderful idea had come to nothing.

I can try again when it's dark, she thought wearily. *But what if*

I still can't get in? And what will the others think when I'm not back for another whole day?

"Oh, Ujurak!" she murmured. "Why did you leave us? We need you so much!"

Lusa was slipping into an exhausted, unhappy sleep when a bird swooped down over her head. Irritably, she batted at it with her front paw. The bird flapped away, then landed on the ground a bearlength in front of Lusa's snout. Blinking at the plump body and brown plumage, Lusa saw that it was a ptarmigan. Toklo had caught plenty of these in the woods on their journey; they made good eating, and this one seemed foolish enough to stay within striking distance of her paws, but Lusa was too tired even to think about catching it.

Then the bird opened its beak and spoke her name. "Lusa."

Lusa stiffened, feeling every hair on her pelt rise. "Ujurak?" she whispered. "Is that you? Am I dreaming?"

The ptarmigan began swelling up, until it was bigger than Lusa. As it grew, its feathers vanished, and brown fur covered its body like a wave washing over the seashore. It stretched upward on its legs and spread its wings as if it would take off again, then bent forward, landing on four paws. Its hard, pointed beak transformed into a soft, furry snout, and Ujurak's eyes gazed warmly at Lusa as he stood in front of her.

"Oh, Ujurak!" Lusa breathed out. "You came! Were you watching me?"

"Of course."

In spite of her joy at seeing her old friend again, frustration bubbled up inside Lusa. "Why do you always have to come and go?" she demanded. "Don't you realize we would suffer less if you just *stayed* with us?"

Ujurak's face was unreadable, but his voice was full of sympathy as he replied. "It's not for me to tell you and the others what to do. This is your journey now."

Lusa knew he was right, but that didn't help the sense of loss she felt that Ujurak wasn't making the journey with them, pawstep by pawstep. But surely if he had appeared now, he knew that they needed him?

"I can't find anything in the forest to heal Yakone," she said. "I've tried everything, but he's just getting sicker. I remembered how the flat-faces healed you after you got the fishhook stuck in your throat, and I . . . I . . ." She trailed off as she realized how foolish her idea seemed now.

Ujurak touched his snout to her shoulder. "Go on," he prompted softly.

"I came here to find a healing den, like the one where the flat-faces took you," Lusa explained in a rush. Pointing with her paw, she added, "It's that big white den over there. I thought I'd find some flat-face herbs there, like the ones they gave you. But I can't get in!" Her voice rose to a wail. "And even if I could, I don't know what I'm looking for!"

Ujurak blinked at her.

He knows it was a stupid plan, Lusa thought miserably.

But then Ujurak nodded. "That could work," he said. "It was a great idea, Lusa, and you're very brave to try it on your own."

"But I failed," Lusa whimpered. "And now Yakone will die.

Unless you can do something to help us?"

Ujurak rubbed his snout against her head. "You look so tired, little one. Just sleep now."

Lusa didn't want to sleep; she was too worried about Yakone. But exhaustion crashed over her like a massive black wave. She saw Ujurak's face, loving and confident, growing smaller and smaller until it faded away and left only darkness.

CHAPTER EIGHT

Kallik

Kallik woke in the night and looked up through the tangled branches that covered the den to see the stars twinkling high above. She could just make out Silaluk, forever running around the Pathway Star, forever fleeing from Robin, Chickadee, and Moose Bird.

Nisa told me that story in the birth den with Taqqiq, Kallik remembered. *It seems like such a long time ago.*

She shifted uncomfortably, feeling the heat that rose from Yakone's body. She wondered if she would ever see the ice again. *Should I have stayed on the Melting Sea with Taqqiq and the other white bears?* she asked herself again.

Guilt flooded over her once more. If she and Yakone had stayed, then Yakone wouldn't have been injured, and they wouldn't be stuck in this den now, like a couple of squirrels, hot and dusty and hungry. . . .

And perhaps Lusa wouldn't have been lost, either. She only went off on her own because she wanted to help Yakone.

Two sunrises had passed since Lusa left. Toklo and Kallik

hadn't dared go very far to search for her, though on the day before they had each made several short forays.

I called for her until I lost my voice, but there was no trace of her.

By the time the sun went down, Kallik had been convinced that the wolves had taken Lusa. What if they had battled over the same prey and they had killed her?

"But there's no sign of a struggle, or blood," Toklo had pointed out. "Lusa wouldn't have given up without a good fight."

Kallik had been unconvinced by his optimism. "You're assuming the wolves caught her nearby," she said. "We don't know where she went. If the wolves got her in this herb valley she was talking about, we wouldn't know."

Toklo looked troubled, unable to argue. "Then she might have met some other black bears, and gone to make her own home," he suggested.

Kallik hadn't even bothered to respond to that cloud-brained idea. Both she and Toklo knew that Lusa would never have left them without coming to say good-bye, especially when they were relying on her to help Yakone.

Now, too restless to lie still, Kallik rose to her paws. Beside her, Yakone stirred uneasily. "Come with me, Kallik," he mumbled. "Not snowing now . . . need to go find a seal hole."

"Yes, we'll do that," Kallik murmured soothingly. She couldn't bear to tell Yakone that he was lying in a dusty forest, a long, long way from his beloved ice. "Sleep for a while first. Then we'll catch a seal."

Yakone settled down again, but his breathing was labored.

Kallik remembered her dream of Nisa and Nanuk, and felt like the bear spirits were circling behind her, just out of sight, waiting.

"You can't take him yet," she hissed.

Still, the bear spirits seemed to crowd closer. Their presence was so real to Kallik that she whipped around to confront them, baring her teeth. But there was nothing to be seen.

The branches above her head rustled, and Toklo poked his nose into the den. "Is everything okay?" he asked.

"Fine," Kallik grunted. "I'm awake, so I'll take over now. You get some rest."

Toklo slid into the den and Kallik took his place outside, staring into the eerily silent forest. *Will the birds and animals ever come back?* she wondered. *Or will more and more wolves come, until they're forced to eat one another, because there's no prey left? Perhaps that's what it will take for the forest to survive.*

Kallik's ears pricked at the sound of a rustle in the bushes. She stiffened, staring in the direction of the sound, and made out the movement of branches and ferns in the undergrowth. Her belly churned at the crackling sound of pawsteps, coming nearer and nearer. Peering into the foliage in an attempt to see what was approaching, Kallik rose to her paws, but stayed where she was. She braced herself for an attack.

Closer and closer came the pawsteps. Kallik bared her teeth and raised one paw, ready to strike. *I'll fight wolves or bear spirits for Yakone's life. He belongs with me now!*

The branches in front of Kallik parted. A small black snout emerged from the bushes. Then, looking around cautiously,

Lusa trotted out. She bounded forward as soon as she spotted Kallik.

"Lusa!" Kallik barked. "Thank goodness! Where have you been?"

Lusa didn't reply at first, just pressed against Kallik and pushed her snout into her shoulder in greeting. As she drew back a pace, Kallik saw that Lusa was carrying some kind of weird pouch in her jaws: It was white, and smelled like flat-faces.

"What's that?" she asked.

Lusa set the pouch down and opened her jaws to reply, but before she spoke, a rustling behind them caught Kallik's attention; she turned and saw Toklo heaving himself out of their den.

"What's all the noise about?" he growled. "I thought—" He broke off. "Lusa! What took you so long?" he demanded, padding up to her. "You were supposed to be back last night. What were you thinking?"

Kallik knew that Toklo was only angry because he'd been so afraid for the little black bear. Lusa seemed to know it, too; she bowed her head.

"I'm sorry," she replied. "I should have told you where I was really going."

"And where was that?" Toklo hissed. "Don't give me any nonsense about herbs," he added, prodding the white pouch. "*That's* not herbs!"

Lusa looked half-scared, half-proud of herself, as she glanced from Kallik to Toklo and back again. "I went to the flat-face denning place to fetch healing stuff for Yakone," she announced.

"What?" Cold horror trickled through Kallik, as if her veins had turned to ice. "How could you—?"

"You fool!" Toklo roared, looming over Lusa. "You could have been killed! I should have come with you."

"But I didn't get killed." Lusa tipped her face up to look at the angry brown bear. "I was fine. And I saw Ujurak!"

The name of their lost friend quieted Toklo. "What happened?" he asked, his eyes wide.

He and Kallik sat down to listen, while Lusa told them how she had traveled to the flat-face place and found the healing den. "I tried and tried, but I couldn't get in," she explained. "When it started to get light, I had to leave and hide. And that's when Ujurak came. He was a bird at first, but he changed into a bear." Her voice softened. "It was so wonderful to see him . . . he's bigger now, much bigger than me."

"What did he do?" Kallik prompted.

"He told me to sleep," Lusa went on. "And when I woke up, this was lying beside me." She nodded toward the white flat-face pouch. "Ujurak must have gone into the healing den to fetch it."

"I guess he must have changed into a flat-face," Kallik said. *Oh, Ujurak! Thank you!*

"I don't know what happened," Lusa admitted. "I didn't see him again. But I know this must be what Yakone needs."

Toklo gave the pouch a dubious glance. "Okay . . . I suppose."

"Is Yakone still in the den?" Lusa asked. When Kallik nodded, she continued, "Let's take this in to him."

Kallik followed as Lusa carried the pouch through the brambles and down into the den. Toklo peered in from the top of the hollow.

"I'll stay out here," he said. "Just in case."

Yakone lay where Kallik had left him. His rasping breath was shallow and painfully fast. He didn't open his eyes as the bears crouched beside him, and Kallik saw Lusa flinch when she smelled his wound. It wasn't hard to see that Yakone was dying.

"I hope this works," Kallik whispered, half to herself. *If it doesn't, there's nothing more we can do.*

"It will." Lusa sounded confident as she pawed at the pouch until it tore, spilling out two things that looked like big seedpods, with flat-face markings on the side.

"Do you know what we have to do with those?" Kallik asked.

Lusa shook her head. "But I guess it's obvious, or Ujurak would have told me." She clawed at one of the pods until it split; a stream of tiny white seeds poured out of it. "I recognize those!" she exclaimed. "The flat-face healer in the denning place gave something like them to Ujurak."

Kallik nodded. "So we have to get him to eat them." She gave Yakone a doubtful look; he was so far into unconsciousness that she didn't think anything would rouse him.

"I know what to do. Toklo!" Lusa called up to the brown bear, who was still sitting at the edge of the den. "Can you find me a big leaf and drop it down here?"

Toklo vanished briefly and reappeared with a large leaf dangling from his jaws. As it fluttered down beside the other bears, Lusa took a mouthful of the white seeds and chewed them up, then spat them out onto the leaf.

"Yuck! Those things taste awful!" Turning to her friend, she added, "Now, Kallik, get Yakone to wake up."

Kallik wriggled up beside Yakone and nudged him. "Wake up," she murmured. "We have some food for you."

At first Yakone didn't move, but as Kallik went on prodding him, he grunted and his eyes flicked open. "You caught . . . seal?" he asked.

"No," Lusa told him. "This is better than seal."

"Nothing . . . better than seal."

"This is." Lusa pushed the leaf wrap next to his jaws. "Try it."

Yakone sighed and looked as if he was slipping back into unconsciousness. Kallik gave him another nudge. "Eat."

"Bossy . . ." Yakone muttered, but to Kallik's relief he picked up the leaf wrap between his teeth, chomped it a couple of times, and swallowed.

Lusa and Kallik exchanged a glance, with identical sighs of relief.

"What's happening?" Toklo called down. "Is it working?"

"Give it time!" Lusa responded. "Besides, we've got this other pod-thing to deal with first."

Edging back from Yakone, Kallik accidentally put her paw down on the other pod, which was long and had a silvery sheen. It split down one side and some green sticky stuff trickled out. Kallik sniffed the pungent smell. "What's that?"

Lusa sniffed it as well. "I don't know."

"I don't think Yakone should eat it," Kallik said doubtfully. "It doesn't smell like food."

Both bears stared at the green goo for a moment; then Lusa gave an excited little bounce. "I know! It looks like chewed leaves, right? So this must be to put on the wound! Toklo, more leaves down here, please!"

While they waited for Toklo, Kallik peeled off the leaves and moss that they had used to wrap Yakone's injured paw, and tried not to flinch at what she saw underneath. The wound was red and angry, blackening at the edges, and greenish pus was oozing out of it. The rotting smell made Kallik gag.

"It's getting worse," she whispered.

"But it'll be better soon," Lusa comforted her.

The leaves Toklo had fetched showered down into the den. Lusa used one of them to wipe away the worst of the pus from Yakone's paw, then slathered the wound with the green sticky stuff and wrapped the paw up in fresh leaves. She gathered up the rest of the white seeds and the pod with the green stuff and placed them tidily at the side of the den. "We'll give Yakone more when he wakes up," she said. "He should soon. . . ."

An enormous yawn cut off the rest of what Lusa meant to say.

Kallik pressed her snout into her friend's shoulder. "Get some sleep," she said. "You must be exhausted after going all that way. And thank you, Lusa . . . it was a terrible risk, and I know you did it all for Yakone."

"Thank me when he's better," Lusa said muzzily as she curled up on the floor of the den. Moments later she was asleep.

Kallik stayed beside Yakone, knowing that it was safe to sleep because Toklo was on watch, but wanting to fix her gaze on Yakone, assessing every breath, every slight movement, to see if he was getting better.

After a while she dozed, and woke to find sunlight seeping into the den. At once she realized that Yakone's breathing was slower and deeper, and the noisy rasping had died away. She reached out to touch his nose and found that it was cool again. As if the touch had disturbed him he shifted, but seemed only to be making himself more comfortable before settling into sleep again.

"He's getting better. . . ." Kallik murmured, hardly daring to believe it.

Once again she was aware of the bear spirits behind her, but now they were quieter, and Kallik sensed that they were watching over Yakone as he healed, instead of waiting to take him away. She didn't look around, wanting to keep her eyes on Yakone, but suddenly she was glad of their presence. They felt comforting now, friendly rather than challenging.

"Thank you for leaving him with me," she whispered.

CHAPTER NINE

Toklo

Toklo headed through the trees to hunt, with Lusa pattering alongside him. Sunlight slanted through the branches and danced on the forest floor. The air was full of the scents of fresh growth, and though Toklo couldn't detect any prey, there was no smell of wolves, either.

They had left Kallik in the makeshift den watching over Yakone, who was still sleeping deeply after the flat-face healing stuff. He was much quieter, his breathing stronger, and his fur didn't feel so hot, but Toklo was still reluctant to allow himself to hope.

Relying on flat-faces is too weird!

"We shouldn't go that way," Lusa said after a few moments. "We'll end up in territory that belongs to another brown bear. I think it might be Old Grizzly's." She shuddered. "I think I saw him the other day, just after I left you. He was *huge!*"

"Okay." Toklo turned in the other direction. He had no desire to steal prey from other hungry bears in the forest.

"Do you recognize this place from when you were a cub?"

Lusa asked as they padded onward.

Toklo hesitated. "I'm not sure," he confessed at last. "One moment things seem familiar, and then the next everything is strange. I've been waiting so long to come back, but I . . . I don't feel like I've come home."

Lusa brushed her pelt comfortingly against his side. "I don't suppose I would recognize the Bear Bowl," she said. "We've been away for much longer than we were ever at our first homes."

But I'm a wild *bear!* Toklo thought. *That's not the same as being born in a flat-face den. This is where I belong, so I should be able to remember it.* He stifled the urge to say so out loud. It might sound rude, especially now that Lusa was a wild bear, too, through and through.

Toklo was beginning to be irritated by the lack of prey, and nervous that they had left Yakone and Kallik alone for a long time, when he heard a faint buzzing. He ignored it, until Lusa exclaimed, "Bees!"

Toklo sighed. "Great. Bees. They'll really fill our bellies."

"Not the bees, fur-brain!" Lusa gave Toklo a poke in the shoulder. "Honey!"

She stood still for a moment, listening until she pinpointed the direction of the sound, then took off through the trees at a trot. Stifling a groan, Toklo followed.

Lusa stopped at the foot of a tree, looking up. A dark hole gaped about halfway up the trunk; bees were flying in and out of it. "Honey!" she repeated, swiping her tongue around her jaws.

While Toklo watched, she raced up the tree trunk and thrust her head into the hole. The sound of buzzing grew louder and more angry, and Toklo heard a faint yelp of pain from Lusa inside the tree. He sighed. *It's not my fault you're getting stung.*

When Lusa withdrew her head from the hole, her snout was covered in golden sticky stuff. Her eyes shone. "It's delicious!" she exclaimed. "Here, Toklo, wait a moment."

Lusa poked one paw into the hole and clawed out a lump of honeycomb, which she dropped to the ground at Toklo's paws. Then she stuck her head back in the hole.

Toklo tasted the honeycomb, letting the sweet honey trickle between his jaws. Then he gulped the rest of it down and waited for Lusa to scramble down the tree. While he waited, he realized that some of the honey was sticking to his snout, while some of it had dripped onto his paws. He licked at it, but it still clung to his pelt and made his fur stick up in spikes.

Lusa dropped to the ground beside him. "Wasn't that good?"

"It was okay," Toklo grumbled, not wanting to admit that he'd enjoyed the sweet taste. "But it's sticking all over my pelt. And you got stung."

"It was worth it!" Lusa insisted, her eyes gleaming.

Toklo huffed. "Let's keep going and find some *real* prey."

To Toklo's relief, he picked up the scent of grouse almost as soon as they set off again. At the same moment he heard the sound of frantic fluttering and spotted the bird trapped in a bramble thicket. With a roar of satisfaction, Toklo pounded toward the grouse. But as he reached the thicket, ready to plunge in, he found himself face-to-face with the brown she-bear he had met in the meadow two days before.

The she-bear thrust her snout at him with a snarl. "Back off! This prey is mine."

Toklo felt his fur bristling with anger. "Yours? I didn't notice any scent marks. This isn't your territory!"

For a moment the she-bear looked disconcerted. "Well . . . no, it's not quite my territory. But I live here and you don't!" she went on, recovering. "So I have the right to hunt wherever I like!"

For some reason, Toklo found her defiance funny, especially when the grouse wriggled free from the brambles and escaped right under their noses. He couldn't stifle a snort of amusement.

"What are you sniggering about, bee-brain?" the she-bear growled.

Before Toklo could reply, Lusa popped up at his side, peering at the she-bear with friendly interest. "Hi," she said.

The brown she-bear reared back, startled. "A *black* bear?"

"Well spotted," Toklo grunted.

Lusa looked from Toklo to the she-bear and back again. "What were you fighting about?" she asked. "Do you know each other from before?"

The she-bear blinked in shock. "Before when?"

"I was born here," Toklo explained. "But then I left. I've traveled a long way since then, and now I'm back."

"Why did you leave?" the she-bear asked, her angry tone

giving way to curiosity. "Where's your mother?"

Like I'm going to tell her everything about Oka and Tobi, Toklo thought. "It's just me now," he replied. He was relieved when the she-bear didn't press him any further; in fact, her eyes softened.

"What's your name?" Lusa prompted.

"Aiyanna," the she-bear replied, and added, "It means 'ever-blooming.' My mother said she called me that because I made her happy, like she was reborn. Then . . . then she died," she ended sadly.

Toklo felt a stab of sympathy, though he didn't let himself show it. *So we both know what it's like to lose our mother.*

Lusa padded up to Aiyanna and rested her snout on the brown bear's shoulder. "I'm Lusa," she said. "And this is Toklo. Can you tell us anything about the wolves?"

Aiyanna shrugged; though she wasn't outwardly aggressive any longer, she still seemed wary. "Not much. They came during the cold season. I guess they were hungry and searching for new hunting grounds. And now it seems like they've decided to stay."

"So what do you do about them?" Lusa pressed.

Aiyanna raised her head proudly. "Like I told your friend, I have my ways of dealing with them."

Toklo guessed that Aiyanna wasn't going to share too many details about her life with strangers. *We're just wasting time.*

"Come on," he said to Lusa. "We have to hunt."

"Okay." Lusa dipped her head to Aiyanna. "It was nice meeting you."

Aiyanna dipped her head in response and stood watching Toklo and Lusa as they strode away and veered uphill, skirting the edge of the meadow where Toklo had first met Aiyanna.

"She's nice," Lusa commented.

Toklo let out a snort. "Not really. She tried to run us off, and we weren't even on her territory!"

"We weren't far off it," Lusa pointed out, snuffling around at the foot of a pine tree. "I can pick up her scent here, so this must be her border."

"Then we'd better stay clear of it," Toklo muttered.

Shortly they came to a stream that gurgled softly downhill, between banks thick with pine needles. Toklo leaped across it and halted in front of a twisted tree with branches spreading upward like the antlers of a deer.

"I know that tree!" he exclaimed, his heart beginning to thump.

Lusa bounded over the stream and came to stand beside him. "Were you here when you were a cub?"

Toklo nodded, as memories crowded in upon him.

Tobi and I stalked that tree, he thought. *We pretended it was a deer, and we killed it and took our prey back to Oka.*

Padding slowly around the tree, he stopped beside a thick patch of fern. *That's the only time I can remember that Tobi played a prank on me! He hid and jumped out at me, and I slipped and fell right into those ferns.* Toklo bent his head, letting the memories flood him. *Tobi laughed and laughed! He wasn't feeling so ill that day. . . .*

For a few moments the pictures were so vivid that Toklo

almost expected to find Oka and Tobi standing beside him. *But it was a long time ago. . . .*

"Are you okay?" Lusa asked, pressing her snout into Toklo's shoulder fur.

"Yes, I'm fine," Toklo replied. "I was just thinking about how I played with Tobi. . . ."

Lusa's eyes were understanding. "Oka was sad and afraid when I knew her in the Bear Bowl," she murmured. "But it's good to know she was happy with you once."

Toklo found it hard to think about Oka and concentrated instead on the memories with his brother that were rushing in on him with all the force of the waterfall where they had hidden from the wolves.

"See that path over there?" He pointed to a narrow path that wound up the hillside between the trees. "It goes past that dead tree up there, and then around a rock, and comes out on a patch of ground below an overhanging rock. There are berry bushes and moss over there. Lusa, that's where Tobi is buried!"

Toklo's heart was pounding even harder now, and he was almost afraid of how clear and strong his memories had suddenly become, and how certain he was that this was the right place.

"Wow!" Lusa exclaimed. "Do you want to go see it?"

Toklo nodded. His paws were carrying him along the path almost before he realized it. He could picture the small burial mound as clearly as if he stood in front of it.

But when he came to the dead tree, its black,

lightning-blasted trunk was marked strongly with Aiyanna's scent. Toklo came to a halt. "This is Aiyanna's territory," he said. For a long moment he hesitated, then turned away. "We can't go there." At Lusa's look of surprise, he added, "I don't want to make her angry for no good reason."

"But it is a good reason!" Lusa protested. "You deserve to see where your brother is buried."

For a moment Toklo stood undecided, still gazing up the path. *It's not far. Aiyanna would never know. . . . But she might pick up my scent, and then she'd think she couldn't trust me.*

As much as he hated to admit it, Toklo had a grudging respect for the she-bear, and for how she had carved out her own territory, even though she was so young. And he didn't want to make enemies where he didn't have to, not if he was planning to find a territory of his own near here.

Sighing, he turned away, heading past Lusa and back down the path. "I'll ask Aiyanna the next time I see her," he decided. "I don't want to get into a fight over this."

Even as he retreated, he felt as if every muscle in his body, every hair on his pelt, was pulling him toward his brother's burial mound. But he remembered Aiyanna's defiant gaze and how ready she had been to fight, even though he was bigger and stronger than her. *If I go to visit Tobi, it has to be with Aiyanna's permission.*

Setting a faster pace, in case he was tempted to go back, Toklo plunged downhill again, following the course of the stream with Lusa scrambling after him. Their path led them through thick green undergrowth, which tugged at their pelts and dotted them with leaves. Toklo began to relax.

"This feels more like home!" he murmured.

"But it's still way too quiet," Lusa pointed out.

Toklo had to admit she was right, although when they reached the valley bottom he could hear more birdsong, and there were hints of prey-scent in the air.

"Maybe the wolves haven't hunted this far yet," Lusa suggested.

Toklo let out a grunt. "If they haven't, it's only a matter of time."

He still hadn't tracked down any prey when Lusa halted, pointing with her snout to a spot on the other side of the stream. "That looks like a place where we might find good herbs for Yakone," she said. "I know we've got the flat-face stuff, but I want the big, soothing leaves that are good for wrapping his paw."

Without waiting for a response from Toklo, she waded across the stream, which was wider and deeper here. Rocks jutted out on the other side; Lusa had to pad along a narrow ledge between the boulders and the water.

"Lusa, watch out!" Toklo called.

Lusa waved a paw before vanishing around a bend, where a rocky outcrop cut her off from sight. A moment later Toklo heard her squeal in shock.

"Lusa!" he called. *Great spirits! What has the bee-brain done now?*

Toklo plunged into the stream and raced after his friend, stumbling and slipping and casting up waves in his haste to reach her. As he skidded around the bend, he spotted Lusa standing safely on dry land, staring at two small brown heads that were peeping over the top of a rock.

"Look, Toklo! Bear cubs!" she exclaimed.

Toklo heaved himself out of the stream and padded over to join Lusa, water pouring from his fur. As he bent his head to sniff the little cubs, both of them bared their teeth, growling fiercely, and showed their tiny claws.

"Stay away from us!" the bigger cub warned him. "We'll fight you if we have to!"

Toklo let out a grunt, admiring the small bear's courage.

"We're not going to hurt you, little ones," Lusa assured them. "Are you here on your own?"

"Yes, we—" the smaller cub began.

Her littermate turned on her. "Shut up!" she growled, and gave her sister a cuff around the ear.

"It's okay," the smaller cub retorted, swiping back at her sister. "Mama told us to look out for wolves, not bears."

The bigger cub rolled her eyes. "Like bears aren't dangerous!"

"Mama went off to hunt," the smaller cub went on, clearly unafraid and happy to chat. "She'll be back soon. She made us hide in case the wolves attack while she's gone."

"Yes," her sister hissed. "That means *hide*, fur-brain!"

The smaller cub ignored her. "I *want* the wolves to attack," she confided. "Then I can show them how strong and fierce I am! Watch!"

Springing up on top of the rock, she reared up on her hind-paws and batted at the air with tiny, soft forepaws. "Take that, wolf!" she squeaked. "Run away, or I'll eat—"

She broke off with a yelp of surprise as she lost her balance and slipped off the rock into the stream.

Her sister leaped up, but Lusa blocked her before she could reach the water to help her littermate. "It's okay," she said. "Toklo will get her."

Toklo leaned out over the stream and gripped the smaller cub's scruff in his teeth when she came up for air. The cub flailed her paws as Toklo plopped her down onto the rock again.

"That was *amazing*!" she squealed. "Did you see me swimming?" She shook herself vigorously, splattering her sister with drops of water.

"Get back under cover," the other cub said, giving her a gentle shove into the hollow where they had been hiding. Looking back at Toklo, her gaze still wary, she added, "Thank you for helping. She's too little to understand. She doesn't even know what a wolf *is*."

Toklo fought with a sudden pang of memory. *I was like that once, protecting my brother.* "You should look after each other," he said. "But I haven't seen any wolves near here, so you should be safe today."

Dipping his head, Toklo was turning away when Lusa protested, "Can't we stay and play with them?"

"Oh, yes!" The smaller cub's head bobbed up again. "Teach us some new games!"

Toklo shook his head. "We need to find leaves for Yakone, and food for all of us," he reminded Lusa. *And when the mother bear turns up, she might not believe that we're only playing.*

As Toklo padded away, followed reluctantly by Lusa, the feelings of amusement and admiration he had felt for the cubs faded, and black depression crept over him.

Bear cubs shouldn't have to hide when their mother goes hunting! They should be able to play, and learn how to hunt for themselves, like Tobi and I did. This should be bear territory, but it's turned into a forest of wolves.

CHAPTER TEN

Lusa

Lusa dug down into the ground and unearthed a pawful of juicy fern roots. "Tasty!" she mumbled as she chewed them.

She was keeping a lookout among the trees beside the den, while Toklo hunted and Kallik watched over Yakone. Three sunrises had passed since Lusa returned with the flat-face herbs, and the white bear still did nothing but sleep. Lusa had given him the rest of the white seeds, and dressed his wound again with the green sticky stuff. There was no more pus oozing out of it, although it still looked red and angry. But Yakone hadn't moved and didn't seem to want to wake up. Kallik was starting to look exhausted with worry, and Lusa was afraid she would get sick, too.

She turned over a fallen tree branch and licked up the grubs that she found underneath, then padded in a wide circle around the den, sniffing the air for wolves and looking for their pawprints.

"Nothing," she murmured with a sigh of relief.

As she approached the den once more, she heard Kallik

calling out, her voice full of excitement. "Lusa! Are you there? Come and see who's awake!"

Lusa scrambled down into the den to see Yakone half sitting up. He was chewing on a squirrel bone from a recent catch of Toklo's, and he looked much better, though he had a confused expression in his eyes.

"How do you feel?" Lusa asked him, exchanging a delighted glance with Kallik.

"Strange," Yakone replied, rubbing one paw over his ears. "Like someone's given me a new head. Everything feels like it's under water."

"And your paw?" Lusa prompted him.

Yakone looked down at the injured paw, still in its leaf wrapping. "I haven't looked yet," he admitted.

"Come on." Lusa gave him a gentle shove. "You know you have to one day. It might as well be now."

"Do you remember what happened?" Kallik asked.

"I remember the trap," Yakone growled with a shudder. "And I know I lost half my paw. But I don't really remember what the wound looks like."

After a moment's hesitation he held out the paw to Lusa, who unwrapped the leaves, feeling slightly worried about what she was going to see. Yakone winced, and started to draw his paw back, as if he was worried, too, then stopped and let Lusa finish.

But this time the bad smell had gone, leaving only the sharp tang of the green sticky stuff. The wound had closed up and looked clean and pale.

"The flat-face herbs worked!" Lusa breathed.

"I told Yakone what you did for him," Kallik said.

"Yeah, thanks for that." Yakone dipped his head toward Lusa. "You were really brave."

Lusa shrugged, feeling hot with embarrassment. "I had to try everything I could to make you better," she told Yakone. "I couldn't have done it without Ujurak."

"I'll thank him, too, the next time I see him," Yakone promised. "If I recognize him!" His gaze flicked to his injured paw and he held it up, examining it with a look of horror in his eyes. "I didn't realize how much of my paw I lost in the trap," he said.

"It's not so bad," Kallik assured him, brushing against him comfortingly.

"But I'm missing two toes!" Yakone hunched his shoulders. "How am I going to cope without them?"

"You should be glad that you're alive!" Kallik told him; Lusa could see that her instinct to comfort Yakone was giving way to frustration. "We defended you against coyotes and wolves, Lusa risked her life going among flat-faces, and you're upset about a couple of toes?"

Yakone met her gaze and heaved a deep sigh. "But how can I hunt with only half a paw?"

"You haven't even tried yet," Lusa pointed out. "Come on, Yakone, stand up and start walking."

Yakone shook his head. "I'm too tired," he said. "Maybe I'll try tomorrow."

Lusa opened her jaws to encourage him, then closed them

again. *He's been so sick; it's bound to take him time to recover.*

But on the following day Yakone still wouldn't venture out of the den. "I feel too shaky," he said. "I need a day or two to build up my strength."

"But he won't build up his strength if he doesn't move," Lusa told Toklo as they shared a squirrel under the tree outside the den. "Somehow he just doesn't want to."

Toklo shook his head, baffled. "That doesn't make sense! He isn't sick anymore, so he must be dying to go hunting."

"I know." Lusa was just as puzzled by Yakone's strange behavior. "He's always been brave and strong. So why won't he try walking?"

"It beats me," Toklo confessed, crunching up the last mouthful of squirrel. "But we can't hang around here forever. Sooner or later, Yakone has to—"

He broke off with a grunt as Kallik exploded out of the den. "He won't listen, and he won't *do* anything!" she complained. "I'm at my wits' end. I'm going hunting." She stormed away into the trees.

"Wait!" Lusa called, bounding after her. "I'll come with you."

Kallik slowed down to let Lusa catch up. "I'm so worried," the white bear admitted. "Yakone is better! His paw has healed, and he isn't hot anymore. But nothing I say to him makes any difference. He won't try to walk."

"Give him another day," Lusa suggested.

"And another day after that? Lusa . . ." Kallik paused.

Lusa touched her nose to Kallik's shoulder. "Go on."

Kallik took a deep breath. "What *really* bothers me . . . Well, what if Yakone's illness has changed him somehow? Made him into an old bear, who doesn't want to hunt or look after himself?"

"But he—" Lusa began, only to break off as Kallik swept onward.

"We won't survive if Yakone has given up! He has to be strong enough to get back to the ice!"

Lusa felt a deep stab of concern. *There has to be a reason Yakone is like this,* she thought. *What is he afraid of? More traps? Coyotes? Wolves? If I could figure out what it is, then maybe I could help.*

That night Lusa curled up to sleep beside Yakone while Kallik was outside, keeping watch for wolves. Toklo was a snoring hump at the far side of the den. *Do all brown bears make that much racket at night?* Lusa wondered, though she had to admit that it wasn't only Toklo who was keeping her awake. Her worry about Yakone was like the stinging of a thousand bees.

Lusa realized that the white bear was muttering in his sleep. At first it was only a low murmur, but gradually she began to distinguish separate words.

"Too slow . . . too slow . . ." Yakone shifted uncomfortably, patting the floor of the den with his injured paw as if he was dreaming of walking. "Can't run . . ." He brought his paw down with a slap on the ground. "Missed it!"

Lusa couldn't help wondering if the fears that Yakone was determined to hide from his friends during the day were coming out now, in his dreams.

"I can't . . . do . . . it!" Yakone's voice was muffled by the leaf mulch beneath him.

Lusa sat bolt upright. Yakone wasn't scared of traps or coyotes. *He's afraid that he'll never walk and hunt properly again.*

"That's it," she whispered to herself. "He's scared to try!"

"No . . . no . . ." Yakone muttered. "Can't hunt . . . leave me . . . too slow . . ."

Surely he doesn't want us to give up on him! Lusa thought, shocked. *Leave him behind, while we carry on without him? He must know that will never happen!*

But Lusa could understand how Yakone didn't want to be their weak link, especially in a place where there were wolves and hostile bears. A stab of pity shot through her. *There has to be a way to show him that he can still walk. . . .*

Lusa slept at last and woke to Kallik's voice, sounding exasperated.

"Yakone, you have to eat something!"

Opening her eyes, Lusa saw Kallik standing over Yakone, the body of a grouse on the floor of the den between them. Yakone gave it a glance, then dropped his nose on his paws and closed his eyes. Lusa could almost taste his misery on the air.

"Please, Yakone!" Kallik begged. "If you won't eat—"

Yakone's eyes flew open again. "Stop fussing!" he snapped. "I'm not a cub. If I can't hunt, I don't deserve to eat."

Kallik recoiled. "Fine!" she hissed. "Starve if you want! Just think about yourself. It's all you ever do." With a snort of fury, she scrambled out of the den.

Yakone let his nose drop to his paws, but Lusa could see the pain in his eyes and knew how much he hated hurting Kallik. Toklo, who had woken during the argument, opened his jaws to speak, but Lusa shook her head at him and beckoned him to follow her out of the den.

"I've got an idea," she told him, when they were both standing outside the den. "I want you to go hunting."

Toklo gaped at her; he was still barely awake, and Lusa could tell he was in a grouchy mood. "Are you bee-brained?" he grumbled. "Kallik has gone storming off to the spirits know where, and you want me to leave you alone with Yakone? No chance!"

"It's daylight. We'll be fine," Lusa pointed out. "And it won't be for long. I just have to find Kallik and tell her—"

"Lusa!" Toklo interrupted. "That'll mean Yakone is left on his own. You can't do that!"

Lusa bit back a hiss of irritation. "Just trust me," she said. "If it worries you, then hide in the bushes over there. Only don't come out, whatever happens or whatever I say. My plan won't work unless Yakone thinks he's alone."

Toklo hesitated, then let out a sigh. "Okay. But if any wolves turn up, you bet I'm coming out!" He plodded off to the thicket.

When Toklo was gone, Lusa picked up Kallik's scent trail and followed it until she reached the edge of a stream. Kallik had flopped down in the shallow water, her eyes half-closed.

Lusa sat on the bank beside her. "Hi," she said. "I have an idea about Yakone."

Kallik gave her a dispirited glance, shaking her head.

"Whatever it is, it won't work. He's ready to lie down and die in that den. I've done all I can."

"Give him one more chance," Lusa urged her. "He's only acting like this because he doesn't want to hurt you anymore."

Kallik half sat up, water streaming from her pelt. "Huh?"

"I think Yakone is afraid of being too weak to keep up with us, or protect us," Lusa explained. "He's afraid to try walking in case he can't." She could see Kallik was unconvinced.

"Well, he's being ridiculous!" the white bear said.

"Just think about how much he gave up to be with us," Lusa reminded her. "To be with you. His family, his home on Star Island . . . He's been so strong, so brave in getting this far. How can he imagine a future when he isn't as strong?"

Kallik blinked. She rose to her paws and clambered out of the stream. "I hadn't thought about it like that. Maybe you're right. I'm going to go to the stupid cloud-brain right now and tell him that it's okay."

"No!" Lusa raised a paw to stop her friend. "Stay here. I'll bring him to you."

Kallik looked bewildered. "How?" she asked.

Lusa gave an excited little bounce. "Just wait and see!"

Charging through the trees, Lusa burst into the den as if all the wolves in the forest were chasing after her. "Toklo!" she gasped. "Come quick! Kallik is trapped under a rockfall!"

But only Yakone was in the den; Lusa was relieved to see that Toklo had obeyed her and stayed hidden in the bushes.

Yakone sat up, alarm in his eyes. "What happened?" he barked.

"Kallik is stuck under a rock," Lusa panted. "It rolled down the bank of the stream on top of her. I can't lift it! You'll have to come and help."

Terror flashed into the white bear's eyes. For a moment he hesitated; then he hauled himself to his paws. Staggering, his chest heaving with deep breaths, he took a pace or two across the den floor. *Yes! You can do it!* Lusa shouted in her mind, though outwardly she remained silent, afraid of distracting Yakone.

Limping badly, but with his jaw set determinedly, Yakone lurched forward and dragged himself out of the den. "Which way?" he demanded as Lusa scrambled after him.

"Follow me!"

Lusa headed back toward the stream where she had left Kallik. Inside she was fizzing with excitement, but she forced herself to go slowly, giving Yakone the chance to figure out how to balance on three and a half paws. He stumbled along, muttering angrily as he tripped over stones or collided with trees, but he kept going. Gradually he picked up speed, still limping, but getting used to the different motion.

As they approached the stream, Lusa heard Kallik's voice. "Yakone! Is that you?"

"I'm coming!" Yakone roared in reply. "Wait there!"

"What?" Kallik asked, appearing from behind a tree.

Yakone let out a huff of relief. "You freed yourself!"

"Freed myself?" Kallik sounded puzzled. "I wasn't stuck anywhere."

Yakone turned to stare at Lusa, who faced him boldly. "I

knew you would be able to walk," she said. "I just had to find a way to prove it to you. I knew you'd do anything for Kallik if she was in danger, so she was the answer."

For a moment both white bears gave Lusa identical glares. Yakone limped a step forward to loom over her. "So that story about Kallik pinned underneath a rock—you made that up?"

Lusa nodded. "Sorry—but it worked, didn't it?"

Kallik's eyes widened. "You told him I was in danger, to get him out of the den? Lusa, that was—was—"

"Clever?" Lusa suggested.

Kallik relaxed and gave a snort of amusement. "I guess it was. Thanks, Lusa."

Yakone still looked upset. "Well, I feel like a real cloud-brain," he muttered. "Lurching along like that . . . and all for nothing!"

"It wasn't for nothing," Kallik soothed him, padding to his side and pressing her snout against his shoulder. "It showed you what you can do. I'm so proud of you!"

A low growl rose in Yakone's throat, and he tossed his head as if he was getting rid of a troublesome fly. But when he looked back at Lusa, his eyes were warm again. "I suppose you're right," he mumbled. "Thanks."

As he finished speaking he staggered, and Lusa realized that despite his ability to walk, he was still weak and frail. She and Kallik moved swiftly to support him on either side.

"No, I can manage," Yakone insisted, drawing away from them. "Let's get back to the den."

He took the lead, testing out his wounded paw to find out

the best way of setting it down. At first Kallik padded close beside him, ready to help him if he fell.

"You have to let him trip, I think," Lusa told her quietly. "You can't support him all the time."

"She's right," Yakone agreed. "I'll tell you if I can't manage, and we'll stop for a rest."

But Yakone kept going all the way back to the den. Lusa could see that he still had a long way to go before he was completely recovered, but he had taken the first important pawsteps.

Kallik fell back to pad alongside Lusa. "Thank you for understanding us all so well," she murmured, brushing her snout across Lusa's head fur. "Sometimes you're as wise as Ujurak!"

CHAPTER ELEVEN

Kallik

Kallik watched Yakone as he lumbered away from her down the path that led to the stream, skirted a bramble thicket, and headed back toward her.

"That was great!" she praised him as he approached her, panting. "You're much faster than you were yesterday."

Two sunrises had passed since Lusa had forced Yakone out of the den. Since then he had hardly stopped practicing with his changed paw.

Thank the spirits! Kallik thought. *And thank you, Lusa.*

"I need to work on turning," Yakone said, halting beside Kallik. He sounded worried, as though he didn't realize how much he was improving. "I can't put as much weight on this paw as I used to. It's making me clumsy and slowing me down."

Kallik nodded. "Why not try running in a circle . . . say, around a tree? That way you're turning all the time."

"Great idea!" Yakone's belly rumbled. "All this exercise is making me hungry."

He limped away toward a pine tree with a clear space

around it. Kallik was glad Yakone had his appetite back. She had been relieved when he had started to eat again, as if he knew he couldn't expect to carry himself around when he was half-starved. Now he was starting to fill out under his loose fur.

Yakone hobbled several times around the tree, and Kallik noticed how his gait had changed; he was taking smaller pawsteps and seemed reluctant to put the maimed paw to the ground, while his hind legs stayed slightly bent, as though they were taking more weight.

At last he stopped and flopped down, sticking his injured leg out to one side. "Stupid paw," he muttered. "It won't do what I want it to do."

Kallik padded up to him and pressed her snout into his shoulder. "Give it time."

Yakone let out an irritable snort. "Time! That's what we don't have. How can I hunt, or fight a pack of wolves or a hostile bear when I'm in this state? What kind of bear am I going to be?"

Letting out a soothing rumble from deep within her chest, Kallik sat beside him. "You won't know until you try. But trust me, you're still a big, scary bear."

"Ha! I wouldn't scare a mouse like this."

"Why don't we try something else?" Kallik suggested, anxious not to let Yakone slip back into depression. "You haven't practiced jumping yet."

"Jumping?" Yakone huffed out a breath. "I'm not sure I'll ever jump again."

"Of course you will," Kallik reassured him. *Traveling will be impossible if he can't jump.* "Look, there's a fallen tree branch over there. See if you can get over that."

For a moment Kallik was afraid that Yakone would refuse. Then he heaved a long sigh and dragged himself to his paws. "You're not going to stop nagging, are you?" he asked.

"Nope." Kallik butted him gently with her head. "That's what I'm here for."

Yakone gave her a long-suffering look, then headed toward the tree branch. As he approached it, he quickened his pace, but he misjudged his takeoff and landed on top of the branch instead of on the other side.

"Fish-breath!" he snorted, disentangling himself from the twigs and dead leaves. He turned to glare at Kallik. "See? I can't jump."

"You jumped just fine," Kallik retorted. "You misjudged the distance, that's all. Try again."

Yakone grunted, then limped away from the branch and turned to practice the jump again. This time he took an extra pace before pushing off, and soared over the branch, his hindpaws just brushing the twigs as he passed over them. He stumbled on landing, but soon recovered.

"Hey, that wasn't bad!" he exclaimed.

"It was great," Kallik told him. "Now do it again."

Yakone turned toward her with a growl. For a moment Kallik thought he was really angry with her, until she saw the amusement in his eyes. "You never let up," he said, swiping playfully at her.

"I thought you said you couldn't fight." A bubble of joy swelled up inside Kallik. "Watch out, scary bear!"

Letting out a roar, she leaped on top of Yakone, and the two of them wrestled happily on the forest floor. Kallik could feel that Yakone wasn't as strong as before, but she knew that his muscles would build up quickly now that he was moving again.

Suddenly Yakone let out a grunt and pulled away from Kallik.

"What's the matter?" Kallik asked, sitting up and shaking forest debris from her pelt.

"Nothing," Yakone replied. "I stubbed my hurt paw, that's all. It's fine."

A stab of alarm pierced through Kallik as she scanned his injury. *The wound isn't bleeding again.*

Yakone touched his snout to her shoulder. "I know you wish you could take some of the pain for me," he murmured.

"I'd take it all if I could," she whispered, leaning into him.

They stayed like that for a moment, drawing comfort from each other, until Kallik heard the sound of voices approaching through the trees. She rose to her paws as Toklo and Lusa appeared.

Toklo had a goose dangling from his jaws; Lusa was bouncing along beside him, clearly excited about something. When she spotted Kallik and Yakone, she rushed over to them.

"We went really far!" she exclaimed. "Almost to the top of the ridge! Did you know there's snow up there?"

Kallik's heart leaped at the thought of being surrounded by

cold, cold snow. She could almost feel it under her pads, the crackling surface breaking to reveal the softness below, and smell its wild, icy scent. "Really? Snow?" she asked.

Toklo nodded. "Yes," he replied, dropping his prey. "There's still some of it left on the peaks, though I don't think it'll be there for long. Come on, let's share this goose. My belly thinks my throat's been clawed out."

Kallik praised Toklo's catch while he tore it into four portions, but the mention of snow had distracted her, and she couldn't summon up much appetite.

"Kallik, you're not eating," Yakone said anxiously. "Are you okay?"

Kallik forced herself to gulp down a mouthful. "Everything's fine," she assured him.

That night in the den, Kallik dreamed that she was back on the ice, crunching over the surface with the black ocean rolling beneath her paws and a cold wind blowing through her pelt. Yakone was beside her, striding along as easily as if he had never been injured. Her brother Taqqiq was with her, too, and their mother Nisa. Kallik was relieved that Nisa no longer seemed interested in taking Yakone away.

Then as Kallik gazed across the ice, she spotted other bears, a little farther away: Nanuk; and Kissimi, the cub she had rescued on Star Island; and all the bears they had met on the Melting Sea. They were padding along beneath the glittering night sky, the stars so bright that they cast an eerie glow over the snow.

This is where I belong, Kallik thought; she felt as if her blissful happiness would spill out around her, because her whole body wasn't big enough to contain it.

"Wolves! Wolves!"

Lusa's voice jerked Kallik out of her dream. Scrambling to her paws, she saw that Toklo and Yakone were awake, too. Lusa was peering down at them from the top of the den; in the dim light Kallik could see that her eyes were wide and scared.

"Wolves!" Lusa repeated. "They're circling the den! They must be able to smell the remains of that goose."

"How many?" Toklo barked.

"I'm not sure." Lusa's voice was shaking. "A lot."

Howling broke out as she spoke, seeming to come from every direction at once. Kallik's heart began to pound.

Yakone started to clamber out of the den, but Toklo blocked him. "No—let them come to us," he ordered. "They'll get trapped in the brambles, and we can take them then. Out there, we'll be outnumbered." Beckoning to Lusa, he added, "Lusa, get your tail down here. We don't have anything to defend but ourselves, so let's stick together."

Lusa slid down into the den and thrust herself into a prickly bush that grew on one side. Toklo took up a position just below the entrance. The howling died down, and briefly Kallik hoped that the wolves had gone, realizing there was no prey in the den.

Then a fearsome snarling ripped the night, and a lean, gray shadow appeared at the opening of the den. Roaring, Toklo leaped upward, lashing out with claws and teeth. The wolf vanished, but a moment later more of them loomed out of the darkness. They were all around the den, trying to force their way through the brambles, letting out furious snarls and yelps as the prickly tendrils tore at their fur.

Kallik drew closer to Yakone, desperately afraid that his injury wasn't healed enough to fight.

"Don't worry about me! I can fight for myself!" he told her, letting out a bellow as he flung himself at the nearest wolf.

Kallik felt a moment's joy at Yakone's recovery of confidence and power before the wolves were upon her, and there was no more time for thought. The night filled up with howling and snapping teeth, the trampling of paws and the crashing of bodies thrusting through the protective undergrowth. The wolves seemed convinced the bears had something they wanted.

Back-to-back with Yakone, Kallik tried to defend the rear of the den. She was battered on all sides by wolves that sprang out of the darkness, their teeth bared as they tried to sink their jaws into her pelt. Her thick fur helped to protect her, but she knew that her white coloring made her a target. The wolves, gray as the shadows, were almost invisible to her, but she struck out at them and felt a fierce satisfaction when her claws connected with flesh.

A wolf leaped on top of her and Kallik staggered, knowing that if she fell, she would feel its fangs in her throat. Recovering, she flung it off and bit down hard on its sinewy gray shoulder. The wolf yelped, tore itself away, and vanished into the darkness. Kallik spat out a mouthful of fur and plunged forward to drive off the next attacker.

Briefly she caught a glimpse of Lusa, lashing out from the

shelter of her bush whenever a wolf got too near. Her black fur hid her, so her attacks seemed to come out of nowhere.

Kallik had no idea how long she stood there in the den, slamming her paws down on any wolf that came within reach. Gradually the night grew quieter, and the wolves weren't attacking so fiercely. But she didn't let herself relax. Determined to keep going, she kept on aiming blows at shadows that seemed to melt into the darkness.

When she felt a paw land heavily on her shoulder, Kallik spun around and reared up, ready to strike down with all her strength.

"Wait!" Yakone exclaimed, pulling out of the way. "It's me. You can stop fighting now. The wolves have gone."

While Yakone was speaking, a roar came from Toklo as he struck a double blow with both forepaws around the head of the last wolf, which turned tail and fled yowling out of the den. "And don't come back!" Toklo bellowed after it.

Kallik relaxed, her gaze traveling anxiously over Yakone. The white bear stood in front of her, scratched and battered, but with the glint of victory in his eyes.

Lusa emerged from the depths of her prickly bush, her fur standing up in clumps but her eyes gleaming. "We survived!" she exclaimed.

"You were great." Kallik pushed her nose into Lusa's shoulder. "I bet those wolves have never been attacked by a bush before! Are you okay?"

"I'm fine," Lusa replied. "I've got more scratches from thorns than wolves!"

"At least you're safe," Kallik said warmly.

"Did you see the size of those wolves' teeth?" Lusa went on.

"We all need some rest until dawn," Toklo said. "I'll take first watch."

"But you need rest, too," Lusa objected.

"Someone has to do it," Toklo said stubbornly.

"The wolves won't come back," Yakone stated. His voice was grim, and with a jolt of relief Kallik realized that he sounded like himself for the first time in so long.

Toklo didn't bother arguing, just turned around and hauled himself out of the den.

Kallik still felt the rush of battle coursing through her and didn't think she would be able to sleep. But as soon as she lay down beside Yakone, darkness swirled around her, and she let herself slide into it. She was so exhausted that she didn't even dream of wolves.

The next thing Kallik knew was a cool dampness in her fur; she opened her eyes to see Lusa dabbing at her scratches with a pad of soaked moss.

"That feels good," Kallik murmured, aware for the first time that her whole body was stinging from the marks of the wolves' claws.

"I don't think any of your wounds are serious," Lusa said. "In fact, none of us are hurt badly. We've been very lucky."

Kallik's gaze flicked to Yakone, who was sitting up, stiffly testing each leg in turn. Blood was trickling from his injured paw.

"Oh no!" Kallik exclaimed. "Your wound has opened up."

"It's nothing," Yakone responded. He swiped his tongue over it. "Look, it's stopping already."

Kallik couldn't help but be a little anxious, but she didn't push it. She could see how much better Yakone felt, beyond any physical pain, because he had proved to himself that he could still fight.

"You were terrific last night," she said.

Yakone grunted. "It wasn't quite the same," he admitted. "I'm still weak from being ill for so long. And my balance is all over the place. . . . I'll have to work on that."

"Yakone, you just fought off a whole pack of wolves," Kallik pointed out. "You should feel proud." Affection welled up inside her as she gazed at him; she was glad all over again that he had decided to come with her.

"I suppose someone ought to hunt," Yakone said, rising to his paws.

"Yes, but it won't be you," Lusa told him sharply. "You rest for now and keep weight off that injured paw."

Yakone looked like he was going to argue, then shrugged and settled down in his trampled nest. "I guess you're right," he admitted reluctantly.

Watching him, Kallik noticed how matted and dusty his pelt was. She was filled with longing to repay Yakone for his loyalty by taking him somewhere safe, somewhere he could feel at home. *He's too generous to admit how much he hates the forest. And he's not strong enough yet to head back to the Melting Sea. But there is somewhere closer we could try. . . .*

"Where's Toklo?" she asked Lusa.

"Somewhere up there," Lusa replied, jerking her head toward the entrance to the den. "He's trying to see if we can repair the barrier."

"I need to talk to him."

Kallik clambered out of the den and found Toklo staring in disgust at the remains of the bushes that had sheltered the den. The whole area was a mess of snapped twigs, trampled undergrowth, and the stench of hungry wolves. As Kallik approached he pushed at a bush that was partly uprooted, but as soon as he let it go, it flopped to the ground again.

"We can't stay here," Toklo muttered. "We'll have to move on."

"I agree," Kallik responded, taking a deep breath to prepare herself for what she was about to say. "In fact, I want to take Yakone up to the peaks, where you and Lusa saw the snow."

Toklo swiveled around from checking the destruction and stared at her, startled. "But there's no food up there!" he protested. "That's why the wolves have come down here. And there are no trees."

"We're snow bears," Kallik pointed out. "We'll find food."

"But this is my home," Toklo began. Clearly he hadn't understood what Kallik was trying to tell him. "At least, this is where I want to find a territory for myself. And now you want us all to go trekking up onto the peaks?"

"No," Kallik responded, already beginning to feel the pain of parting. "I know this is where you want to live. But you don't need me or Yakone to do that. And we don't belong in the forest."

Toklo gazed at her with a mixture of anger and hurt flaring in his eyes. "I lived with you on the ice for moons!" he protested. "You haven't gone hungry in the forest, have you?"

"No," Kallik admitted, realizing that he still didn't understand. "But we're not comfortable here. And Yakone can't fight wolves every night. If the wolves have left the peaks, then we should go there." She paused, waiting for what she was saying to sink in, but Toklo just studied his paws. "Besides," Kallik went on, "we'll attract too much attention down here. Our white pelts stand out too much. It's better for brown and black bears to stay in the trees, where they can hide in the shadows . . . while white bears go where there's snow."

"I won't leave the forest," Toklo said stubbornly.

"I don't expect you to." Kallik's voice was quiet. "Yakone and I will go alone."

Toklo looked up at her again; Kallik saw that at last he had realized what she was suggesting. "You mean . . . we'll split up?"

Kallik nodded. "Yakone and I came with you from the Melting Sea to help you find your home. And you've found it."

Toklo blinked. "So you're leaving?"

"Yes. I haven't talked to Yakone yet, but I think we should live among the peaks until he's strong enough to go back to the Melting Sea."

"But what about Lusa?" Toklo challenged her. "Don't you want to stay and find a home for her, too?"

Kallik looked around her, gesturing with one paw. "Look at all these trees. This is where Lusa belongs, just like you." She paused. "Toklo, we always knew our journey together would come to an end sometime. I think this is it."

CHAPTER TWELVE

Toklo

Toklo felt his vision blur as he stared at Kallik. There were too many emotions swirling inside him to say anything. *This might be the place where I was born, but it's full of wolves and hostile bears, and it just doesn't feel like home.* He found it hard to admit, even to himself, but he wasn't ready for his friends to go yet. He couldn't imagine living without Kallik—or even Yakone.

"I'm going hunting," he growled. Swinging around, he headed into the trees.

The forest was full of the scent of wolves; Toklo felt that the stench was lapping at him like greasy water, clinging to his fur. He was surrounded by an eerie silence, as if every scrap of prey had been killed or frightened off in the attack the previous night.

I've had it up to here with wolves, and white bears, and everything!

As if he could outrun his own dark thoughts, Toklo picked up his pace until he was racing through the trees, crashing through bushes and tearing his pelt on trailing tendrils of bramble. A roaring sound ahead of him alerted him just in

time, and he skidded to a halt at the edge of the ravine where
he and his friends had found shelter behind the waterfall.
Struggling to keep his balance on the brink of the precipice, Toklo heard an amused rumble from behind him. He
whipped around to see the brown she-bear, Aiyanna, watching him from behind a bush.

"I haven't crossed any of your scent marks," he snapped at
her.

"I know," Aiyanna replied mildly. "I was just watching you
nearly break all your legs."

Toklo opened his jaws for a stinging retort, but before he
could speak, Aiyanna turned and padded away, vanishing into
the dense undergrowth. An unexpected pang pierced him as
he watched her go.

*It's been such a long time since I had a brown bear as a companion. I miss
Ujurak so much. . . .*

Sighing, Toklo gazed down into the ravine. Movement
flickered among the stones at the bottom, and he made out a
rabbit, hopping from one clump of grass to the next. Seeing it
reminded him of the hollowness of his belly; his feelings about
losing Kallik had distracted him for a while.

Cautiously Toklo clambered down into the ravine, testing
each rock before he put his weight on it. Spray from the falls
made the surface slick, and Toklo's heart was thumping by the
time he made it to the bottom. During the climb he had lost
sight of the rabbit, but he pinpointed it again by scent and
crept up on it using the boulders beside the stream for cover.
Sharp satisfaction ran through him as he leaped on his prey

and killed it with a heavy blow to the head.

Toklo didn't like the idea of climbing back up the rocks with the rabbit in his jaws, so he took the longer route out of the ravine, trudging up the track that he and Kallik had used with Yakone when they first arrived. Heading back to their den, he spotted Lusa digging up some ferns, but when she had exposed the roots, she only sniffed at them, as if she didn't feel like eating. She turned around as Toklo padded up to her, and he saw the unhappy look in her eyes.

He dropped the rabbit at her paws. "Kallik talked to you, didn't she?" he guessed.

Lusa nodded miserably. "I can't believe she and Yakone want to leave us. Did we do something wrong? Was it unfair to expect white bears to live under trees?"

"We lived for moons and moons on the Endless Ice," Toklo pointed out. "*And* we didn't complain about it."

"Well, we did complain a bit," Lusa said. "And with Yakone being injured, Kallik must feel very vulnerable and homesick." She hesitated, scrabbling her forepaws among the fern roots, then added tremulously, "Toklo, when they've gone, will you still want me around?"

Toklo was surprised that she should even need to ask. "Of course, you bee-brain!" he replied, giving her a friendly shove.

Lusa met his gaze steadily. "But you know that when we reach places that each of us can call home, our journey together will end. We'll all end up alone eventually. Except for Kallik and Yakone. They'll still have each other."

Toklo admired the little black bear's courage in facing what he had been trying to ignore for so long. He rested his muzzle on Lusa's head. "You won't be alone," he promised gruffly. "Not if I can help it."

Picking up the rabbit, Toklo headed back to the den with Lusa trotting companionably by his side. Before they had gone far, Toklo heard a familiar buzzing and smelled the sweet scent of honey. Looking up, he spotted bees flying in and out of a hole in an oak tree. He nudged Lusa. "Honey!"

Lusa glanced upward and tasted saliva building in her jaws. "I'm going to get some!" she said, beginning to climb.

Toklo spotted a dead branch lying on the forest floor, withered leaves still clinging to it. Setting his prey down, he lifted the branch by one end and waved it about in the air, distracting the bees and clearing Lusa's way to the hive. Lusa climbed up the tree and stuck her paw into the hole, clawing out great lumps of honeycomb, which plopped stickily to the ground. Then she scrambled down again and plunged her snout into the sweet treat.

"Delicious!" she mumbled. "Hey, Toklo, thanks for waving that branch. I hardly got stung at all."

"You're welcome," Toklo responded, licking the honey and trying not to get it all over his fur this time.

Lusa looked up, with honey dripping from her snout. "We make a great team!" she said.

Toklo blinked. "Always, little one," he murmured.

CHAPTER THIRTEEN

Kallik

Kallik shifted uneasily in the den, unable to sleep. She knew that as soon as the sky paled into the new dawn, she and Yakone would leave.

"I want to do what makes you happy," Yakone had said when they discussed the plan the night before. "I know it's hard to say good-bye to friends."

"But we have to part sometime," Kallik responded with a sigh. "If we wait too long, all the ice will have gone from the Melting Sea."

"Then if you're sure," Yakone said, leaning his head toward hers, "that's what we'll do."

She *had* felt sure, but now every breath that Kallik took was bringing her closer to the parting with Lusa and Toklo.

It feels so strange to be saying good-bye to them forever.

Restless and fretful, Kallik let her mind drift back to the long path they had traveled together, out to the Endless Ice and back.

I'll never forget all we did. . . . That time we had to go underground to rescue Toklo when he fell down the hole. And the time when we stampeded the caribou to destroy the flat-face oil rig, and all the spirits danced for us in the sky. She let out a long sigh. *I can't believe it's over. . . .*

"Are you okay?" Yakone's whisper surprised Kallik; she thought he was asleep. "I know you're upset about saying good-bye to Toklo and Lusa," he went on, moving closer so that he could stretch out a paw and touch Kallik's shoulder. "You don't have to leave them because of me. I'm healing quickly now. Why don't we stay with them until I can get all the way back to the Melting Sea?"

Kallik felt that her heart would overflow with love for Yakone; he was being so generous! And for a moment she was tempted to take him up on his offer. "No," she murmured at last. "What about the wolves? You won't mend if you have to keep fighting them off."

"Poor Toklo!" Yakone said. "He must feel like his home has been taken over by wolves."

"Yes," Kallik agreed. "But Toklo will have a better chance of establishing his own territory if he doesn't have to worry about a couple of white bears blundering around. And I know he'll look after Lusa."

But even as she spoke, knowing that they were doing the sensible thing, her heart ached at the thought of leaving her best friends behind.

"I know what they mean to you," Yakone told her, pressing his snout against Kallik's shoulder. "You've been together for so long. You know," he added teasingly, "you seemed so weird to me at first, when you popped up on Star Island with a black bear and a brown bear who had no place being on the ice." His tone became serious again. "But now I know why they're so precious to you. And they've become precious to me, too. They've saved my life several times over."

Kallik sighed again and huddled closer to Yakone, taking comfort in his strength. Eventually she managed to sleep, and woke when sunlight was breaking through the undergrowth at the edges of the den. The other bears were stirring around her.

Kallik rose to her paws. "I'm going to hunt one last time," she announced. "I'll catch some prey for you two before we leave."

Instantly Toklo rose and stood beside her. "I'll come with you."

"And me!" Lusa bounced up.

"What about you, Yakone?" Toklo asked. "Are you coming?"

The white bear shook his head. "My paw is aching a bit," he replied. "I'd better rest it if we're going to be traveling later. You go."

As Kallik climbed out of the den, she glanced back at Yakone, knowing perfectly well that there was nothing wrong with his paw. *He wants the three of us to have one last hunt together.*

With Toklo in the lead, the friends set out into the glowing green forest. Sunlight slanted through the branches and poured over the ground like golden rain. Kallik began to understand why Toklo and Lusa loved woodland so much. To her, the branches felt suffocating after the endless skies above the ice, but there was beauty in the dappled sunlight and the dancing beams.

It's not the right place for white bears . . . but it's a good place.

Before they had gone very far, Lusa halted, sniffing. "I can smell a bird," she murmured. "It's somewhere on the ground, over there," she added, pointing with her snout into a clump of bushes.

Without a word, Kallik and Toklo began to circle around so that they could approach the bushes from different directions. *This is so natural for us now,* Kallik thought with an inward sigh. *And this is the very last time. . . .*

Lusa prowled up to the bushes, not bothering to hide her approach. Before she had covered half the distance, the bird—a grouse—burst out of the thicket, wings flapping frantically, only to realize its escape was cut off by Kallik and Toklo. Landing with a thud on the ground again, the grouse headed away from the bushes, one wing trailing as if it was broken.

She's trying to lead us away from her nest, Kallik thought. Bounding forward, she caught the grouse with a clean blow on its neck, and it fell limply to the ground.

"Good catch," Toklo grunted, padding up to sniff at the prey.

Meanwhile Lusa had dived into the thicket and backed out again, carrying an egg in her jaws. "There's another!" she announced happily, and plunged back into the bushes.

Kallik carried the bird, while Toklo and Lusa each took an egg carefully in their jaws as they headed back to the den.

They found Yakone resting in the shade of a pine tree and settled down to share their meal.

Our last meal together, Kallik thought.

"Lusa . . . Toklo," she began. "Being with you . . . it's been . . ." She couldn't go on.

"It's okay," Lusa murmured, resting her head for a moment against Kallik's flank. "We know."

In the silence, Kallik felt how precious their friendship was to each one of them.

At last, when all the food was gone, Yakone stood up and gave Kallik a gentle nudge. "Come on, it's time," he said.

Kallik realized he was trying to make the parting easier for her by taking charge. She was grateful to him, but she knew that nothing could make it better. She rose to her paws. "I guess this is good-bye, then."

Toklo ducked his head awkwardly. "Take care. Watch out for wolves."

"We'll never forget you." Lusa padded up to Kallik and Yakone in turn and brushed her muzzle against their pelts. "May the spirits be with you."

"You too." Kallik felt as thought a huge paw was squeezing her heart until it would burst. "And we won't forget you, either."

"Good-bye." Yakone dipped his head to the other two. "I've learned so much from you."

With a last look at her friends, Kallik turned and padded into the trees beside Yakone.

As they headed up toward the ridge the forest was quiet, but it felt peaceful rather than threatening. Kallik was more aware than ever of the beauty of lush growth and dancing sunlight, but at the same time she knew she would never belong there. Even though she hated saying farewell to Lusa and Toklo, she was itching to feel the crunch of snow beneath her pads.

A rustle in the bushes behind her alerted Kallik, and she turned to see a young deer burst out into the open and run straight past her. Her muscles tensed for the chase, but then she relaxed and watched it vanish behind a bramble thicket.

Yakone hadn't moved, either. "I think the trees are sending us prey to tempt us to stay here," he said with a snort of amusement. "But we have to save our strength for the climb."

Kallik nodded. "I know. I hope Toklo catches it."

She padded on beside Yakone, following the slope of the hill through the forest. Eventually they reached a narrow shoulder of land, where they struck upward to reach the ridge. She walked slowly for Yakone's sake, taking a last look around and noting the landmarks that had become so familiar.

We've been here long enough to get used to the forest by now. There's the bush like a crouching bear . . . and the stream where Toklo and I caught a ptarmigan . . .

"Yakone," she said in sudden panic, "do you think we'll still be able to find food in the snow? After all, the wolves couldn't find any. . . ."

Yakone touched his snout briefly to her shoulder. "At least we won't be competing with the wolves for prey," he pointed out. "They're all down here in the forest."

"You're right," Kallik agreed. "And our white pelts will

blend in better up there. Hunting will be more natural for us. We'll be fine."

Sunhigh had passed by the time Kallik and Yakone emerged from the trees and faced the bare, rugged shoulder of land that led up to the Sky Ridge. Twisted thorns, distorted into weird shapes by the wind, dotted the landscape, but the bulk of the forest lay behind them. The ridge itself was barely visible, a thin line of snow blurred by distance. Kallik knew they still had a long way to go.

We need to take it steadily and not put too much strain on Yakone's injured paw.

After so long in the forest, Kallik had become used to the enclosing trees, and the open sky above the bare rocks made her feel exposed, as if hostile eyes might be watching her. At first she led the way along the edge of the forest, but Yakone kept tripping over roots, letting out grunts of pain if he stubbed his wounded paw.

I'm being silly, she thought, struggling with anxiety. *Sooner or later we have to travel in the open.*

"Let's go this way," she said aloud, heading away from the edge of the forest and along a spur of rocky ground that led up to the ridge.

Her heart beat rapidly as she and Yakone forged their way along the spur under the empty sky. Then Kallik realized that the sky wasn't empty after all; high above their heads, a small black shape was circling lazily.

"An eagle!" she gasped.

Fear was making her paws clumsy, and watching the eagle,

she slipped on a loose rock. Scrabbling to regain her balance, she would have fallen down the mountainside if Yakone hadn't been there to block her with his solid body.

"Careful!" he exclaimed.

"Sorry," Kallik said. "I was watching that eagle. Is it going to attack us? We should hide," she added, looking wildly around for shelter.

"Kallik." Yakone turned her to face him. "Calm down. We're white bears. We're far too big for an eagle to carry us off. Besides, my paw has healed well enough that I can take care of myself. There's no reason to hide. If the eagle does attack, it would make excellent prey!"

Kallik huffed out a long breath. "Of course. Sorry."

"Let's take a rest," Yakone suggested. He pointed with his snout to where the ground had fallen away into a hollow, with a small pool at the bottom. "You need to relax."

Kallik padded down the rocky slope and took a long drink from the pool. The water was icy and refreshing, and her racing heart began to slow down. "I know what my problem is," she confessed, sitting down beside Yakone. "I'm used to looking after all four of us, thinking ahead and planning where to hunt and rest, and what dangers to beware of. Toklo and Lusa would do that, too. We were all responsible for one another's safety."

Yakone brushed his muzzle along her shoulder. "I know. And it's great that you did that," he told her. "But you need to trust me now, too." His voice took on a faint note of challenge. "You're not the leader, and you're not on a quest that I've just joined. This is *our* journey home now, equally shared."

Kallik nodded. "I know."

"Although," Yakone went on, his expression lightening as he gave Kallik a friendly shove, "my paw is killing me. Maybe you could do some hunting for us?"

"Sure."

But the whole mountainside was empty, without the sight or sniff of prey. Neither bear wanted to stray far from the rocky path, so they contented themselves with some green shoots from a bush that grew beside the pool.

Lusa would love these, Kallik thought, with a renewed pang of loss.

"I'm looking forward to hunting on snow again," Yakone said as he swallowed the last mouthful. "But I suppose it's too much to hope for a seal up in the mountains!"

The two bears set out again and kept on walking toward the Sky Ridge as the sun slid down the sky. The air grew thinner and colder as they climbed higher, and Kallik could scent snow on the air. She longed to keep going, but when the sun had gone and twilight was gathering, she realized that Yakone was limping more than usual.

"It's time we stop for the night," she said, halting and looking around.

Not far away a rocky outcrop jutted from the ground, surrounded by a few scrubby thornbushes. Kallik and Yakone found a sheltered spot in the middle of the rocks and curled up there together. Yakone fell asleep almost at once, but sleep eluded Kallik as she thought of Toklo and Lusa. *I hope they're safe and well fed.*

The howling of wolves drifted up from the forest below. Kallik stiffened, then realized they were too far off to be a threat.

"You'd better stay away from Toklo and Lusa," she muttered.

Kallik slept at last. Cold seeping through her pelt woke her in the pale light of a new dawn. She turned to rouse Yakone, and her heart started to thump faster when she saw she was alone. She sat up, forcing down panic, then heard the sound of pawsteps on the rough ground outside their shelter. A moment later Yakone appeared, squeezing through a gap between two rocks.

"Guess what?" he announced cheerfully. "I can see snow!"

Excitement welled up inside Kallik. She pushed her way into the open and looked up to where the last of the trees petered out and the mountains continued in jagged peaks of rocks and snow, outlined against a wide blue sky. The night before it had been too dark to see them. But Kallik's excitement faded as she and Yakone set out again. The slope quickly became much steeper, and she found it was a struggle to keep on trudging upward. She could see Yakone was having the same trouble.

"It feels like a long time since we had to walk every day," she panted, "even though it's only been half a moon. We're not fit anymore!"

Just before sunhigh, they reached the last of the trees. Kallik felt a momentary pang of uncertainty as she gazed out at the bare, snowy expanse ahead of her. *I know I can hunt in trees now,* she thought. *Should we have stayed down there?*

A bird called from one of the trees behind her, and Kallik was tempted to turn back and catch it. *No,* she decided, her doubts giving way to determination. *I'm a white bear. That's not where I find my food.*

"I don't like the look of the rocks up ahead," Yakone pointed out. "They seem more like a cliff than a hillside. How are we going to get up there?"

Kallik's heart sank as she saw that Yakone was right. A sheer cliff ran right across their path, stretching into the distance in both directions. "We'll have to walk along until we find a way up," she said, not liking the idea at all. "It could take forever."

"Let's take a closer look," Yakone suggested. "The wolves got down here somehow, so there must be a path. . . ."

He padded right up to the foot of the cliff and searched carefully along it, sticking his snout into cracks and around boulders. Kallik watched him, afraid that he was wasting his time. She was beginning to get impatient when Yakone turned back to her. "Over here!" he called.

Kallik scrambled up the last few bearlengths of the slope to join him, and saw a narrow shaft cut into the cliff. It was almost as steep as the precipice itself, but rocks jutted out all the way up.

"Those would make good pawholds," Kallik murmured, half to herself.

Snow had drifted into crevices and at the side of the shaft, but it had been trampled by the passage of many paws.

There was a strong reek of wolf.

"This must be the route the wolves used," Yakone said, sounding pleased to be proved right. "But the scent is old and stale. . . . I guess it's been a long time since they came down to live in the forest."

With Yakone in the lead, he and Kallik began to climb the shaft. Kallik thought that it felt like an old, steep riverbed with the water long gone. The stones were slippery with melting snow, and some of them were loose. Kallik was worried about how Yakone would manage, and braced herself to stop him if he fell backward. But the white bear heaved himself up steadily, never pausing until they emerged at the top of the cliff.

"Thank the spirits!" Kallik panted as she scrambled out of the shaft. Her legs were shaking with the effort, and she paused to take a look around. Steep slopes swept upward in front of her, leading to the ridge. On the open ground the snow was thin, but it grew thicker farther up the slopes and lay in deeper drifts in hollows and in the shelter of rocks. The top of the ridge was a clear-cut white outline against the sky.

While Kallik stood there, Yakone plunged forward and hurled himself into the nearest snowdrift, snuffling at it and throwing snow up in the air to fall in clots onto his pelt. *He's acting like a cub!* Kallik thought with a huff of amusement. Racing across the ground, she hurled herself into the snow beside Yakone, rolling over in it and reveling in the cold.

I'd forgotten it was like this, she thought joyfully. *It's so crisp, so icy, and it reminds me of home.*

Then she sat up, suddenly struck by the differences from the snow she was used to. This snow didn't lie over a frozen sea, and it didn't have the salty tang that was so familiar to her. It felt strange to scrape down and hit stones and rock so quickly.

But it's still wonderful! Kallik decided. *Now I'm sure we did the right thing coming up here.*

CHAPTER FOURTEEN

Lusa

Lusa's heart swelled with grief as Kallik and Yakone headed off through the trees. Unable to face losing them, she rose to her paws and slunk furtively after them, keeping them in sight and ducking behind bushes when they stopped to look around.

"I know I'm being ridiculous," she murmured to herself. "I'm just not ready to say good-bye." *I wonder what Ujurak would think about us splitting up,* she added silently.

Slipping between two pine trees, she startled a young deer, and her heart thumped as the creature raced into the open, right past the two white bears. Lusa crouched behind some ferns and froze, hoping desperately that Kallik and Yakone wouldn't chase the deer straight back toward her. Peering out, she saw them halt briefly, then ignore the prey and keep going.

After that, Lusa was more careful, staying farther back and almost losing the white bears when she had to struggle through dense undergrowth. Emerging into a clearing, she looked up and realized that she couldn't see them anymore.

"No!" she exclaimed, springing forward in a frantic dash along their scent trail.

Lusa burst into the open on the rocky shoulder of the hill. The two white bears were a long way above her already, climbing upward toward the thin line of snow that was just visible on the horizon.

When Kallik and Yakone were no more than two white dots against the hillside, Lusa suddenly felt very alone in the huge forest. "Good-bye and good luck," she whispered as she gazed after them. Then she hurried back to Toklo.

The brown bear was sitting on the edge of the den and rose to his paws when Lusa appeared. "I thought you'd gotten lost," he said gruffly. "We need to move on."

"Why?" Lusa asked.

"Because it's too dangerous to stay in this den now that the wolves know we're here. Without Kallik and Yakone, we won't be able to defend ourselves if they come back again."

Lusa felt small and useless. "Can't we get branches and build up the walls of the den?" she suggested.

"No," Toklo replied curtly. "I'm not going to make myself a captive and hide from wolves as if I was in an eagle's nest! I'll find us somewhere different to live instead."

Not waiting for Lusa to respond, he stomped off through the trees, and Lusa had to scamper to catch up. Toklo was heading upward in the opposite direction from where Kallik and Yakone had gone. *He can't stand to follow them,* Lusa thought. *I know he's hurting inside, but he'll never let any other bear see it.* She wished she could comfort Toklo and share her own sadness that the white bears had gone. *But we always knew we wouldn't be together forever,* she reminded herself. *And if Toklo and I have found a place we can live, then Kallik and Yakone deserve to go back to the ice.*

Looking around at the quiet forest, Lusa felt a tremor of doubt about making it her home. *Where are all the black bears? We haven't seen a single one! Have the wolves chased them away?* Then she remembered how surprised Maniitok and Aiyanna had been when they saw her. *Black bears can't be living in this forest, if the brown bears have never seen one before.*

Lusa couldn't imagine being on her own and having to compete with wolves for food and shelter. But if this wasn't the end of her journey, she couldn't think where it might be. *Back in the Bear Bowl? No . . . I'm a wild bear now!*

Lusa's thoughts were interrupted by a snort of satisfaction from Toklo. He had his nose down on a scent and set off to track it through the trees. Eventually he halted a couple of bear-lengths from a thick clump of berry bushes. Lusa repressed a sigh as she thought how long it would be before the season of delicious berries.

Toklo's eyes gleamed as he stared at the bushes. "The prey's in there," he growled, and added abruptly, "Circle around and guard the other side. And don't even think about letting it escape."

Lusa bit back a sharp retort at being treated like a cub with still-wet fur. She just did as she was told, setting her paws down quietly as she skirted the bushes and crouched on the far side of them, ready to grab the prey if it broke into the open. Her nose twitched as she caught a familiar scent beneath that of the prey. *Another bear?* she wondered. She assumed the scent must be old, for Toklo readied himself without fear or apprehension.

Instead, a roar of fury from Toklo split the silence. *Something's wrong!* Lusa thought, springing forward and bursting into the thicket. She almost collided with Toklo, who was clawing at the remains of a dead animal: just bones and a few scraps of the creature's pelt remained. The air beneath the branches was heavy with the scents of deer and wolves.

"Prey-stealers!" Toklo was almost too enraged to speak. "This deer should have been *ours*!"

Lusa nosed at the bones. The wolves had already stripped the meat away, and all Toklo had picked up was the scent of the remains. Though Lusa and Toklo chewed the bones for a few moments, there was nothing left to fill their bellies.

"The wolves shouldn't even be here!" Toklo huffed, throwing his bone to one side. "*Bears* live in this forest, and the prey should belong to them."

While he was speaking, Lusa was taking a closer look at their surroundings. As well as the scraps of deer carcass and the pawprints of the wolves, she spotted different prints, and teeth marks on the remains of the deer that were too big to have been made by a wolf. Looking further, she found torn tufts of gray fur, and a spattering of blood on the ground.

"Look at this, Toklo," she said. "I think the wolves fought with a bear here. And I think the bear won. It got to eat some of the deer, anyway."

Toklo examined the traces she showed him and looked up

with a grunt of satisfaction. "Good job, bear, whoever you are!"

Lusa felt daunted at the thought of a bear so powerful that it could fight off two or three wolves, but she was relieved that Toklo's bad mood seemed to have passed and he was looking cheerful once more.

With Toklo in the lead they set out again, until they came to a part of the forest where the undergrowth grew too dense to force their way through. *Is Toklo going to walk the whole length of the mountains?* Lusa wondered irritably, tugging herself away from a bramble tendril that had snagged her fur. "Don't you think we should stop for the night?" she asked aloud.

Toklo stopped trying to force a passage through the thickly growing thorns. He looked around, blinking, and seemed to realize for the first time that the sun was setting; the little light that seeped through the covering branches had turned to scarlet.

"I suppose so," he said grudgingly. "We need to find a place for a den."

To Lusa's relief it wasn't long before she spotted a thicket of vines. *At least there's nothing here that's going to prick me!* She and Toklo hollowed out a makeshift den among the twining stems, turning around to make a space big enough to lie down in.

"It seems so quiet without Kallik and Yakone," Lusa remarked as she curled up to sleep.

Toklo let out a snort. "At least it's easier to find food and shelter without them."

You don't mean that, Lusa thought, gazing affectionately at the brown bear. *You miss them just as much as I do.* Looking up through the vine branches, she gazed at the stars until she found Arcturus. "I hope Kallik is watching you, too," she whispered to the bright star. "And Ujurak, I hope you're watching over all of us."

CHAPTER FIFTEEN

Toklo

Toklo stumbled through dense fog, so thick that he couldn't even see his own paws. Voices echoed around him, calling his name. Sometimes he thought the voice was Kallik's or Yakone's, sometimes Tobi's or Ujurak's, and sometimes all of them together. Bewildered, he swung around, trying to figure which direction the sounds were coming from.

"Where are you?" he called. "I can't find you!"

He was still staggering along in confusion when something slammed into him from behind. Barely managing to stay on his paws, he turned to see Nanulak, the half-brown, half-white bear they had met on the Island of Shadows.

"You!" Nanulak growled, his eyes on fire with rage. "It's all your fault!" He reared up on his hind legs and batted at Toklo with his forepaws.

"What's all my fault?" Toklo tried to block Nanulak's blows, but he didn't want to hurt the smaller bear. "I don't know what you mean."

"No bears like me!" Nanulak snarled, ripping his claws

through the pelt on Toklo's shoulder. "No bears want me, and it's all your fault! You said I could stay with you."

As Toklo fought the enraged bear, the others who had called out to him loomed up through the fog and stood around, watching. None of them lifted a paw to help him. Toklo had never felt so lost, so abandoned.

While Toklo tried to fend off Nanulak's attack, he felt something poke him from behind. His paws still thrashing at Nanulak, he whirled around with a snarl, expecting to see another hostile bear ready to pounce upon him. Instead, he saw Lusa, her eyes wide with terror as she prodded him awake. Moonlight showed Toklo that he had rolled deeper into the thicket and become tangled up in brambles. Letting out a growl of annoyance, he tore himself free.

"Shh!" Lusa whispered. "I can hear wolves! I think they're attacking another bear."

Shaking off the last shreds of his nightmare, Toklo sat up and listened. At once he realized that Lusa was right. Not far away he could hear the howling and snarling of wolves, and a furious roaring that had to come from a brown bear. Toklo's heart grew cold at the clamor of voices and the crashing of paws in the undergrowth. "It's not a fair fight," he said. "There are a lot of wolves out there!"

Lusa had already sprung to her paws. "We have to help!"

Toklo pushed his way out of their den, and with Lusa following hard on his paws, he scrambled through the dark forest toward the sound. He was aware of passing scent markers, and halted, stunned by a powerful memory like a blow from a massive paw.

Do I know the bear that lives here?

But Toklo had no time to think about that. He shook his head and continued on into the territory. The noise of the attack was growing louder and louder. The brown bear was roaring in defiance, still fighting, but clearly overwhelmed by the sheer number of the wolves.

Racing around a stand of pine trees, Toklo caught sight of the attack at last. The brown bear stood on his hindpaws at the bottom of a hollow, with wolves circling him and darting in to strike him with claws and fangs.

What's going on? Toklo asked himself. *They're not fighting over prey.*

The bear was huge and powerful, but Toklo saw in an instant that he was lame in one of his hind legs, unbalanced and lashing out in desperation rather than placing his blows with careful thought.

Reaching Toklo's side, Lusa let out a gasp. "That's the bear I saw before!" she exclaimed. "On the way to the flat-face place."

"Is he Old Grizzly?" Toklo asked. "The bear Maniitok warned us about?"

"I think he must be," Lusa replied, "but I didn't exactly ask him his name!"

With a bellow of rage, Toklo charged down the slope and hurled himself into the shadowy tangle of wolves. Lusa popped up beside him, bravely snapping at the lean shapes that swirled around them.

Toklo was thankful that he had space to fight the wolves here, unlike the attack in their den with Kallik and Yakone. *Now I can* really *show these mangepelts how dangerous a bear can be!*

In the shadows cast by the trees, it was hard for Toklo to see clearly, but he could make out the massive form of the brown bear. He was old and shaggy, and blood was pouring out from many wounds; the reek of it was everywhere. But he fought grimly on, sending wolves reeling with blows from his huge paws.

The brown bear was too busy fighting to notice Toklo and Lusa, and there were too many wolves for Toklo to reach him. Toklo concentrated on clearing a path to the big bear, slapping wolves out of the way with powerful swipes. But there were so many wolves! As soon as Toklo had shoved one away, another appeared to take its place. Lusa was holding her ground bravely, but three wolves leaped upon her at once, and Toklo had to turn to help her. He waded to her through a sea of gray bodies and caught the nearest wolf by the throat, ripping his claws through pelt and flesh. It slumped bleeding to the ground. Toklo slammed his paw into the side of the second wolf's head, and the third fled, yelping.

"Thanks!" Lusa panted.

Toklo saw with relief that she wasn't badly hurt. Ignoring her protests, he got his shoulder under her and boosted her up onto the lowest branch of a nearby pine tree. "Stay there!" he roared, and turned back to the battle.

The old bear was staggering as if his strength was coming to an end. Toklo tried once more to reach him, but more wolves pressed around him, leaping onto his back and snapping their fangs perilously close to his throat. Toklo felt like he was being smothered in wolves. *I'm going to lose this fight. . . .*

Just as the wolves threatened to throw Toklo off his paws and crush him to the ground, he felt their weight being yanked off his back. A fierce bellow sounded close to his ear, and he turned to see that another bear had joined the fight.

Aiyanna!

She was smaller and lighter than Toklo, but she fought nimbly, whirling around to face one wolf after another, raking them with her claws until they drew back. There was no time for Toklo to thank her. He fought side by side with her, their fighting styles matching well as they drove off the wolves.

"Look!" Aiyanna pointed with her snout at a shaggy gray wolf that was bigger than the others. "That's the pack leader. We need to target him!"

Together Toklo and Aiyanna battled their way through the mass of wolves until they reached the big gray wolf. Aiyanna darted forward and dealt him a blow over one ear. As the wolf turned toward her, snarling, Toklo leaped on him from behind and fastened his fangs in the wolf's shoulder. Caught between the two bears, the pack leader tore himself free and fled. Dismayed howls rose from the rest of the pack, and though a few of them still fought on, most followed the lead wolf. It didn't take long for Toklo and Aiyanna to convince the remainder that sticking around was a bad idea.

"Good riddance!" Toklo grunted, delivering a farewell blow to the hindquarters of the last fleeing wolf.

As he stood, chest heaving in the middle of the trampled clearing, Toklo realized that the moon had set and the light of dawn was creeping into the sky. He padded over to Lusa, who had jumped down from the tree, and checked her over for injuries.

"I'm fine," Lusa assured him, sounding annoyed that he had put her up in the tree to begin with. "What about the old bear?"

Toklo turned to see that Aiyanna was approaching the other brown bear. "Old Grizzly?" she said softly. "Are you hurt?"

Toklo blinked. So this *was* the ferocious bear Maniitok had told them about. He didn't look particularly fearsome right now, exhausted and bleeding.

"What are you doing here?" Old Grizzly snapped at Aiyanna, showing his teeth. "This is my territory!"

Toklo let out a long, hissing breath, pushing down an angry response. He was battered and scratched from his battle with the wolves, and his nose was full of the stench of blood and fear. "We're saving your pelt, you ungrateful old mangefur," he muttered as he strode over to join Aiyanna.

The she-bear was sniffing at Old Grizzly's wounds, and he was trying to slap her snout away. "I don't need your fussing," he protested. "And don't call me Old Grizzly. I have a proper name, you know." Seeing Toklo, he fixed him with a furious glare. "Who are you?" he demanded. "Another trespasser?"

"Come on, Chogan," Aiyanna said, her tone pleading. "You know you would be wolf prey by now if it wasn't for us. You should be thanking us."

The old bear, Chogan, growled something inaudible. Toklo couldn't make out what he said, but he was sure it wasn't thanks.

"You know you're not going to fight us," Aiyanna went on. "You're too badly hurt to be fighting anything bigger than a squirrel."

"You think so? Just try me!" Chogan challenged her.

Aiyanna gave an exasperated sigh. "Why are you always so bad-tempered?" she asked. "You've got some older wounds on you, I can see. Why don't you learn to stay out of trouble?"

Chogan only replied with a snarl.

"Older wounds?" Toklo remembered the evidence of the fight that he and Lusa had found the day before. "Was it you who fought some wolves over a deer?"

The older bear drew himself up with a touch of pride. "Yes, that was me," he replied gruffly. "I drove off those mangy beasts—four of them!" Rounding on Aiyanna, he added, "What do you think of that?"

"I think the rest of the pack came back to get revenge," Aiyanna retorted. "Perhaps you should have left them alone with their catch."

"And let them take over the whole forest?" Chogan said. "Never!"

"He's right," Toklo told Aiyanna. "Someone has to stand up to the wolves."

"You're a stranger, so keep your snout out of our business," Chogan barked at him. His gaze flicked past Toklo to Lusa, who had padded up quietly and was listening wide-eyed to the exchange. "Oh, now I know who you are," Chogan continued. "I've heard about the black, brown, and white bears who've moved in. Where are the white bears?" he added with a sneer. "Have you fed them to the wolves?"

Toklo opened his jaws to snarl a furious reply when Lusa jumped in. "They're safe," she told Chogan.

Chogan gave a surprised grunt. "So are *all* of you trespassing on my territory? Didn't you notice my scent marks, you stupid young bears?"

"We're *not* trespassing," Toklo pointed out. He wanted to give this ungrateful bear a good wallop around his ears, but he restrained himself. "We came to save your hide, or have you forgotten?"

Chogan shrugged that off. "Just go," he snarled. "Find a home of your own, if black and brown bears are living together these days."

"I don't think Toklo is used to scent marks," Aiyanna suggested. "He's been sniffing around my territory, too."

Toklo bristled. *I only wanted to see where Tobi is buried.* "Come on, Lusa," he said. "We're leaving."

Aiyanna padded after them as they climbed the slope out of the hollow; Toklo was aware of Chogan's angry gaze boring into his back until he was hidden by the trees.

"I can't believe how ungrateful he was!" Lusa exclaimed.

"He's a miserable old bear," Aiyanna said. "Everyone knows

to leave him alone. He's been here longer than any of us can remember, and no bear ever threatens his territory."

"I'm not surprised," Toklo muttered. "No one would want to put up with the stink of his mangy pelt!"

Toklo and Lusa padded together with Aiyanna until they crossed the scent marks of Chogan's border.

"You fought well," Toklo told Aiyanna, though he couldn't help thinking that if Kallik and Yakone had still been here, they wouldn't have needed her help. "Is *that* how you deal with wolves?"

Aiyanna nodded. "One of the ways. Anyway, I have to be going," she added. "Good luck on your journey." She veered away into the undergrowth with a farewell flick of her ears.

Toklo watched her go, feeling vaguely dissatisfied. Aiyanna seemed to assume that he wouldn't stay here in the forest, and he didn't want to argue with her. *This place doesn't feel like home,* he thought. *It's just somewhere I once passed through, like so many other places. Yet where else would I go?* And he wondered how he and Lusa would even be able to carry on, now that Kallik and Yakone had gone.

Both Toklo and Lusa were sore and stiff after the battle and took the rest of the day slowly. They didn't venture far from their new den and hunted only long enough to catch a couple of small birds. The sunlight had not entirely gone when they squeezed back into their makeshift den and settled down to sleep.

Toklo felt troubled, and still uncertain about what he should do next, as he curled up and tucked his nose into his pelt. Drifting toward sleep, he could smell the wolves again, dried blood, and the scent of the old bear, Chogan. Again the fugitive memory flickered, the one that had stirred when he crossed Chogan's scent marks. This time, bright images flashed into his drowsy mind.

Toklo was standing beside his brother Tobi at the edge of a rocky river. Their mother, Oka, was facing a huge grizzly, who was forcing them to leave his territory. Toklo felt scared and angry at the same time. He drew back his lips and snarled at the huge bear. "Don't you be nasty to my mother!" he growled.

Oka pulled him back and placed herself between Toklo and the grizzly. "Hush, little one," she said. "Now run!"

Pushing Tobi ahead of him, Toklo prepared to flee across the stepping-stones that would take them to the other side of the river.

The huge grizzly loomed over them. "Get off my land!" he roared. His scent drifted over the young Toklo.

In his dream, Toklo flinched. The memory was so strong: the chattering sound that the river made as it flowed around the stepping-stones; the hard, cold feeling of the stones on his pads; the scent of the bear who was driving them out.

Toklo sat upright, his eyes wide, staring into the darkness. *It's the same scent! Chogan is the bear who chased us out of his territory!*

CHAPTER SIXTEEN

Kallik

Light reflecting from the snow woke Kallik. She poked her nose out from the shelter of the boulders where she had slept curled up beside Yakone, and looked around. Snow-covered slopes swept upward to the ridge, the surface glittering under the rays of the sun. The rocks cast long, blue shadows. Kallik could see there had been a snowfall in the night; her pawprints and Yakone's had filled up and were barely visible.

Rising to her paws, Kallik ventured out into the open and drew a breath of delight as wind sliced through her pelt. The air was clean and sharp, and high above, no more than a dot in the sky, an eagle was circling. Kallik remembered her panic at the sight of the eagle the day before, and let out a huff of amusement. As she padded forward, Kallik reveled in the crunching of snow underpaw. The sensation was familiar and welcoming, and yet . . . *I know this isn't home.* She was too conscious of being high up in the air, instead of on top of a frozen sea. *The smells aren't right . . . and I miss the taste of seal.* Then she reflected that this was never meant to be her home. *I ought to enjoy it without expecting too much.*

As Kallik stood looking back the way they had come, watching the sun burn off the mist and the forest rolling out below, Yakone limped up beside her.

"It's great up here, isn't it?" he said. "That was the best sleep I've had for moons."

Kallik nodded. "Yes, it's wonderful."

But she couldn't help glancing into the trees and wondering if Toklo and Lusa were safe. *I'm sure I heard wolves last night....*

"Let's explore," Yakone suggested.

Kallik murmured agreement and led the way in a widening circle around the boulders where they had spent the night, trying to spot likely places for prey, or rocks to hide behind if any hostile creatures attacked.

After a few moments Yakone bounded ahead of Kallik and threw a pawful of snow into her face.

"Hey!" Kallik exclaimed. "I'll get you for that!"

"Catch me first!" Yakone retorted.

Racing through the snow, Kallik outpaced Yakone and used her hindpaws to shower him with snow. The crystals glittered on his pelt. Kallik drew a deep breath and wondered when the last time was that she had felt so light-hearted. Yakone shook the snow off his pelt and charged toward her, but before he reached her he halted with a yelp of pain, raising his injured paw and swiping his tongue over it.

Kallik's playful mood vanished. "Are you okay?" she asked.

"I stubbed my paw on a rock," Yakone explained. "It's nothing."

"You'd better rest for a bit," Kallik said, relieved to see that the wound hadn't started bleeding again. "Why don't you go back to the boulders where we slept, and I'll hunt?"

"Okay." Yakone set off, limping more heavily than before, while Kallik looked around for prey.

The eagle was still circling, but now it was much lower and seemed to be concentrating on one particular spot. Kallik remembered how birds of prey hunted over the ice, and headed over to where the eagle was circling. He must have his eye on something. As she drew closer, she spotted an old hare hobbling at the edge of the snow line. Kallik crept closer, grateful for how her white pelt blended with the snow, and set her paws down lightly to avoid a crunching sound. Instead of trying to track the hare and maybe giving herself away, she kept an eye on the eagle, tracing the prey's position by the bird's keen circling movement. Just as the eagle folded its wings for a dive, Kallik plunged forward, her forepaws sinking into the hare's body. The shadow of the eagle swept over her, and it let out a harsh cry.

"Sorry," Kallik murmured. "It's mine now!"

Picking up the hare in her jaws, she carried it back to Yakone. "It's not the plumpest prey I've ever caught," she apologized as she dropped it by his paws, "but it'll have to do." *And I'm hunting on snow again,* she added to herself, glowing with satisfaction.

When she and Yakone had shared the hare, Kallik checked on his injury to make sure it was still healing.

"I'm fine now," Yakone told her. "It doesn't hurt at all."

Kallik could see that the wound must still be very tender, but the remaining toes were beginning to close together over the gap. "I think you'll be okay," she said.

"Let's go exploring again," Yakone said, rising to his paws. "I want to see what's on the other side of the ridge."

"Okay," Kallik agreed. "But stay away from buried rocks!"

Side by side Kallik and Yakone climbed the final slope and stood on the ridge, the wind buffeting their fur. The slope beyond was even steeper, broken by the dark line of the forest, then falling down to a broad, flat plain. They ventured down a little way, picking out a path between scattered boulders.

"We can't stay here for long," Kallik said after a while. "It's good, but it's not the right place for white bears."

"True," Yakone agreed. "As soon as I'm strong enough, we'll head for the Melting Sea, right?"

Kallik paused before replying, feeling loose scree under the snow and heading across the slope until she found firm ground again. She stood with Yakone on a flat ledge and spotted a river winding its way across the distant plain until it was lost among the trees.

"The other bears will be glad to see us," she said thoughtfully. "I'll see Taqqiq again, and we'll be able to keep those other cloud-brained bears in check." The prospect should have filled Kallik with joy, and she wondered why she didn't feel the excitement she had expected to be reunited with her brother. Then she gave her pelt a shake. *It's just that I'm missing Lusa and Toklo.*

"We might even arrive as the sea starts freezing again."

Yakone sounded quite happy with the plan. "Just in time for snow-sky."

"Yes, that would be good," Kallik responded.

Moving on, they came to the head of an old waterfall that was now filled with snow and rocks and bushes.

"Come on," Kallik said, taking the lead again. "It looks like there might be a chance of prey down there."

They began to clamber down; Kallik hoped they would find prey before they got anywhere near the tree line. The distant forest looked dark and forbidding and suffocating, even after such a short time in the open. "I can't believe we ever survived down there!" she exclaimed.

"Neither can I," Yakone agreed. "We—" He broke off, scenting the air.

At the same moment Kallik heard the sound of pawsteps and spotted a mountain goat scrambling over the rocks. "Over there! Quick!" As both bears headed after it, she added, "I ate goat when we were traveling across Smoke Mountain. It's delicious!"

Kallik and Yakone stalked after the goat, which was unaware of their presence, cropping tufts of grass that poked up through the snow. But before they were close enough to make the catch, Yakone stumbled over a rock and sent a shower of pebbles sliding down the hillside. The goat jumped up and fled along the ridge, with Yakone and Kallik bounding after it. It dodged among the rocks, then swerved down toward the shelter of the trees.

Kallik raced after it, her belly rumbling in anticipation of a feast, and plunged into the undergrowth beneath the trees. The goat was trapped in a bramble thicket, tugging vainly at the tendrils that entangled it and letting out terrified bleats. Kallik was about to spring on it when a furious roar sounded from farther in the trees.

Halting, Kallik turned to face the sound. A light brown she-bear was looming in front of her. "Prey-stealer!" she growled. "What are you doing? Why—?" She broke off suddenly, her jaws gaping in astonishment. "Great spirits! What color are you?"

Kallik backed away. The she-bear was enraged, and much bigger than her. "I'm sorry," she said. "I didn't realize this was your territory. I'll leave."

But before she could move, Yakone limped up behind her and stood at her side. "No. We found that goat first," he asserted, glaring at the she-bear.

"Yakone, don't," Kallik said, touching his shoulder with one paw. "We're on her territory. We shouldn't fight her over a goat."

"But it's *our* goat," Yakone protested.

"What are you doing here?" the brown bear demanded, her tone still hostile. "This isn't your place."

"We've come from a long way off, and we're going back soon," Kallik replied politely.

The she-bear grunted as if she wasn't sure she believed what Kallik told her. "Well, you'd do better to stick to the snow," she told the white bears. "You show up like clouds down here among the trees. And leave my prey alone," she added.

While she was speaking, a couple of small brown cubs bounced out of the undergrowth and started wrestling in the shade of a clump of ferns.

"Oh! Are they yours?" Kallik asked, captivated by the lively little creatures.

Instantly the she-bear moved to block her, as if she expected Kallik to attack her cubs. "Get out of here!" she snarled.

"Okay, we'll go," Kallik said with a sigh. She led the way out of the trees, and Yakone followed her with dragging pawsteps, casting frequent glances over his shoulder.

"We could have taken that goat," he complained. "Why did you back down? You're much braver than that."

"No, we couldn't have," Kallik flashed back at him. "We don't stand a chance when it's just the two of us, and you're injured. It would be different if we still had Toklo and Lusa with us."

Yakone halted and glared at her. "So you don't feel confident with just me around?"

"It's not that at all!" Kallik protested, wondering how they had slid so suddenly into an argument.

"Then what is it?" Yakone demanded. "You can go back to your friends, if that's what you want."

"No, I want to be with you," Kallik told him, taking a pace toward him. "Back where we belong."

I don't even care where that is, she thought. *Wherever Yakone is, that's where I belong.*

CHAPTER SEVENTEEN

Lusa

Lusa struggled out of sleep to hear pawsteps stomping around outside the den. Poking her head out through the vines, she saw Toklo pacing up and down, muttering to himself. "What's the matter with you?" she called. "I thought every bear in the forest was charging past."

Toklo turned toward her, and Lusa's irritation faded as soon as she saw how ruffled and sleepless he looked. "Is something wrong?" she asked more quietly.

At first Lusa thought Toklo wasn't going to reply; he turned his head away and worked his forepaws in the debris of the forest floor. "I remember Chogan," he said eventually.

"You mean from when you lived here before?" Lusa said in surprise.

Toklo nodded. "Tobi and I were born on his territory," he began. "I never knew his name—he was just 'the big bear.' Oka used to warn us about how fierce he was. She told us to stay away from him, but you know how fluff-brained young cubs can be."

Lusa stifled a huff of amusement, not wanting to interrupt Toklo's story.

"Once, Tobi and I went hunting," Toklo went on, "and we met the big bear. Great spirits, I had no idea that a bear could be so huge and scary. We ran away and hid, but our hiding place turned out to be his den!"

"What happened?" Lusa gasped.

"He terrified us out of our fur," Toklo snorted. "But he let us go in the end. Only then he found the den where we'd been living with Oka, and she knew that we had to leave. The big bear drove us out . . . and Oka almost had to fight him before we could cross the river."

"That was Chogan? Wow!" Lusa said. "And he didn't recognize you!"

"Well, I've changed a lot since then," Toklo pointed out. "But he's still a bully, and unfriendly, and determined to live on his own." Alarm prickled through Lusa's pelt as Toklo bushed up his fur and showed his claws. "Chogan forced my mother to leave when Tobi was too weak for such a long journey," he continued. "But I was born on his territory, so I have as much right as he does to live and hunt there."

"Are you going to try to drive him out?" Lusa asked anxiously.

Toklo shook his head. "I don't know." He slumped to the ground, looking worn out. "I don't know if I want to live here when wolves are taking over the forest."

Lusa had never seen Toklo looking so defeated. She sat down beside him, wishing she could comfort him. "We could always keep traveling," she suggested. "These mountains are huge! I traveled for moons from the Bear Bowl before I found you and Ujurak." She pressed her muzzle against Toklo's shoulder. "There will be a place for you somewhere else."

Toklo turned his head to look at her. "What about you, Lusa? Where are you going to live?"

A jag of fear struck through Lusa like a wolf's fangs.

"I . . . I want to find some black bears," she replied. "That might be far away from here, but I know there must be a place that's safe for me."

Toklo's only response was a grunt.

Lusa gazed at him miserably for a moment longer, then rose to her paws and headed off to look for food. On her way down the hill she spotted some butterflies dancing in the sunlight, and a couple of baby rabbits nibbling the long grass under a tree. She thought about catching one of them for Toklo, but they looked so peaceful that she couldn't bring herself to attack. *And they'd hardly make a mouthful anyway.*

When the rabbits had hopped away, Lusa investigated the spot where they'd been nibbling and found a patch of juicy green shoots. She felt happier as she sat down and started to chew.

Then bear scent wafted toward her, and she heard the sound of pawsteps in the undergrowth. Scared that it might be Chogan, she scrambled up the tree out of the way and peered down from the shelter of a leafy branch.

Instead of Old Grizzly, two small cubs bounced into view, followed by a she-bear who had to be their mother. Lusa recognized the cubs as the two she had met beside the stream when she was with Toklo.

"You'll never catch anything if you charge around like that," the mother bear was saying. "You have to be very quiet and sneak up on your prey before it knows you're there. Now, can you scent anything?"

Both cubs stuck their noses in the air and sniffed.

"Rabbit!" the bigger cub exclaimed.

"But I can't *see* any rabbits," her smaller sister said, with a disappointed look.

"You don't have to see prey to track it," their mother told them. "You can follow its scent trail. But just for now, you see that rock over there? The one with all the moss covering it? Let's pretend that it's a rabbit. I want to see you stalking it. Fala, you go first."

The bigger cub crouched down to the ground and began to creep slowly toward the rock. Lusa was impressed by how lightly she put down her paws. But before Fala reached her prey, a frond of fern brushed across her face, and she sneezed.

"Bee-brain!" her little sister huffed. "Your rabbit just ran away!"

"Well, never mind," their mother said as Fala plodded back to her side, dejected. "Things go wrong, even for experienced hunters. Now it's your turn, Flo."

"Watch me!" the little cub said, wriggling her haunches. "I'll show you how to catch a rabbit."

She started well, too, but the moment a butterfly fluttered past, she was distracted and reared up from the grass to bat at it with her forepaws.

"Now who's a bee-brain?" Fala snorted with disgust.

Toklo and Tobi must have been just like this, Lusa thought.

"Listen," the mother bear went on, gathering her cubs closer to her. "This is important. What have I told you about wolves?"

"They're big and scary," Flo replied, her eyes wide.

"And they'd eat us," Fala added.

"Right," said their mother. "So what do you do if wolves come?"

"Run away fast!" said Fala.

Flo nodded. "Run away if we even scent a wolf."

Lusa shivered. The charming scene beneath her had suddenly turned darker. She could imagine what wolves would do to these little cubs if ever they caught them.

"And what else could you do?" the mother bear prompted.

"We're small," Fala said thoughtfully. "So we could squeeze into tiny spaces where the wolves couldn't get at us."

"Very good!" her mother praised her. "And do you remember what I told you to do if wolves chase you?"

"Split up!" Flo said.

"Because . . . ?"

"Because then one of us might survive." Fala was serious now, shrinking closer to her mother.

"That's right." The mother bear gathered her cubs to her side and held them. "I couldn't bear to lose both of you, my darlings."

Perched in her tree, Lusa suddenly felt cold. She was

reminded that the sunlit forest could be a harsh place, where cubs died and bears fought with one another for territory. And that was even before the wolves had come. *Nowhere's safe all the time,* she thought.

The mother bear rose to her paws, briskly ruffling her cubs' fur with one forepaw. "That's enough of that," she said. "Come on, let's find some real prey!"

"Yes, I'm *starving!*" Flo exclaimed.

Once the bears had disappeared down the hill, Lusa jumped to the ground. Still acutely aware of how hard life could be, she tracked the young rabbits by their scent and killed one of them before it could escape down its burrow.

When she returned to the den with her prey, Toklo was nowhere to be seen. Lusa buried the rabbit under some loose stones and dragged out the crushed vines from their previous night's nests. She had pulled up some ferns for fresh bedding and was checking them for thorns when she heard a bear approaching. Distracted by her task, she hadn't noticed the pawsteps until the bear was almost on top of her.

Spinning around, Lusa expected to see Toklo. Instead, the newcomer was the she-bear Aiyanna. "Oh, it's you!" Lusa exclaimed.

"Sorry if I startled you," Aiyanna said, dipping her head. "Is this where you live now?"

"For the time being," Lusa replied, still a little wary of the she-bear.

Aiyanna stepped forward as if she was going to enter the den.

"It's very cramped in there," Lusa said, diverting her but trying to sound polite. "Why not sit out here? Have a fern root; they're very good."

Aiyanna picked up a root and chewed it. "Where's Toklo?" she asked after a moment.

"Hunting," Lusa barked. "But he'll be back soon."

Aiyanna let out a snort of amusement. "Are you scared of me?"

"No!" Lusa retorted. *Maybe just a bit.* "But you haven't done anything to show that you're a friend yet."

"I saved you from the wolves, didn't I?" Aiyanna asked, sounding faintly annoyed.

"No, you helped us save Chogan from the wolves," Lusa pointed out. "What do you know about him, anyway?"

Aiyanna shrugged. "Not much. When I came here with my mother from the other side of the ridge, Chogan made it pretty clear that we weren't to go anywhere near his territory. He never got along with the other bears around here."

"Toklo used to know Chogan when he was a tiny cub." Somehow, without intending it, Lusa found herself sitting beside Aiyanna and telling her part of the story Toklo had told her. "Chogan forced Oka, Toklo's mother, off his territory, along with her cubs, Toklo and Tobi."

Aiyanna snorted. "Sounds like Chogan," she commented. "So where's Tobi?"

"On your territory."

Aiyanna looked startled. "What?"

"He wasn't strong," Lusa explained. "He died when he was

still a cub. His burial mound is under an overhanging rock on your territory. Toklo tried to see it, but you wouldn't let him."

"He never said that's what he wanted to see!" Aiyanna protested.

Lusa shrugged. "Well, he wouldn't tell you, would he?"

"So what did Toklo do after Chogan drove him away?" Aiyanna asked. "And what happened to Oka? She isn't one of the she-bears I've met around here."

Lusa knew that Toklo might not approve of her sharing his whole story with Aiyanna. But the brown she-bear seemed so sympathetic that before Lusa knew it, the words were tumbling out.

She told Aiyanna how Oka had abandoned Toklo after his brother died, because she thought he would die, too, and she couldn't face losing both of them. "So she was brought to the Bear Bowl—"

"What's a Bear Bowl?" Aiyanna interrupted.

"It's a place where bears live and flat-faces go to look at them," Lusa explained.

Aiyanna rolled her eyes. "Flat-faces are weird."

"Yes, well . . . That's where I met Oka. She was so sad, and so scared for the cub she had left behind. I promised her I would escape and find Toklo, and give him a message from her. And I did that, and then we met Kallik at Great Bear Lake, and ended up traveling all the way to the Endless Ice."

"Wow!" Aiyanna stared at Lusa in astonishment. "You guys have been everywhere!"

Lusa realized she might have said too much. *But Aiyanna is really easy to talk to.* "Yeah, we've been traveling for a whole sun-circle," she admitted. "But now it's time to go home."

"And that's why Toklo came here? Because it's where he was born?"

Lusa nodded. "But everything is different," she said. "The wolves have taken over the forest, and there's no room for a new territory."

Aiyanna murmured agreement. "I fought hard to win mine." Rising to her paws, she pointed her snout farther up the hill. "Come with me," she invited.

Lusa got up and followed Aiyanna through the trees until they came to the edge of a rocky river that tumbled down from the mountains. Aiyanna padded along the bank until they came to a spot where they could cross the river by step-ping-stones.

"Careful!" Aiyanna warned. "They can get slippery."

Lusa hopped across warily, wondering where Aiyanna was taking her. As Aiyanna jumped onto the opposite bank, a waterbird took off with a loud alarm call and flapped away into the trees. Aiyanna bounded up to the place where it had appeared.

"I've had my eye on this for a day or two," she said.

Lusa ran over to her and saw a nest with three speckled blue eggs. Her jaws began to water at the thought of crunch-ing them up.

"Come on, we'll take them back to your den," Aiyanna said.

It was difficult to carry three eggs between them, especially crossing the river, but finally, by passing them back and forth to each other, they made it back to the den among the vines.

"These are for you and Toklo," Aiyanna said, surprising Lusa. "Just to prove to you that I can be a friend."

"Thank you," Lusa responded. "That's really good of you."

Aiyanna dipped her head. "I'll see you around," she said, and disappeared into the trees.

Lusa watched her go, warmed by the she-bear's generous gesture. *Maybe the forest isn't such a hostile place after all,* she thought.

CHAPTER EIGHTEEN

Toklo

When Lusa had set out hunting, Toklo slumped to the ground, resentment seething in his belly. *Lusa wants to leave, Kallik and Yakone have already gone . . .* he thought dejectedly. *This is the forest where I was born, but now it's overrun by wolves and the bear that drove me out with Oka and Tobi.* He closed his eyes. *There's nothing I can do . . . nothing.*

Then a familiar scent wreathed around him, and Toklo's eyes flew open. "Ujurak?" he whispered. He looked around, but he was still alone. No familiar brown-bear shape appeared from the undergrowth, but the scent was still there. Toklo felt as if it was stirring him to do something.

Maybe Ujurak is reminding me that I'm never alone, not when he's watching out for me from the stars.

Toklo rose, feeling energy returning to his limbs, and began searching for his friend. "Ujurak! Ujurak!" he called. There was no answer, but a ptarmigan emerged from a thicket and began pecking around in front of him.

"Ujurak, is that you?" Toklo asked uncertainly.

The bird looked at him, its head cocked on one side, then fluttered off into a bush with a disdainful *chack*. Toklo stood looking after it, feeling stupid. *I'm glad Lusa didn't see that!*

But the thought of Ujurak had given him strength. "I'll go find Chogan and confront him," he murmured aloud. "I'll tell him who I really am and make him pay for driving out a she-bear and her cubs all those moons ago!"

Tingling with energy now, Toklo ran through the trees. Birds flew up from under his paws, but he ignored them. When he reached the edge of Chogan's territory, he marched boldly past the scent marks. Striding onward, he began to realize that some things about this part of the forest looked familiar. *That spring between those mossy rocks . . . Tobi and I used to drink there. And I remember when lightning blasted that tree. Tobi and I were so scared! And that boulder shaped like an eagle . . . Oka taught us how to stalk rabbits there.*

When he was well beyond the boundaries of the territory, Toklo halted. "Chogan!" he roared. "Chogan, where are you?" His words echoed around the forest.

Toklo waited; at last he heard the sound of heavy pawsteps crashing through the undergrowth, and Chogan thrust his way into the open. He halted when he saw Toklo, fixing him with a hostile glare.

"What do you want?" he demanded gruffly. "Get off my territory!"

Toklo ignored the old bear's challenge. "Did you once know a bear called Oka, who had two cubs?"

Chogan hesitated, and Toklo braced himself in case the

old bear preferred to fight instead of talk. But after several moments he replied grudgingly, "Yes, I knew Oka. That was a very long time ago."

"I was one of her cubs," Toklo told him. Anger swelled up inside him as he remembered the scene by the river, and how scared he and Tobi had been. "I should have let the wolves tear you apart for what you did to my mother and brother."

Chogan stared at him in disbelief. "*You* were one of those cubs?"

"Yes, I'm Toklo. My brother Tobi died because you forced us to leave our home." As he spoke, Toklo's rage spilled over and he rushed at Chogan, his paws flailing. "You killed my brother, and sent my mother mad with sadness! Why didn't you let her stay?"

Chogan blocked Toklo's attack and swung a powerful forepaw at him, raking his claws down Toklo's shoulder. Toklo veered away from him, then darted back and caught Chogan a blow on the side of his head, following it up with a scratch down his side before leaping back out of range. Chogan bellowed with fury and reared up on his hindpaws, splaying out his forepaws as he advanced on Toklo.

That's a move Oka taught me, Toklo thought. *I wonder if she learned it from Chogan.*

"This is my territory," Chogan growled. "I share it with no bear. I should never have let Oka give birth here; that was my only mistake."

Toklo waited until the huge bear was almost upon him. Then, ducking under the outstretched paws, he hurled himself at one of Chogan's hind legs. The big bear lost his balance, then tottered and fell to the ground with a crash that shook the forest. Toklo narrowly avoided being crushed under the big bear's weight. Slipping aside, he spun around and leaped on top of Chogan, pinning him to the ground with a claw at his throat.

"It was definitely a mistake," he hissed into the old bear's ear. "Because I've come back to take revenge! If you're so determined to live alone, why did you let Oka give birth to us here, you old wolf-breath?"

Chogan's gaze met Toklo's, his eyes glittering with fury. "Because I'm your father," he replied.

Toklo lurched backward. "Wh-what?" he choked. "You're my *father*?" He felt his heart thudding painfully, and for a moment he couldn't think what to say. "Then why did you drive us away?" he asked eventually.

Chogan rose stiffly to his paws and gave an indifferent shrug. "Because this is my home, not yours. Your mother should have taught you to fight for your own territory."

"I taught myself!" Toklo retorted. "And my mother's name is Oka. At least show enough respect for her to use it."

Now that the fight was over, and Chogan wasn't losing to a younger, smaller bear, the rage in his eyes died away, to be replaced by amusement. He circled Toklo, peering at him. "You turned out well," he said. "I could be proud of a son like you. I guess I did the right thing."

Chogan's approval meant nothing to Toklo. Instead, it stung like thorns in his fur. "You have no right to claim credit for raising me," he growled. "I grew up well *in spite of* having a lazy, arrogant father who abandoned my mother. If I ever have cubs, I'd want to watch them growing up close by, and teach them skills to hunt and survive."

Chogan tossed his head. "You'll be grateful to me one day," he sneered.

"Never!" Toklo told him, trying to put all the contempt he felt into the single word. "I have a different family now. I don't need you, and I never did. I'm strong because of who I am, not because of you!"

"Strong, huh?" Chogan's gaze traveled arrogantly over Toklo. "You think you're strong? Let's fight again, and I'll show you just how strong you are!"

Toklo felt fury building inside him. But he didn't want to fight this miserable old bear. "You're my father!" he spat. "Just because you showed no mercy to my mother doesn't mean I can't show mercy to you."

Rage flared in Chogan's eyes. "I don't need your pity!" he snarled. "Fight me. Go on! Show me what you're made of! Any son of mine would have clawed my ears off by now."

"I won't fight unless I have to." Toklo forced himself to speak calmly because he knew that Chogan was trying to make him lose control. "And you know why? Because I'm not like you."

"You'll end up regretting that you let me live to fight another day," Chogan growled. "Now get off my territory! You never belonged here, and you still don't!"

He let out a furious snarl at Toklo, who paused for a

moment to show that he was only leaving because he wanted to. Then he turned and padded away without once glancing back to look at Chogan.

As Toklo stumbled back across the scent line, he was dazed and shaking. Old Grizzly was his father! He remembered how terrified he had been of Chogan when he was a cub, but how he had still admired him and wanted to be like him when he grew up.

Not anymore, he realized. *It's good to be strong and fierce, but not to drive out weaker bears.* Throughout his long journey with his friends, each of them had protected the others and cared for them. *That's better than fighting every other bear, and always being alone.*

Toklo halted and looked back at the territory that had once been his home. "I came such a long way to find this place," he murmured. "Instead, I found the bear who was responsible for destroying my family." He let out a long, tremulous breath. "My own father."

CHAPTER NINETEEN

Kallik

Kallik and Yakone were heading back to the boulders where they had made their den. The sun was going down, staining the snow with scarlet light and casting their long shadows across the slope.

"The hunting is good up here," Kallik mumbled around the hare she was carrying.

Yakone just nodded; his jaws were full of the ptarmigan he had caught.

"Prey is coming back now," Kallik went on, as she dropped her hare at the edge of the den. "It's great!"

"Yes," Yakone agreed, settling down to eat. "Those lazy wolves ought to come back. There's more than enough food for them!"

Kallik still worried about Lusa and Toklo, fighting with the wolves in the forest for every mouthful of prey. A stab of guilt pierced her that she and Yakone had abandoned them.

Still, she comforted herself, *it was the right decision. Yakone is getting his strength back up here. We've been able to walk so far along the ridge!*

The day before, they had stood at the very top of the rocks, looking out at the horizon. In one direction lay the huge flat plain that led toward the Melting Sea. In another, the mountains led all the way to the Endless Ice.

"I can't believe we traveled so far!" Kallik had told Yakone. "Sometimes it was really scary—once we had to swim across a huge river, and I was convinced Lusa wouldn't make it. I practically had to carry her across on my back."

"You were very brave," Yakone replied.

Kallik shrugged. "I didn't feel brave at the time. And some things were wonderful," she went on, "like at Great Bear Lake, where we joined in the ceremonies for the Longest Day. I've never seen so many bears all in one place!"

"Really?" Yakone sounded even more impressed. "We celebrated the Longest Day on Star Island, too, but it was just us."

Kallik felt a pang of sadness that she would never see Star Island again. *Kissimi will be growing big now,* she thought, remembering the cub she had rescued. "Do you miss your home, Yakone?" she asked.

The white bear nodded. "I do, but not as much as I'd miss *you* if I left you to go back there." He hesitated, then added, "But someday I'd like to see them again: Aga, and Illa, and even Unalaq."

"Your brother?" Kallik asked, wondering how one mother could give birth to an awesome bear like Yakone, and a bear like Unalaq, who had done everything he could to make trouble for the travelers.

"Yes . . . he wasn't always such a fish-brain," Yakone said.

"We had some good times together when we were cubs. We used to make burrows in the snow and see who could stay down there the longest. And I used to have races with him and Illa."

"Who won?" Kallik asked.

"Illa, usually. She's fast! And in snow-sky, when the sun hardly rose at all," Yakone added, "we used to hunt seal by starlight. That was awesome!"

The sun had gone down while they were speaking, and stars began to appear overhead. Kallik searched for the brightest star of all, knowing that it pointed out the path to the Endless Ice.

It must have been great, living on Star Island, she thought. *I wish we hadn't needed to leave so soon. I spent all that time traveling to the Endless Ice, and then I never really got to experience it.*

Yakone was gazing at the bright star, too. "I think I can smell the Endless Ice on the wind," he said, a teasing note in his voice.

"Oh, sure!" Kallik gave him a shove. "And I can smell the seals underneath it!"

Yakone's gaze drifted back to the sky, where more and more stars were appearing. "Do you think Ujurak is up there watching us?" he said.

"I know he is," Kallik replied, tracing out the pattern of her friend's constellation. "He'll always watch over us until we find our homes."

Now Kallik dragged her thoughts away from the night before as she sank her jaws into the flesh of the plump hare.

Soon we'll set out again, she thought. *And Ujurak will be with us, every step of the way.*

As sunrise followed sunrise, Kallik realized that even up on the ridge the snow was disappearing. Their snowy den among the boulders was shrinking, and the surface of the rocks felt hot to the touch. The open ground between the snow line and the edge of the forest grew wider each day.

"Soon all the snow will be gone," Kallik said sadly as she emerged from the den one sunrise.

Yakone followed her out. "I'm feeling stronger every day, so who cares if there's snow here or not? We'll be leaving soon, right?"

"Yes," Kallik replied. "Back to the Melting Sea." But somehow the prospect didn't excite her as much as it once had. *What's wrong with me?* she wondered. "I keep remembering that goat we saw on the other side of the ridge. My jaws are watering just thinking about it. I'm hungry."

"Then let's hunt," Yakone said.

Side by side the two white bears climbed to the top of the ridge, where Kallik picked up a goaty scent once again. "I can smell it, but I can't see it," she muttered.

Yakone was scanning the slopes on the far side. "Down there," he said, pointing with one paw.

Kallik followed his gaze and saw a mountain goat perched on a sheer cliff face several bearlengths farther down. "Great spirits, how did it get there?"

Yakone watched the goat for a moment, then glanced

around, assessing the landscape. "You go down toward the trees," he suggested to Kallik, "and I'll chase the goat down to you."

"Great plan!" Kallik agreed. "But be careful!"

She headed down toward the forest, circling low to stay out of sight so she wouldn't alert the goat. Once she was in position, she looked back to see Yakone scrambling down the rocks, and faintly heard him roaring to startle the goat. The mountain goat sprang away, racing down the slopes to where Kallik was waiting. Letting out a snarl, Kallik charged toward it. Panicking, the goat turned back toward the snow line, but Yakone was there, ready to intercept it.

Before Kallik could close in to make the kill, she heard a growl behind her. She whirled around to see the brown she-bear who had driven them out of the forest a few days before. Her two cubs were just behind her, staring round-eyed at Kallik.

"You're trespassing *and* stealing prey!" the she-bear accused her.

"No, we're not!" Kallik protested. "We're hunting above the tree line!"

Refusing to argue, Kallik spun around again and headed back up the slope to where Yakone was now chasing the goat toward the abandoned waterfall. The brown she-bear followed with her cubs hard on her paws. Ignoring her, Kallik raced after Yakone, her muscles burning as her paws flew over the barren terrain. Reaching the waterfall, she began climbing after Yakone over the rock-strewn snow, with the goat leaping lightly ahead.

Nearly there . . . Kallik thought grimly, trying to force every last scrap of speed out of her legs.

But when they were almost upon the goat, Kallik heard a dreadful creaking noise, as if the ground beneath her paws was groaning. She lurched backward. At first she thought her paws were slipping on the rocks slick with snowmelt.

No! The whole world is falling away!

Kallik was swept off her paws as all the snow, boulders, and dead branches in the old waterfall slid down the mountain in a terrifying avalanche. Rocks crashed into her sides; a mixture of snow and earth covered her head and carried her down with it, tumbling her head over tail. She fell in a chaotic darkness, with only flashes of light here and there to tell her she wasn't blind. Down, down, down . . . Kallik thought the battering and falling would go on forever.

At last Kallik thumped against something solid. She felt like every bone in her body was broken. Her mouth was full of grit and snow, and though her eyes were open, she couldn't see anything.

I have to climb out . . . she thought groggily, but she didn't know which way to dig. Then she felt something dripping on her paw, and realized that it must be snowmelt from the debris covering her. Now that she knew which direction was up, Kallik dug determinedly with her forepaws, even though all her muscles were shrieking in protest.

At last her head broke through the covering of rocks, earth, and snow. She spat out a mouthful of damp soil, blinked her stinging eyes, and looked around.

The avalanche had cut a swathe of destruction across the lower slopes of the ridge and into the forest. The surface looked like a solid, choppy sea. Uprooted bushes, boulders, and chunks of ice had punched down through the trees; some trees had crashed down and been carried along, while others leaned sideways, supported by others. The force of the avalanche had been spent, but the massive devastation it left behind made Kallik's head reel.

"Yakone!" she called out, her voice no more than a croak. "Yakone, where are you?"

There was no sign of the white bear. Terrified, Kallik dragged herself out of the snow and stumbled across the surface of the avalanche, calling and searching. Her panic mounting, she finally spotted a small uprooted pine tree with a tuft of white fur clinging to a branch.

"Yakone!" Kallik gasped, starting to dig with huge scoops of her forepaws.

At first she found nothing but earth, snow, and debris. But every so often she would stop and listen with her ear pressed to the snow, and at last she heard a groan come faintly from below. Kallik dug even more frantically and let out a cry of relief as she revealed a patch of white fur. Yakone raised his head, shaking off loose twigs and shards of ice.

"Wha' . . . happened?" he rasped.

"You're alive!" Kallik exclaimed.

Grunting with pain, Yakone hauled himself upward. Kallik grabbed his shoulder in her jaws and pulled, and at last he managed to free himself from the avalanche and stagger to the solid ground beyond. Looking him over anxiously, Kallik could see that he was battered, that his pelt was filthy, and that his wounded paw was bleeding again. But he didn't seem badly hurt.

As they stood panting at the edge of the snowfall, Kallik heard a tiny wail coming from farther into the forest. Glancing around, she spotted one of the small brown cubs standing at the edge of the undamaged trees.

"Mother! Yas!" he barked.

Forcing her aching limbs into motion, Kallik bounded down to join the little cub. "What's the matter?" she asked.

The cub was too upset to be afraid of her. "My mother and my sister, Yas," he whimpered. "I've lost them! They were swept away when the ground started to fall."

Horror seized Kallik at the thought of more bears being trapped in the devastation. "Don't worry!" she assured the little cub. "We'll find them!".

She began scrabbling around among the debris, but that set off another snowslide that almost carried the cub off his paws. Only Yakone, coming up from behind to grab him by the scruff, saved him from being swept away.

"We have to think this through," Yakone said, setting the cub down gently, well away from the edge of the avalanche. "Little one, do you know where your mother and sister were standing? Can you pick out a tree that was close to them when they fell?"

The cub peered across the waste of snow and ice. "Over

there," he said at last, pointing with his snout toward an uprooted oak that lay half-buried with its roots in the air.

The bark on the part of the tree trunk that Kallik could see looked like an angry bear face. With a sharp pang, Kallik remembered Lusa's bear spirits, and how distressed the black bear would be that their trees had been destroyed. *Take care, spirits,* she prayed silently. *Travel safely to the stars.*

The tree the cub had pointed out was right in the middle of the snowfall.

"How are we going to get out there?" Kallik asked, giving Yakone an uncertain glance. "We'll just sink back into the snow if we try it."

Yakone shook his head. "I don't know, but there has to be a way."

"Please don't leave my mother and sister to die," the cub pleaded.

"Of course we won't," Kallik said. "Yakone, what if we lay something on top of the snow? That way we could spread out our weight."

"It might work," Yakone murmured, measuring the distance with a glance. "Let's see what we can find."

Kallik spotted twigs sticking up at the edge of the churned-up earth and hauled out a long branch. "This would do, but we need to find more."

Gradually the white bears built a path of logs and branches out toward the uprooted oak. Then Kallik crept along it, with Yakone just behind her, ready to drag her out of the snow if the support gave way. The branches creaked, and some of them snapped under the weight of Kallik's paws, but they kept her on top of the snow and earth. At last she reached the oak tree and leaned carefully off the edge of the wooden path to dig with her front paws.

"Can you find anything?" Yakone called from behind her.

Kallik shook her head. "There's no sign of them near the surface," she reported. "Let me listen."

Crouching down, she pressed her ear to the snow. Yakone edged his way to her side and felt the surface gently with one paw.

"I think there's something under here," he said. "Can you hear anything?"

"I'm not sure. . . ." Kallik strained to listen, remembering how skillful Yakone was at sensing what was underneath snow. "Wait. Yes . . . I can hear tiny little scrabbling sounds. Dig down here!"

Lifting each pawful of snow out as gently as they could, Kallik and Yakone scooped a hole, shoring up the sides with branches as they went.

"This reminds me of how my mother built the walls of our den when I was a cub," Yakone said.

Kallik nodded. "Me too. But she didn't have to do it in the middle of an avalanche!"

"What's happening?" the little cub yelped from the edge of the snowfall. "Oh, please hurry!"

"We *can't* hurry," Yakone called back. "But don't worry— we're doing our best!"

Kallik began to despair as they dug farther and farther into the chaos of snow and ice and rocks. *We should have found something by now. This can't be the right place....*

Then, instead of more snow, her paw landed against soaked fur. Peering into the hole, she spotted a sodden brown flank. "Yakone! Here!" she exclaimed.

With delicate scrapes, Kallik shifted the snow from around the body until she revealed a tiny cub, even smaller than the one who waited under the trees. She fastened her teeth gently in the cub's scruff and drew her out. The little bear felt icy cold and had no sign of life in her at all.

Please, spirits, let her be alive! Kallik prayed.

Leaving Yakone to keep on digging, Kallik carried the cub to the edge of the snow.

"Yas! Yas!" her brother shrieked, jumping up and down. His eyes bulged as Kallik laid the little body down beside him. "Is she dead?" he whimpered.

"Let's hope not," Kallik responded, though she feared the worst. "Come on, lick her and rub her fur to get her warm again."

The cub crouched over his sister and started to lick her vigorously. "Wake up, Yas," he encouraged her.

Kallik licked and rubbed, too, and at last the she-cub let out a faint squeak. Her eyelids flickered, and she coughed up a mouthful of melting snow.

"Oh, thank the spirits!" Kallik exclaimed. "You keep licking her," she instructed the male cub. "I'll help Yakone dig your mother out."

When Kallik had edged back over the path of branches, she

saw that Yakone had already dug down deeper and uncovered the mother bear. Kallik helped him to clear more snow and debris from around her, shoring up the walls with branches like before. While they were working, the mother bear coughed and raised her head feebly.

"Wapi? Yas?" she murmured.

"Your cubs are safe," Kallik reassured her. "Now we have to get you out."

The bear tried to get to her paws, but only flopped down into the hole again with a groan. "I'm sorry. I can't climb out," she said.

"And she's too heavy for us to lift," Yakone murmured to Kallik. "What are we going to do? It's already getting dark."

Kallik had been so absorbed in rescuing the brown bears that she had hardly noticed the sun setting. Now twilight covered the slopes, the snow shining eerily in the light of the first stars.

"Rest for a bit," Kallik said to the mother bear.

"But I need to see my cubs. Are you sure they're not hurt?" The brown she-bear made another massive effort to get up, only to sink back again.

"Stay where you are," Kallik urged. "I'll bring the cubs to you." She padded back along the path to the cubs. "We've found your mother," she told them. "She's fine, but she needs to rest. I'll take you to her. We've made her a sort of den."

The male cub, Wapi, jumped up and down, letting out a shrill roar of delight. His sister Yas still looked shaky, but her eyes shone.

Kallik nudged Wapi ahead of her along the path, then picked up Yas by her scruff and followed. Wapi jumped down into the hole with his mother, and Kallik lowered Yas down after him. The mother bear drew them to her, and they snuggled into her fur.

"This isn't safe," Yakone said quietly to Kallik.

"We can't keep them apart," Kallik responded. "If the hole starts to collapse, we'll get the cubs out of there."

The two white bears settled down at the top of the hole, alert for every creak and shift of snow. Beneath them the mother bear nuzzled her cubs and licked them all over, fluffing up their fur. At last she looked up at Kallik and Yakone.

"I'm feeling better," she announced. "I think I could try getting out now."

"Okay," Kallik said. "Let us take the cubs first."

With Kallik's help the two cubs scrambled out of the hole. Yas was strong enough to walk now, and Kallik led them both along the path of branches to make sure they reached the edge of the avalanche safely. Then she returned to Yakone and the mother bear. Looking down into the hole, Kallik saw that the she-bear had risen to her paws.

"Stand back," she said. "I'm going to climb out."

Kallik and Yakone retreated a bearlength and heard scrabbling sounds as the mother bear clambered upward. Her head and her forepaws appeared out of the hole; Yakone stepped forward and bent over to grab her by the neck and pull.

But at the same time the snow began to shift again. The hole started to collapse inward, while the mother bear was only halfway out. Kallik leaped forward, but the branch path broke beneath her paws and she found herself floundering in loose snow. Finally reaching the brown bear, she boosted her upward and shoved her toward the edge of the devastation.

"Go! Go!" she roared.

Kallik caught a glimpse of Yakone guiding the she-bear onto the remains of the branch path; he was gazing back at her with a look of horror in his eyes.

"Go!" Kallik repeated.

Her roar was cut off as a falling boulder struck her and carried her off her paws. Struggling to regain her balance, she was dragged down in a fresh storm of snow and earth and uprooted trees. She heard Yakone roar, "Kallik!" but in a moment she couldn't see him anymore.

Paws flailing, Kallik slid down with the avalanche. She was sinking into the snow when she slammed into a tree that was wedged across the flow. Desperately she sank her claws into it and clung there, her eyes tightly shut, as the rest of the world slid past her like thunder.

At last the movement stopped and silence fell, broken only by Yakone's voice. "Kallik! Kallik, are you okay?"

Dazed and bruised all over, Kallik opened her eyes. Across a sea of snow and rocks and branches, she saw Yakone standing with the brown bear family beside him.

"Stay there!" Yakone called. "I'm coming to get you."

"No!" Kallik didn't want to put him in danger. "I can make it."

Still clinging to the tree, she worked her way along to the

end, then launched herself at a boulder that was sticking up out of the devastation. From there she scrambled over a few branches and finally reached solid ground beside Yakone. He bent over, grabbed her shoulder, and helped her for the last couple of pawsteps.

"I thought you were dead," he whispered, his voice shaking.

Kallik's whole body was one vast ache, but everything seemed to be working. "I'm fine," she said.

The brown she-bear stepped forward and dipped her head to the white bears. "Thank you," she said. "If it wasn't for you, Yas and I would be dead, and Wapi left to fend for himself. I am Izusa," she added. "I'll always remember what you did."

Kallik exchanged an embarrassed glance with Yakone. "It wasn't anything," she mumbled.

"You risked your lives for us," the she-bear went on. "You're white bears; you didn't have to do that."

"The color of your fur doesn't matter," Kallik responded. "We would never have left you to die."

She felt a surge of relief as Yakone pressed himself against her side. "No," he said. "Bears stick together, whatever happens."

CHAPTER TWENTY

Lusa

Lusa was dozing in the den when she heard pawsteps approaching. She stuck her nose out and saw Toklo coming toward her through the undergrowth. She drew in a horrified breath when she saw how battered and scratched he was.

"What happened?" she barked, scrambling out of the den and bounding to his side. "Was it wolves?" She was shocked at the fury smoldering in Toklo's eyes as he turned to face her.

"No," he growled. "It was my father."

Shock froze Lusa's paws to the ground. For a moment she could only gape at him. When she spoke, her voice was a strangled squeak. "Your *father*?"

Toklo nodded. "You remember I told you that Chogan was the bear who drove my family out? I went to confront him about what he'd done." He spat every word as if he was trying to pour out all his hatred for the big bear. "We fought. I told him I was Oka's cub, and that's when he told me he was my father."

"Who won the fight?" Lusa gasped.

Toklo snorted. "I did."

Excitement was swelling up inside Lusa. "You thought you had no family left!" she exclaimed.

Toklo fixed Lusa with a long look. "You're my family," he said at last. "No one else."

Lusa felt a pang in her heart, of pity and affection for Toklo. "Go into the den," she said. "I'll find some herbs for those scratches."

When she came back from a quick foraging expedition and was chewing up the herbs to put on Toklo's wounds, Lusa said, "Don't you want to talk to Chogan? Maybe what happened wasn't as simple as you've always thought."

Toklo shook his head. "Lusa, I know you were close to your family in the Bear Bowl, so it's hard for you to understand that some kin-bears aren't friends." A trace of anger crept into his tone. "Don't try to change my mind."

"Oh, Toklo . . ." Lusa stopped smoothing the herb mush onto his scratches and leaned her head against his shoulder. "Please try to forgive your father. It would be worth it to have some real family again."

A low growl rose in Toklo's throat. "Chogan is dead to me."

I wish I could do something for him, Lusa thought, though she knew she couldn't go on pushing him.

Toklo ate the rabbit Lusa had caught and one of Aiyanna's eggs, then tried to sleep, but he tossed and turned all night.

At dawn Toklo finally slipped into deeper sleep. Lusa decided to leave him in peace for a while. Creeping out of the den, she headed for her favorite patch of green shoots. The sky was overcast; Lusa relished the cool shadows of the forest and the freshness of the dew that misted her pelt as she pushed through the undergrowth.

When she had eaten enough green shoots, Lusa dug for maggots among the roots of a tree, licking up the tasty grubs until her belly was comfortably full. *I'll see if I can catch something for Toklo,* she thought. *He'll be hungry when he wakes up.*

Spotting a squirrel nibbling something at the foot of a tree a few bearlengths away, she stalked carefully toward it, but at the last moment a breeze sprang up, carrying her scent toward her prey.

The squirrel jerked upright, then swarmed up the tree with Lusa hard after it. But once it reached the cover of the leafy boughs it vanished; Lusa decided it must have leaped into another tree.

"Seal rot!" she hissed.

She was about to climb down and search for some other prey when she spotted movement in the undergrowth. Thin, dark shapes were slinking through the forest like ominous fish. Their scent drifted up to her.

Wolves!

Lusa dug her claws into her branch and clung on, hardly daring to breathe. She couldn't forget the horror of almost being dragged out of a tree by coyotes. *We've only heard wolves hunting at night before,* she thought. *Why are they out in daylight? Maybe it's because the day is so dark.*

As she crouched among the leaves, trying to track the wolves by the movement of ferns and bushes, Lusa heard another sound. Two high voices were raised in excitement, and the little cubs she had seen the day before tumbled into the open, play-wrestling with each other.

"You're a grouse and I caught you!" Flo squealed.

"Okay." Fala shook off her little sister and stood up. "Now you be a grouse and I'll stalk you."

"No, I don't want to practice anymore," Flo objected. "I want to do it for real."

"Yeah," her sister agreed. "Let's find a big deer and catch it for Mother!"

Oh, please don't make so much noise! Lusa willed the cubs. *There are wolves close by.*

To her relief the little bears were quiet as they padded across the open ground beneath her, sniffing at the air as they tried to locate prey. They were moving away from the wolves, and Lusa began to hope that they would escape.

But then Flo noticed the dug-up earth where Lusa had been foraging for maggots. "Look!" she yelped. "Grubs! Come on, Fala—they're so good!"

Lusa heard a rustle in the undergrowth and knew with a cold shock of horror that the wolves had heard them. She caught a glimpse of the dark shapes slinking toward her, their lean gray backs just visible over the tops of the ferns. The cubs had no idea they were there, and stayed happily at the foot of the tree, munching the maggots and playfully swiping at each other.

Lusa wanted nothing more than to stay in the safety of her tree, but she knew she couldn't stay there and let Fala and Flo be torn apart by wolves. Gathering her courage, she leaped down and raced over to the two cubs.

"Wolves! Climb the tree!" she ordered.

At first the two cubs didn't seem to have heard what she said.

"Where did you come from? Are you a bear-squirrel?" Fala asked curiously.

"Or a bird?" Flo barked. She gave Lusa a friendly nudge. "Hey, wait. I know you! We saw you by the stream!"

"Listen!" Lusa's terror was growing. "Wolves are coming. You have to climb this tree."

Now the cubs' eyes widened, and they exchanged a frightened glance.

"We don't know how to climb," Fala protested. "Mother told us to run away if wolves came."

"It's too late!" Lusa said, glancing over her shoulder to where she could see the betraying movement of the ferns. "If you run, they'll catch you. Wolves could outrun you in their sleep!" She didn't wait to argue anymore. She shoved Flo up the tree, ignoring the little cub's squeak of protest. "Put your paw in that knothole," she directed. "Push with your hind-paws. That's right. Now sit on that branch and hold on!"

Lusa could hear the wolves growling softly, their pawsteps crunching through the bracken. "Go!" she barked, boosting Fala up the trunk next.

Thankfully, she saw that Fala had gotten the idea of how to climb and quickly scrambled up the tree to join her sister on the branch.

At the same moment the first wolf launched itself from the undergrowth, racing across the clearing with massive strides. A second wolf was close behind. Lusa hurled herself up the tree behind the cubs, with teeth snapping at her hindpaws.

"Go higher!" she gasped when she reached the branch where the cubs were crouching. "Go! I won't let you fall!"

Wailing with terror, the two cubs clambered farther up the tree, clinging to the trunk as they gazed down at the ravenous wolves. Two of them circled the tree, their jaws gaping and their tongues lolling. Now and again they jumped up, raking their forepaws down the bark. After a few moments they lay down, their forelegs stretched out and their heads alert as they gazed with angry yellow eyes at the bears huddled in the tree. Lusa thought these wolves looked young; they were smaller than the ones that had attacked Chogan, but they were still dangerous.

How long can we stay up here? Lusa wondered. She could see that the cubs were already getting tired. *They won't be able to hang on much longer.*

Then Lusa heard new pawsteps approaching, and a voice called out, "Fala! Flo! Where are you?"

"It's our mother!" Fala gasped.

Oh no! Lusa thought. *The wolves will hear her!*

Already the wolves had risen to their paws, their ears pricked as they sniffed the air. The mother bear called out again; she was getting closer.

"I have your cubs up here!" Lusa shouted. "Look out! There are wolves!"

There was a loud crackle and the mother bear launched herself through the undergrowth, her teeth bared in a ferocious snarl, her claws out, ready to slash at the wolves as she hurtled toward them. The wolves leaped at her. The she-bear rose on her hindpaws and swiped at them, but she couldn't fight both of them at once. One of them fastened its teeth in her hindquarters while the other sprang up and grabbed hold of her shoulder, pulling her down to all four paws again.

"Oh no!" Flo whimpered. "The wolves will eat her!"

"No, they won't," Lusa said. "You two just hold on tight!"

Her heart thudding in panic, Lusa jumped to the ground and hurled herself on the nearest wolf. It let go of the she-bear with a growl and turned on Lusa; they rolled over and over together, paws flailing and teeth snapping. Lusa felt a sharp pain in her shoulder as the wolf's jaws closed on it.

She caught a glimpse of the mother bear on top of the other wolf, clawing at its throat. The wolf let out a howl of pain, struggling to get up. Then Lusa lost sight of the brown bear, as the wolf atop her bore down with burning eyes and parted jaws.

Oh, Arcturus, help! Lusa prayed, battering the wolf with both forepaws.

Suddenly a huge brown paw thumped down on the wolf's shoulder, tearing it away from Lusa. She staggered to her paws to see the other wolf vanishing into the undergrowth, yelping as it went. The she-bear threw a couple of stinging blows around the head of the wolf that had attacked Lusa, and it fled after its packmate.

Lusa and the she-bear were left looking at each other. Lusa's chest heaved as she fought for enough breath to speak.

"Thank you," the brown bear began. "I—"

"Mother! Mother!" Shrill cries came from the tree where Lusa had left the cubs. "We're up here!"

The she-bear padded over to them and stood at the bottom of the tree. "You can come down now," she panted. "It's safe."

"But how do we get down?" Fala asked, while Flo wailed, "We're stuck!"

"It's okay!" Lusa called to them. "I'll come help you."

She climbed quickly up the tree to the two frightened cubs and began coaxing them down from branch to branch, showing them where to put their paws.

Fala made it to the lowest branch, then launched herself to the ground in a mighty leap. "I'm a squirrel-bear!" she announced.

Her mother sniffed her all over, making sure she wasn't hurt. "Thank the spirits!" she said. "Maybe we should practice tree climbing, too."

Meanwhile Lusa was guiding Flo's paws into cracks and knotholes in the tree bark, but the little cub hurried too much, and her paws slipped. She let out a screech as she plummeted through the leaves.

"Flo!" Her mother darted forward and managed to break her fall with her shoulder.

Flo rolled over on the ground, her paws waving in the air. "I can fly!" she squealed.

While Lusa was climbing down the tree, the mother bear

gathered the two cubs together. "What have I told you about going too far from our den?" she scolded.

"But we were going to catch a deer for you," Fala told her.

"And we were fine," Flo added. "That funny black bear saved us. I think she's a squirrel."

Lusa dropped down to the ground and padded over to the brown bears. "My name's Lusa," she said.

The brown she-bear looked her over with friendly interest. "I'm Makya," she said. "And these are Fala and Flo. I think you must be the black bear they told me about, the one who spoke to them by the stream one day?"

"That's right," Lusa said.

"Thank you for saving my cubs," Makya murmured, her eyes clouding with emotion. "Things have been so hard since the wolves came down into the forest. They came early in snow-sky, and even though the weather's getting warmer now, they don't seem to want to go back."

Lusa nodded. "My friend Toklo is really angry that wolves have taken over the forest."

"Every bear is angry," Makya agreed. "When we woke up from the longsleep, the wolves had already taken most of the prey. It's getting harder and harder to find food, and it doesn't help when new bears arrive," she added with a growl.

She means us, Lusa thought sadly. "I won't be staying here much longer," she said.

Makya paused, seeming to realize she had been tactless. "Well, thank you again for what you did," she said briskly. "Fala, Flo, we need to be getting back to the den." She dipped her head to Lusa. "Perhaps we'll meet again."

"Yes, come and see us," Fala invited.

"You can teach us to climb trees!" Flo said excitedly.

"Maybe," Lusa said, though she wondered whether Makya would want her around.

As she watched the brown bear family head off into the undergrowth, Lusa struggled with a surge of feeling. *The wolves are endangering the lives of every bear in the forest. And yet Makya and her cubs still have each other. And Toklo has his father, even though he wants nothing to do with him. Plus, he has Aiyanna. She's way nicer than Toklo will admit. But I have no one. Where are all the black bears?*

Lusa was struck by the memory of playing with black bears in the woodland beside Great Bear Lake. *There were more black bears there than I've ever seen in my life!* They hadn't all been friendly, but some of them had treated her like family, helping her to learn how to survive in the wild.

Lusa glanced up at the sky. Today the sun was covered by cloud, but when it was shining, it was almost at its highest. It must be nearly the Longest Day, which meant bears would be gathering at Great Bear Lake once more. Excitement flooded through Lusa, and she felt a tug at her paws. If she could find her way back to the lake, she would find the black bears again!

Yes, that's the answer!

Lusa's courage wavered for a moment. It was a long, long journey, yet again. But she knew it was what she had to do.

My journey will end only when I find other black bears to live with. And I know where I can do that. . . .

CHAPTER TWENTY-ONE

Kallik

The hare streaked across the slope, with Kallik hard on its paws. It wore its brown burn-sky pelt, making it easy to spot against the remaining patches of snow. Kallik had to look harder when it darted onto a stretch of bare rock, so she switched to her forest hunting skills, stalking it slowly until she was close enough to leap and make her kill.

"Good catch, Kallik!" Yakone bounded up to her. His gait was still uneven from his damaged paw, but Kallik could see that he was so much fitter and stronger than before.

The two white bears settled down together to share their prey. Up here on the ridge, Kallik could enjoy the warmth of the sun on her pelt, for the wind was still crisp and cold, and she realized that the snow would never vanish entirely.

As she watched Yakone basking with his eyes half-closed, he let out a grunt, as if he had just decided something. "It's time to leave," he said.

Kallik stared at him, her belly lurching with shock. "Really?"

Yakone opened his eyes and met her gaze. "I'm well enough

to travel," he said. "If we stay here, it will just get hotter. There's no reason not to leave."

Kallik looked down at her paws. "I suppose . . ."

"This was always our plan, wasn't it?" Yakone reminded her gently.

Kallik was silent for a moment, struggling with her doubts. Then she looked at Yakone. They had been through so much together—she owed him the truth, even if it wasn't what he wanted to hear. "I don't know if I want to go back to the Melting Sea," she confessed in a rush. "I want to see Lusa and Toklo again. I'm not ready to leave them, not when they haven't found their new homes. Toklo still doesn't feel comfortable here, and Lusa hasn't found any more black bears."

To her astonishment, Yakone nodded. Leaning over, he touched Kallik's shoulder with his snout. "Why didn't you tell me before?"

"I was afraid you'd be angry. I'm sorry."

"And I'm sorry, too," Yakone responded. "I worried that we were doing the wrong thing by leaving them so soon. I should have talked to you."

Kallik blinked affectionately at Yakone, happiness warming her like the sunlight. *We've been honest with each other just in time.* "So we'll go back and find Toklo and Lusa, and help them get settled," she said.

Yakone looked at her with his head tilted to one side. "And then?"

Kallik hesitated, then remembered this was the time for telling the truth. "I thought we might go back to the

Endless Ice, to Star Island."

Yakone's eyes shone. "Home!" he exclaimed, then added less certainly, "At least, *my* home. Are you sure that's what you want?"

Kallik nodded. "I will always miss my brother, but he has his own life now. I left the Melting Sea to find the Endless Ice, but I never had a chance to appreciate it. Now that I know it really exists, I want to go back, to stay for longer—perhaps forever."

Yakone nuzzled her shoulder. "I'll be honored to take you home with me."

The white bears were well rested now, their bellies full from the hare. Kallik rose to her paws. "Then let's go."

Before they headed down to the forest, they climbed the last few bearlengths to the very top of the ridge and looked down on the other side, where the destruction of the avalanche was still visible.

"I hope Izusa, Wapi, and Yas are still safe," Kallik said.

"They will be." Yakone gave a snort of amusement. "We'll probably go down in legend as the mysterious white bears who dug them out of a snowfall!"

With a last look at the far slopes, Kallik turned and padded beside Yakone back over the ridge and toward the familiar forest. Wind buffeted them, whipping up the snow into sharp little flakes. Kallik hesitated for a moment at the top of the scree that led down the cliff; it looked too much like the old waterfall where they had been trapped by the avalanche. Then she told herself she was being stupid. *It couldn't happen twice—could it?*

Letting Yakone take the lead, she half climbed, half slid down the narrow gully, trying to grip the rocks with her paws. Her heart thumped every time a pebble shifted under her weight, and she let out a huff of relief as they reached the bottom.

Heading down the lower slopes, Kallik was aware that the air was growing hotter and dustier. Her mouth was dry, and she longed for a drink of cool water. *But what matters is that I'm going to see Lusa and Toklo again!*

The white bears followed the rocky, exposed shoulder of the hillside as far as the edge of the forest. Confronted by the dark, rustling trees, Kallik felt a moment of disquiet; this still wasn't a natural place for her to be.

"Toklo and Lusa will be amazed to see us," Yakone said, padding up beside her.

"I hope they haven't moved on," Kallik said, realizing for the first time that her friends might have left the forest. *This is Toklo's home,* she reminded herself. *But then, there are the wolves. . . .*

Kallik broke into a run, scrambling down the last part of the rocky shoulder and plunging into the trees. But once she was surrounded by the soaring trunks, she felt disoriented.

"Everything looks the same," she muttered. "How are we supposed to find our way in here?"

"We just need to look more carefully," Yakone suggested.

Taking a deep breath, Kallik forced herself to slow down and look around more closely. As her eyes adjusted to the gloom, she started to recognize some of her surroundings.

"I'm pretty sure I've seen that before," she said to Yakone, pointing with her snout at a buckthorn bush. "And the crooked tree that looks a bit like caribou antlers."

Yakone nodded, though Kallik saw that he was looking confused, too. It took a while before they were sure of where they were, and were able to follow faint paths through the undergrowth until they reached the den among the brambles.

"Toklo! Lusa!" Kallik called out. "We came back!"

There was no reply. The broken branches and torn vegetation from their battle with the wolves still lay strewn around the outside of the den. When Kallik peered through the remaining brambles, she saw that the den was empty; Toklo's and Lusa's scents were cold and stale.

"I can smell fresh wolf scent," Yakone reported. "They've been back here since we left, I'm sure of it."

Kallik shuddered. "Do you think the wolves came back and drove Toklo and Lusa out?" she fretted. "They might be hurt. We have to find them!"

She began looking around for any blood or tufts of bear fur that would tell her there had been another attack. But all she found were a few scraps of rabbit fur and a scattering of feathers.

"Okay, there's no fresh scent here," Yakone said. "But there's no blood, either. If Lusa and Toklo left, they were walking, and uninjured."

His words comforted Kallik a little, but she knew that she wouldn't feel real relief until she was reunited with her friends. "We have to find them," she repeated determinedly.

Together Kallik and Yakone trekked through the forest in ever-widening circles around the abandoned den.

"Maybe we should split up to cover more ground," Yakone suggested.

Kallik shook her head. "No. I'm not going to risk losing you, too."

The forest seemed dark and threatening as they continued their search. Kallik felt like hostile eyes were watching them from every tree and clump of bushes. Her ears were pricked for the slightest sound, and she sniffed the air, hoping to pick up her friends' scents.

But it was Yakone who first noticed a new smell. "Wolves!" he hissed, shoving Kallik into the shelter of a bramble thicket.

Kallik caught the scent, too, along with the reek of blood, and poked her head out cautiously to see what was happening. Two young wolves limped past, slinking along with their tails between their legs. Patches of bare skin showed where their fur had been torn out, and they were both bleeding from deep scratches.

"It looks as if they met their match," Yakone remarked as they emerged from hiding once the wolves had gone. "I'd say a couple of fierce bears, wouldn't you?"

Kallik nodded. "And what two fierce bears do we know who have been fighting wolves?" she asked, suddenly optimistic. "Come on!"

She led Yakone back along the wolves' trail, following the scent and the smears of blood in the undergrowth. It led to a clearing where the earth had been churned up under a tree.

The air was filled with the scents of bears and blood, and tufts of fur were scattered on the ground. Kallik's hope suddenly vanished, replaced by the chill of fear.

"What if—" she began.

"Kallik! Yakone!" A voice full of amazement and joy interrupted Kallik, and Lusa bounded out from behind a tree. "You're back!"

"Lusa!" Kallik ran up to her friend and began checking her all over for injuries. "What happened?" she demanded. "Don't tell me you fought off those wolves by yourself!"

Lusa shook her head. "No. They were hunting a couple of brown bear cubs. I got the cubs to safety in a tree, and then their mother and I fought the wolves."

"That was very brave, saving those cubs," Kallik said when she was satisfied that her friend wasn't badly hurt. She gave Lusa's ears an extra lick.

"What was it like on the ridge?" Lusa asked, wriggling free. "And why are you back here?"

"It was fine up there," Kallik replied. "But Yakone is strong enough to travel now."

All the happiness drained out of Lusa's face. "Then you'll be leaving the forest?"

"No, not exactly," Yakone told her. "We want to stay with you and Toklo until you find your homes, and then we'll go back to the Endless Ice."

Lusa's eyes stretched wide. "Wow!" she exclaimed. "Well, I've just decided where I want to go," she continued. "I'm going back to Great Bear Lake, to find black bears to live with." She blinked at Kallik. "I love being with you two, and Toklo, but in the end I need to be a black bear."

Kallik's admiration grew as she listened to Lusa's plans. "That's even braver than fighting wolves!" she said.

Lusa shrugged. "I don't feel brave," she confessed. "It's a long way to Great Bear Lake."

"But we can go with you!" Kallik said. Her paws tingled with excitement at the thought of traveling with Lusa again. "The lake is on the way to the Endless Ice, more or less."

"Yes, of course," Yakone agreed. "I've never been to the Longest Day gathering. I'd love to see what happens."

"Oh, thank you!" Lusa flicked her stubby tail in delight. "It's settled, then."

"I guess we can leave soon," Kallik said. "Toklo will stay here, I suppose."

"I'm not sure. This is his home, but it's not as simple as that," Lusa said.

"Why? What do you mean?" Kallik asked.

Lusa huffed out a long breath. "You know the bear who Maniitok called Old Grizzly? Well, Toklo and I helped him fight off some wolves, and Toklo remembered that back when he and Tobi were cubs, Old Grizzly drove them and their mother out of his territory."

"That's terrible!" Kallik gasped.

"But that's not all," Lusa went on. "Toklo went to fight Chogan—that's Old Grizzly's name—and challenged him about what he did, and it turns out that Chogan is Toklo's *father*."

Kallik exchanged an astonished glance with Yakone. She was too stunned to speak.

"Toklo is still very angry with Chogan for driving them out," Lusa said. "I suppose he'll stay here in the forest because it's where he was born, but he doesn't seem settled or happy."

Kallik knew how much Toklo had dreamed of returning to his own forest and carving out a territory there. She felt so sorry for him that his dreams had been tainted like this. "Is there anything we can do?" she asked.

Lusa's eyes darkened. "Well, there is one thing. . . . I've had an idea! And there are more bears than just Toklo who'd thank us for it."

Yakone tipped his head to one side. "What do you mean?"

Lusa braced her shoulders. "We have to find a way to get rid of the wolves!"

CHAPTER TWENTY-TWO

Lusa

Lusa felt warm with relief as she led Kallik and Yakone through the darkening forest to the vine thicket. *It's going to be pretty cramped with all four of us,* she thought, *but at least we're together again. And Toklo will be so pleased to see them!*

"Toklo!" she called as they padded up to the den. "Come see who's here!"

Toklo pushed his way into the open, then halted, staring, as he spotted Kallik and Yakone. "What are you doing here?" he asked gruffly. "Are you on your way to the Melting Sea?"

Lusa was shocked that he sounded so unwelcoming. "Toklo!" she began, but the brown bear cut her off with a glare.

"We've said good-bye already," he muttered, turning away.

Lusa felt a stab of sympathy. Did Toklo think he was about to lose the white bears all over again?

"Actually, we're going to the Endless Ice," Kallik corrected him. "And on the way we'll take Lusa to Great Bear Lake."

Toklo gave a grunt of surprise. "I see you've all made your plans."

"You've found your home," Lusa pointed out. "Now we have to find ours." She stepped forward and rested her muzzle against his shoulder. "But not yet. Not until you feel this is truly your home."

Toklo looked startled, then glanced around at his friends. "I don't know if I can stay here," he admitted. "It isn't what I expected."

Kallik padded up to Toklo's side and pressed her muzzle into his shoulder. "I know the forest isn't as good as you remembered," she said. "But what if we got rid of the wolves?"

Toklo looked at her like she had gone crazy. "We can't kill them all!"

"I don't mean kill them," Kallik explained. "Actually, it was Lusa's idea." She turned to Lusa. "I've been thinking about what you said, and there could be a way to do it. The prey is coming back to the ridge as the snow melts, so the wolves don't need to be down here in the forest anymore."

Toklo gave a contemptuous snort. "So what are you going to do?" he snapped. "Ask them to just go away?"

Kallik looked at Yakone. "You remember that shaft we had to climb up to get to the top of the cliff? What if we got the wolves up onto the ridge, and then found a way to block the route back?"

Lusa saw that Yakone was starting to look excited. *He thinks Kallik's plan might work!*

"Kallik's right," the white bear said, turning to Lusa and Toklo. "That narrow shaft is the only way up or down a sheer cliff that stretches for skylengths. If the wolves can't get down it, then they'll be stuck up there, forced to get used to their old territory again."

Lusa blinked. "Assuming we could get the wolves up there in the first place, how would we block it?"

"With an avalanche!" Kallik exclaimed.

Lusa stared at her, remembering the terror she had felt during the avalanche on Star Island, where Ujurak had died to save their lives. "You're not serious?" she whispered.

"On the other side of the ridge there's an old waterfall that's pretty much like the shaft," Kallik told her. "We were hunting a mountain goat there the other day, and something started an avalanche. It felt like the whole mountain was sliding down . . . snow and rocks and trees. We were both buried."

"We had to dig ourselves out." Yakone took up the story. "Then we discovered that a brown she-bear and one of her cubs were caught in it, too, so we searched for them and got them out."

Lusa listened to the tale with growing horror. "Wow!" she gasped. "You could have died."

"We almost did," Yakone said somberly.

"But we didn't, and we're fine." Kallik briefly touched her nose to Lusa's shoulder. "Anyway, if we started an avalanche on *this* side of the ridge, inside the shaft, we could block it off and trap the wolves on the ridge."

Lusa nodded. "It's a fantastic idea!"

"But how are you going to round up the wolves?" Toklo cut in with a challenge in his voice. "They'll never do what you want."

Lusa and the white bears looked at each other blankly for a moment. Lusa shivered at the thought of trying to make the wolves do anything, much less leave a rich hunting ground.

"We could leave a trail of dead prey," Yakone suggested.

Toklo shook his head. "That wouldn't work. Wolves only eat one piece of prey at a time, so they wouldn't follow a trail."

"Then we'll have to lie in wait for them every night," Kallik said, "and chase a few of them at a time, until all the packs have gone up."

Lusa shook her head. "No, they'd just come back down again before the shaft is blocked."

The bears settled into a gloomy silence. The shadows thickened around them, and in the distance the thin howl of a wolf echoed through the trees. Night had fallen, and the hunters were out.

Lusa began to fear that their plan would come to nothing. *How can you make packs of ferocious wolves do what you want?* Then an idea stirred in her mind. "Suppose we could trap all the wolves first?" she began uncertainly.

"Come on, Lusa. How—" Toklo began.

Kallik silenced him with a gesture of one paw. "Go on, Lusa."

Lusa found some sticks among the debris under a bush and began laying them out on the ground. Her idea grew clearer as she spoke. "Imagine this is the ravine with the waterfall. What if we got them all in there, and then attacked them from the sides—here, and here," she added, scraping little hollows in the earth to demonstrate. "Once the wolves are weak and scared, we could chase them up to the ridge." She dusted off her forepaws. "Job done."

Her friends examined the outline she had laid on the ground. Lusa was relieved to see that even Toklo was looking interested.

"How do we get the wolves into the ravine?" he asked.

"That would be difficult," Kallik agreed. "And would we have enough strength left to attack the wolves and chase them up the mountain?"

"We could get other bears to help," Lusa pointed out. "Makya and Aiyanna and Maniitok would all love to get rid of the wolves. Surely some of them would join in."

"Yes," Yakone said encouragingly. "An ambush worked for those rowdy bears on the Melting Sea, so I don't see why it couldn't work here."

"Don't forget what happened when we tried to ambush the coyotes," Toklo warned him. "We had to jump onto the firesnake to escape. And this time there'll be many more wolves than bears."

"So we'll have to be extra clever," Lusa said. Mention of the coyotes gave her an unpleasant flutter in her belly, but she wasn't willing to give up her plan. "What if we put traps in the ravine? Not to kill the wolves or cut their paws off, but to give them a shock and make them scared of us. We could use sticks to trip them up, and brambles to slow them down."

"Tripping up the wolves is too good for them," Toklo growled.

"These wolves have as much right to find food and shelter

as we do," Lusa retorted. "Just not here, where the forest belongs to brown bears. They'll survive up on the ridge, if we can get them back there."

Toklo grunted. "Okay."

"We can't do any more until we've had another look at the ravine," Yakone said. "We need to make sure it's right for what we want to do."

Toklo grunted. "And that will have to wait until tomorrow." He glared through the walls of the thicket and curled his lip. "The wolves have the forest tonight, but not for much longer!"

Lusa woke as the first rays of the sun pierced the branches. At first she was confused by the warm press of furry bodies around her, then she remembered. *Kallik and Yakone came back! And we're going to chase the wolves out of the forest!* She sprang to her paws. "Wake up! Let's go check out the ravine!"

With Toklo in the lead, they hurried through the forest and across the grassy slope that led to the top of the ravine, heading toward the path that Toklo, Kallik, and Yakone had used when Yakone was too injured to climb.

"Look!" Lusa said when they were all standing on the edge and looking down at the pool and rocks below, bathed in sparkly dawn sunshine. "It's going to work perfectly. We'll set traps down there to confuse the wolves, and then we'll drive them down the track into the ravine."

"I can find a fallen tree and drag it across the track to block them in," Toklo offered.

"But we don't want them blocked in," Kallik objected. "They have to be able to get up to the ridge."

"The tree won't hold them for long," Lusa noted quickly, seeing that Toklo was starting to look offended. "But it *will* help scare them."

"What if they flee the other way, down the stream and back toward the SilverPath?" Kallik asked.

Toklo grunted thoughtfully. "Maybe *that's* where I should put the tree," he suggested. "And I could hide there and roar if any of the wolves head that way."

"Perfect!" Lusa said, her spirits lifting as the details of the plan came together. "But let's have two trees, one downstream *and* one to block the track."

Toklo nodded. "You got it."

"The rest of us can drop stones and branches down on top of them once they're in the ravine," Yakone suggested.

"But remember we don't want them badly hurt," Lusa warned. "They have to be able to run."

"We'll just use small stones and branches," Kallik said. "And we don't need to aim for the wolves. Stuff falling out of the sky will confuse them, even if it doesn't hit them."

"That should work," Yakone agreed. "As soon as the wolves know they're beaten, we let them escape, and chase them all the way up to the ridge."

"But it's almost a day's climb up there, and we'll all be exhausted," Toklo noted, turning to gaze across the open grassland to the trees beyond.

Lusa gave him a friendly nudge. "That's why we'll need

the other bears to help us. I'll ask Makya, and you can ask Aiyanna."

Toklo let out a snort. "Aiyanna won't help," he muttered. "She seems safe from the wolves in her territory."

"She'll help," Lusa assured him. "She's kinder than you know, and she doesn't want the wolves here any more than you do. Makya should know where we can find Maniitok, too," she added. *Better not mention Chogan,* she told herself. *Toklo won't work with him, and he wouldn't want to help us anyway.* "If there are enough of us," she went on, "we can line up through the forest to pick up the chase when someone else gets tired."

"And Yakone and I will be at the very top to start the ava-lanche!" Kallik's eyes gleamed. "Lusa, I really think this is going to work!"

Lusa nodded. "We'll do it at nightfall tomorrow," she said. "The moon will be full then. The wolves are used to hunting in darkness, but we're not, so we'll need the extra light."

"But we still don't know how we're going to get the wolves into the ravine to begin with," Toklo growled.

Lusa couldn't come up with an answer. Frustrated, she could see her plan melting away.

"I could lure them," Kallik offered after a moment. "They'll easily spot my white pelt in the darkness."

Lusa froze with horror. "No way!"

Yakone shook his head. "Absolutely not. Remember what happened when I lured the coyotes."

"But that worked, sort of," Kallik argued.

"I don't care. You're not doing it," Yakone retorted.

Kallik was looking furious, but before she could speak, Toklo stepped between them. "Calm down, both of you," he said. "It wouldn't work this time anyway. It only worked with the coyotes because they were all together."

"So what can we do?" Lusa asked.

"I'll catch a really good piece of prey," Toklo replied. "A deer, if I can find one. I'll lay several scent trails through the forest, all leading to this ravine. The wolves will follow the scent of prey, and the deer will be down there in the ravine waiting for them."

Lusa butted Toklo affectionately with her head. "That should work!" she told him.

Yakone nodded. Kallik looked disgruntled for a moment longer, then relaxed and murmured her approval.

"Okay," Lusa said. "There's a lot to do and not much time to waste. Let's get down there and set some traps."

She led the way down the track into the ravine and looked around. *What can we use that will scare the wolves but not hurt them too much?*

"Thorns." Kallik spoke as if Lusa had uttered her question aloud. "We can pull thorns off the bushes and scatter them about at the bottom of the track. The wolves will get them stuck in their pads."

"Great idea!" Lusa said. "I can do that."

"And we can loosen stones on the edge of the stream," Yakone suggested. "It'll do the wolves good to get a soaking!"

Toklo let out a snort of amusement. "I'm beginning to look forward to this," he said. "What about brambles in the shadows of the rocks, where the wolves will trip over them?"

"And I'll collect stones and branches to throw down at them from the top," Kallik said.

"Great! Let's get to it," Lusa directed.

She padded over to a straggly thornbush growing at the foot of the ravine wall. It was hard to grip the thorns in her teeth to tear them off, and she kept snagging her pelt on the branches. But she was determined, and gradually built up a pile of thorns beside the bush.

When she turned away to transport her thorns to the bottom of the track, she spotted Yakone working patiently at the stones beside the stream.

"Don't walk too close to the edge," he warned her. "Half these stones will give way if you put your weight on them."

Toklo padded past with a bundle of brambles trailing from his jaws and deposited it in the shadow of a rock. Even in daylight Lusa could hardly see that it was there.

"The wolves are going to get such a shock!" she said.

Toklo nodded. "You've got a good heap of thorns there," he told her, pointing with his snout at the pile she had gathered. "But don't scatter them until we leave. We don't want them stuck in *our* pads!"

"I never thought of that!" Lusa exclaimed.

When the rest of the traps had been set, Yakone and Toklo padded up the track. Lusa scattered the thorns around the area at the bottom, where the wolves would have to pass, then followed them.

At the top of the ravine, Kallik had been busy. She had

collected a huge pile of branches and another of small stones, and heaped them up close to the edge of the cliff.

"Good work!" Lusa exclaimed.

"I haven't finished," Kallik said, dragging another branch onto the pile. "I need to go over to the other side and collect some there, too."

"I'll help you," Yakone offered.

"Oops!" Lusa felt a stab of guilt. "You can't go down the track anymore. I've trapped it with thorns."

"Not a problem," Yakone responded. "We'll just cross the stream above the waterfall and get to the other side that way."

Leaving him and Kallik to their task, Lusa padded beside Toklo back into the forest. The sun had slid behind clouds, and it was cool beneath the trees. "I'm going to find Makya and ask her to help us," she said. "And you should go see Aiyanna."

Toklo glared at her. "I suppose you won't stop nagging until I do," he grumbled. "I hope when I see you next I still have my ears."

He headed off into the trees, making for Aiyanna's territory. Lusa watched him go, then turned her pawsteps toward the clearing where she had met Makya's cubs and saved them from the wolves. *I should be able to follow their scent trail from there and find their den.*

Lusa kept alert as she trekked through the trees. With the sky overcast, she knew that the wolves might be hunting in daylight. *I don't want to meet them now, not when we're so close to getting rid of them.*

But the forest was quiet, except for a few birdcalls from

high in the branches. When Lusa reached the scene of her fight with the wolves, the only scents were stale. She quickly identified the scent trail that Makya and her cubs had left and followed it through a wide stretch of fern and across a small stream. The scents grew stronger once she had crossed the water, and soon she came upon a sheltered glade where Makya and the cubs were settled in the shade of a maple tree, sharing a grouse.

Makya looked up as Lusa stepped out of the undergrowth. "Oh, it's you," she muttered. "What do you want?"

You might be a bit more welcoming! Lusa thought, trying to hide her indignation. *If it wasn't for me, your cubs would be in a wolf's belly!*

Before she could say anything, the two cubs sprang up and raced across the glade toward her. "Lusa! Lusa!" they squealed.

Flo was running so fast that she tripped over her own paws and rolled over in the grass. Fala was still chewing a mouthful of grouse, and she had a feather stuck on her nose.

"Come and eat with us," she said, swallowing. "There's plenty for all of us."

Lusa didn't think a grouse was enough to share between four. *Maybe that's why Makya sounds so unfriendly.* "No thanks, I'm not hungry," she responded, even though the scent of prey was making her jaws water. "I just want to talk to your mother."

She padded over to Makya, who gave her a grudging nod as Lusa sat down beside her. "Well?" she prompted.

"My friends and I have a plan to trap the wolves and send them back up to the ridge," Lusa announced.

Makya stared as if Lusa had grown an extra set of ears. "And

I'd really like it if prey came and jumped into my mouth," she responded.

"No, I mean it," Lusa insisted. "I think it'll really work." Quickly she outlined the plan, and the preparations she and her friends had already made. The cubs came to sit beside her and listened, their eyes growing round with excitement as she spoke.

"I suppose it *might* work," Makya conceded, reluctantly. "But why are you telling me about it?"

"We want your help," Lusa told her. "We need as many bears as possible to chase the wolves up to the ridge."

"Yes!" Fala bounced up and down. "No more wolves!"

Makya gave her cub a gentle cuff over the ear. "That's enough!" she said. To Lusa she added, "I'm sorry, but I can't help. I can't put myself in danger. Who will look after my cubs if I die?"

"Look," Lusa said. She didn't want to frighten the cubs, but she realized this was no time to be gentle in her words. "Your cubs are in danger every day from the wolves. Don't you want to raise them in a place where you don't have to be scared to let them out of your sight? Remember how worried you were earlier, when you couldn't find them?"

"Mother, please!" Fala said. "It would be really great not to have to be scared of the wolves."

"Yes," Flo added. "Lusa, we want to help!"

"No," Lusa said. "You two have to stay safe. Makya can't be worried about you when she's chasing the wolves."

"Who said I'm going to chase them?" Makya demanded.

She reached out a paw to touch Fala's head and then Flo's. Her gaze softened. "Okay," she agreed heavily. "I'll come to the ravine at dusk tomorrow. But I'm still not convinced. If it looks like the plan will go wrong, I'm out of there."

"Thank you," Lusa said. "I need to find Maniitok to ask for his help, too," she added. "Do you know where he lives?"

Makya shook her head. "Maniitok is only found when he wants to be," she replied. "But you could try the stream beside the lightning-blasted pine tree." To Lusa's surprise, she rose to her paws. "I'll come with you. The cubs could do with stretching their legs, and I haven't seen Maniitok in a while."

Makya led Lusa through the trees, with Flo and Fala bumbling around their paws or darting off into the undergrowth to investigate rustling or strange scents.

"Stay close to me!" Makya told them sharply.

Lusa assumed it would be quite some distance to the pine tree, but Makya took her down a narrow gully in the forest lined with moss-covered rocks. A trickle of water ran down the bottom. "I've never been this way before," Lusa said.

"I know this forest better than the hairs on my belly," Makya told her.

"You'll know where to send the wolves, then," Lusa said.

Makya's only reply was a grunt.

The gully led the bears to the stream, where the trickling rivulet poured down in a tiny waterfall. The lightning-blasted pine was only a few bearlengths away.

"I can't see Maniitok," Lusa said, looking around.

"Oh, he's here all right," Makya told her. "I can sense

him. He'll be hiding somewhere, watching us, the crafty old mangepelt." She raised her voice. "Hey, Maniitok!"

Several moments passed, and Makya called again. At last the ferns near the pine tree parted, and the old bear shambled into the open. Lusa had a moment's misgiving as she looked at him. *I'd forgotten how old he is. Will he have the energy to help us?*

"Hello," Maniitok said to Lusa as he padded up. "Are you still here?" He sounded surprised. "I thought the wolves would have chased you off long ago, with those weird white bears."

"No, we're going to chase the wolves off instead," Lusa told him. "Will you help?" Quickly she outlined the plan for him.

Maniitok pricked his ragged, gray-tinged ears. "Chase the wolves back to the ridge?" he said when Lusa had finished. "In my day I was the fastest bear in the forest! No one could catch me!"

Lusa glanced doubtfully at the old bear's scrawny frame and bowed legs. "Then you'll help?" she asked him.

"I'll be there," Maniitok promised. He lurched up onto his hind legs and batted the air with his forepaws. "See that?"

"We're not asking you to fight the wolves single-pawed," Lusa told him, hiding her amusement.

Maniitok glared at her. "I may be old, but there's a good few fights left in me yet. I've fought more bears like this than you've eaten squirrels." He dropped back onto all fours, breathing hard.

"Thank you." Lusa dipped her head. "We'll see you at the ravine in two sunsets."

Saying good-bye to Maniitok, Makya led Lusa back along the gully. "I really didn't think you'd get him to join in," she told Lusa, sounding impressed. "I always thought he didn't care about anyone else."

"Perhaps he was just waiting to be invited," Lusa suggested.

"I'll see you at the ravine," Makya said as they returned to the glade where Lusa had found her.

Lusa said farewell to her and the cubs, who were even more excited now, and hurried back to the den among the vines through gathering twilight. The other bears were already there, sharing a grouse and a squirrel.

"Hey, I asked Makya and Maniitok, and they're both going to help," she announced.

"That's great," Yakone said, while Kallik pushed Lusa's share of the prey over to her.

"What about Aiyanna?" Lusa asked Toklo. "I see you've still got your ears!"

The brown bear looked slightly embarrassed. "Yeah, she'll come," he replied, swallowing a mouthful of squirrel. He sounded more enthusiastic than before. "She said she thought it was a brilliant plan."

Lusa hid her amusement. *It seems like Aiyanna convinced him when I couldn't.*

While the other bears settled down to sleep, Lusa slipped out of the den and climbed a tree. From the topmost branches she gazed up at the dark-blue sky, tracing the pattern of Ujurak's stars.

"I hope you think we're doing the right thing," she whispered. "It would be so much easier if you were with us."

No answer came from the bright shape overhead, but Lusa still felt comforted, because she knew their friend was watching over them.

CHAPTER TWENTY-THREE

Kallik

Snow swept Kallik off her paws, tumbling around her in a chaos of white. She flailed her paws helplessly, unable to find anything solid to cling to. The thundering roar of the avalanche filled the whole world. Kallik was falling, falling . . .

She woke with a jolt to find herself lying next to Yakone, squashed uncomfortably in the tiny den. *We won't have to live here for much longer,* she thought with relief. *Once we've chased off the wolves, we'll leave for Great Bear Lake, and then the Endless Ice.*

Excitement fluttered inside Kallik like the beating wings of a bird. She somehow knew that this was the path she was supposed to take, instead of going back to the Melting Sea. *And maybe I'll see Taqqiq at the Longest Day gathering.*

But none of that could happen until they had driven the wolves back to the ridge. Kallik began to work out how she and Yakone would create the avalanche. They'd have to go up to the ridge that day, to have everything in place for the attack on the wolves at nightfall. *We'll need to pile up snow and rocks and branches, and put them in position so we can get them going quickly. Perhaps we can roll one boulder into place, or shove in some branches so they hold it all. . . .*

Kallik halted in her planning, her limbs stiffening as she realized there was a terrible problem. *If Yakone and I are going to set off the snowfall, we'll need to be at the top of the shaft. But then we'll be trapped on the ridge, just like the wolves!*

Kallik prodded Yakone in the ribs to wake him. The white bear raised his head, blinking sleepily. "Huh?"

"Yakone," Kallik whispered. "I've just thought of something. . . . We'll have to be at the top of the shaft to start the avalanche. But then we'll be trapped, just like the wolves!"

Yakone rolled over, instantly awake. "I see what you mean." He thought for a moment. "We could trek along the ridge until we find another way down."

"But that cliff stretches for skylengths!" Kallik protested. Discouraged, she rested her snout on her paws. *It's all starting to go wrong. . . .*

Yakone was silent for a few moments. "What about Izusa?" he said at last. "Do you think she would help?"

"She might," Kallik responded, beginning to feel slightly hopeful. "But don't forget, we're going to be driving the wolves closer to her territory. She won't like that. In fact, she might not be supportive of this plan at all."

"Yes, but wolves have always lived on that ridge," Yakone pointed out. "And we know there's enough prey for them up there now. I don't think the wolves have ever been much of a problem for Izusa before."

"I hope you're right," Kallik said.

"Getting Izusa's help is the obvious solution." Yakone's voice was persuasive. "She already lives on the other side of the ridge. If she sets off the snowfall, she won't be trapped away from her home."

Convinced at last, Kallik sprang to her paws. "Let's ask her!"

Her movement disturbed Lusa and Toklo, who looked up drowsily. "Now what?" Toklo grunted. "It's not even sunrise!"

Kallik quickly explained the plan to them. "I know it's a long way to Izusa's territory, but I can make it if I set off now. It's our best chance, and we need all the help we can get."

"Do you think she'll agree?" Lusa asked.

Yakone nodded. "We saved her and her cubs from the avalanche. She owes us." He rose to his paws. "Okay, Kallik, let's go."

"No, you stay here and I'll go," Kallik said. "I can manage this on my own, and you need to save your strength for driving the wolves away."

"What?" Yakone's voice was indignant. "Are you worried I can't keep up? My paw is fine now."

"This has nothing to do with your paw," Kallik told him. "You're the only bear strong enough to help Toklo with the fallen trees."

Yakone grunted. "Okay," he said grudgingly. "Just be careful."

"I will." Kallik touched her nose to Yakone's shoulder. She lifted her head and looked at Toklo. "I'll be back in time to take my place on the hillside, ready to take over chasing the wolves."

Toklo narrowed his eyes. "Are you sure that gives you long enough to speak with Izusa and build the avalanche?"

Kallik nodded. "I'll go as fast as I can. Don't worry, I'll be back before the wolves make it up to the ridge."

"Good luck," Toklo growled. "You'll need it!"

Leaving the den, Kallik headed toward the ridge, climbing easily through the trees in the cool air. Dawn was still some way off when she set out; later the sun rose in a clear sky, sending shafts of golden light into the forest. Kallik slowed down as the warmth of the day increased, but she kept going, pausing only to drink from a stream until she emerged from the trees near the rocky shoulder that led to the ridge.

By this time the sun had already passed its height. Picking up the pace, Kallik bounded across the open land until she came to the bottom of the shaft. *This will be perfect,* she thought, looking around as she scrambled upward. *So steep and narrow—it'll be easy to block.*

At the top of the shaft Kallik stopped to rest, enjoying the stiff, chilly breeze and the scent of snow. After a few moments she spotted a hare nibbling the tough upland grass and leaped upon it before it realized she was there. She gulped her prey down, aware for the first time of how hungry she was.

Revived by the food, Kallik rose to her paws again and trekked to the top of the ridge. On the other side she could see the line of destruction left by the avalanche, and she used it to guide her to the edge of Izusa's territory. As she plunged into the trees, Kallik realized that she was getting tired, but she was determined not to stop until she found the brown she-bear. It didn't take long. Before Kallik had traveled many bearlengths into the forest, Izusa burst out of the undergrowth with a fierce bellow. "Get out! This is—"

She broke off and halted when she saw who it was. "Kallik," she said more calmly. "What are you doing here?"

Wapi and Yas peered out from behind their mother, and Izusa signaled to them with one paw to stay back, as if she still didn't entirely trust Kallik.

"I've come to ask for your help," Kallik said, and she explained what was happening in the forest on the other side of the ridge, and about their plan to drive the wolves back.

"I knew the wolves had gone down there," Izusa said when she had finished, "but I didn't realize how much trouble they'd caused." She let out a snort that was half-amused, half-annoyed. "You don't seem too bothered about sending them back to trouble *me*."

"The ridge is the wolves' real home," Kallik pointed out, feeling guilty. "And there's plenty of prey here for everyone now."

Izusa nodded reluctantly. "True. I admit it's been peaceful without the wolves, but they've never been that much of a problem for us before. They know not to mess with me," she added, showing her teeth.

"Once we've driven them back up here, they'll be even less likely to mess with you, or any bear," Kallik said.

Izusa nodded. "You could be right. . . . Tell me what you

want me to do to help. But I'm not sure if I'll be much use. My cubs can't travel all the way to the forest, and they're too small to be left alone." As she spoke she turned to Wapi and Yas and drew them both closer to her. "They've been scared to venture far since the avalanche," she explained.

"You won't have to go as far as the forest," Kallik said. "If we chase the wolves up the shaft, could you set off the avalanche from the top? Just a small one. One you can control, but big enough to block the shaft."

Izusa stared at her. "There's no way you could make that work!" she gasped.

"Yes, we can," Kallik encouraged her. "The shaft is narrow, and before I go I'll pile up snow and rocks and stuff at the top so that it takes only a tiny movement to bring it all down."

Izusa blinked. "But will it be safe, with all those angry wolves around?" she said at last.

"I think they'll be more scared and exhausted than angry," Kallik assured her. "They'll just want to find a place to shelter."

Izusa glanced down at her cubs, then back at Kallik. "Okay," she said reluctantly. "After what you did for me and my family, I'll give it a try."

"Thank you!" Kallik said with feeling. "I know it's a big risk for you. I wouldn't ask if it wasn't important."

Izusa huffed. "I hope not!" she teased with a flash of humor.

"We were just going to eat," Wapi piped up. "Would you like some deer? Or do white bears eat snow?"

"No, we eat prey like you," Kallik replied.

"Then you're welcome to share ours," Izusa said. "Come on—our den is just through here."

Kallik followed her through the undergrowth to a den underneath an oak tree. The carcass of a deer was lying there, already partly eaten.

"Help yourself," Izusa said.

Kallik enjoyed the food, and the antics of the cubs, who became more playful as their confidence around her grew. *Spirits, keep them safe when the wolves return,* Kallik prayed. She had faith in her plan—she had to, it was the only solution for the bears on the other side of the ridge—but she knew it had its flaws.

They ate quickly, and Kallik could tell that Izusa wanted to make a start on the trek over the ridge before she had too long to think about it. There were still a few shreds of meat left on the deer bones when the brown bear called to her cubs.

"Wapi! Yas! Come on, we need to go!"

Kallik led the way up to the ridge, soon breaking free from the trees and scrambling over sun-warmed rocks to the summit.

"We've never been this high!" Yas squeaked. "We're right above the clouds!"

"And there's so much snow!" Wapi barked, jumping into a drift and popping out again with white flakes clinging to his furry muzzle.

"Don't play silly games," Izusa warned.

The stiff breeze buffeted their fur as they reached the very top of the ridge.

"Help!" Wapi squealed. "I'm being blown away!"

His sister leaped on top of him, and both cubs fell over and rolled down the snowy slope until they came to a halt beside a boulder with snow clinging to their pelts.

"We're white bears now!" Yas announced.

When they reached the shaft, Izusa studied it for a while, then turned to Kallik, shaking her head. "I still don't see how we're going to fill it with snow," she said doubtfully.

"We won't use just snow," Kallik explained. "We need rocks and branches as well. Let's collect as much as we can to start with."

Izusa and Kallik began to drag branches and fallen logs over to the shaft. Together they rolled bigger boulders between them, while the cubs helped by fetching twigs and smaller stones. When Kallik thought they had enough, she began to build a barrier across the top of the shaft, using the longest branches as the foundation, and piling rocks and smaller branches on top.

"Will there be enough space for the wolves to get by?" Izusa asked, watching Kallik with interest.

"Yes, I'm leaving a gap," Kallik puffed, hoping that it was wide enough for the wolves to get past without setting off the snowfall too soon.

When the barrier was in place, Kallik drew on all her knowledge of snow to make small trial avalanches by rolling boulders across the slope. "It has to go *this* way," she muttered to herself as the snow cascaded down to pile up on top of the barrier.

At first Izusa kept Wapi and Yas well away from the moving snow, but after a while she seemed to get the idea of what Kallik was doing. "Can I help?" she asked.

"Sure," Kallik replied. "If you crouch down there, you can block the snow. Then when I say 'Now!' shove it in that direction." She pointed slantwise across the slope, to the top of the barrier.

Kallik controlled the flow of snow down to Izusa by letting just a little slip at a time. When there was a good pile behind the brown she-bear, Kallik exclaimed, "Now!"

Izusa stepped aside, still blocking the snow so it couldn't move straight down. The whole mound of snow slipped slowly down at an angle to settle on top of the barrier.

"We can do that!" Wapi announced. "Crouch down again, Mother, and we'll send more snow down to you."

With an amused glance at Kallik, Izusa took up her position, and the cubs began jumping into snowdrifts built up by Kallik, loosening the snow and sending it down to their mother in tiny avalanches. Suddenly Wapi let out a grunt of surprise. Kallik looked up to see him and Yas vanish into a drift that was bigger than they had expected. A huge wall of snow began to slide down the slope, heading straight for Izusa.

"Look out!" Kallik shouted.

She scrambled across the slope to stand beside Izusa and take some of the weight of the oncoming snow. It struck the two bears in a cloud of snow-spray; Kallik was swept off her paws and slid several bearlengths down the mountainside. She started to panic. *I'm heading straight for the cliff top!* Then almost at once her own barrier stopped her, leaving her winded and buried up to the neck in snow. Looking upward, she spotted Izusa floundering to the edge of the loose snow, and the two cubs, farther up still, bouncing up and down with excitement, having freed themselves from the drift.

"We sent you a *lot* of snow!" Yas squealed.

"Yes, you did," Kallik panted as she hauled herself out. Her momentary fear gave way to amusement. "Good job. But don't be quite so eager next time, okay?"

At last Kallik thought that they had piled up enough snow behind the barrier. "Look at this," she said to Izusa, pointing to a long branch that stuck out at one side. "That branch is holding everything together. You can release the snow by moving it, but be careful not to touch it until all the wolves have gone past."

Izusa nodded. "Got it. So I'll hide behind one of the boulders until they're all up here, then move the branch, releasing the snow and starting the avalanche."

Kallik suddenly realized how much she was asking of the brown she-bear. It was a dangerous task, with no benefit to Izusa at the end of it. "Are you sure you want to do this?" she asked. "Your cubs need you. I can manage." *If I get trapped up here, I'll find Yakone and Lusa again somehow.*

Izusa shook her head. "I said I'd help, and I will."

"Yes!" Yas and Wapi shouted, jumping up and down. "We're going to make an avalanche!"

Their mother turned toward them with a fierce glare. "*You* are not!" she said. "You won't be anywhere near."

Both cubs gave her identical mutinous looks.

"I mean it," their mother told them. "I'll make you eat leaves for a moon if you disobey me."

Yas's eyes went wide. "You wouldn't!"

"Just try me," said Izusa.

Ready to leave now, Kallik dipped her head to Izusa. "Thank you so much," she said. "I'll never forget how much you've helped. Be ready at dusk, and we'll chase the wolves up to you as fast as we can."

"I'll wait all night if I have to," Izusa responded. She hesitated, then asked, "Kallik, why are you doing so much to help these bears, when you don't live here?"

"Because it's the right thing to do," Kallik replied. "I traveled for a long time with one of those bears, and I'll do anything to help him find a safe home, just as he helped me find mine."

Izusa nodded, and with a final good-bye Kallik turned, slid carefully past the barrier, and plunged down the shaft. Racing across the hillside, she took one look back to see Izusa and the two cubs watching her from the top of the cliff. Then she made the best speed she could, to get back to her friends before dusk fell and the attack began.

CHAPTER TWENTY-FOUR

Lusa

The sun had gone down, and twilight had fallen on the forest. Lusa waited tensely at the top of the ravine, with Toklo and Yakone beside her. *Had Kallik made it up to the ridge to speak with Izusa? Was the avalanche in place?* Lusa could tell from the shadows in Toklo's and Yakone's eyes that they were wondering the same thing. There was no way of knowing if the snowfall was ready. They just had to follow through with their part of the plan, and hope that Kallik had had enough time.

Toklo had positioned a fallen tree a few bearlengths downstream, to cut off the wolves' retreat that way, and another lay ready to block the path to the ravine once the wolves had passed it.

"What happened to the other bears?" Toklo asked, glancing around. "They should be here by now."

Lusa had a moment's misgiving, afraid that the others would let them down at the last moment. Then she spotted movement on the grassy slope that led up to the forest. Makya and her two cubs appeared out of the gloom and padded to her side.

"Here we are," Makya announced.

The two cubs were buzzing with like a tree full of bees, as though excited to be surrounded by strong, grown bears.

"You two have to stay back and out of the way," Toklo instructed them. "This is going to be dangerous."

Fala and Flo shared a disappointed glance, then both nodded solemnly.

"You can help by throwing stones and twigs down on the wolves," Lusa comforted them. "Not to hurt them; we just want them to be scared."

"And once the wolves come out of the ravine, you hide," Makya told them severely.

As she spoke, there was more movement on the slope, and Maniitok appeared. He was bouncing on his hindpaws, ready to fight, with forepaws slashing at the air. "When do we start?" he asked.

"Soon," Lusa promised him, surprised once again at how nimble the old bear was. "We're just waiting for Aiyanna."

"I'm here," Aiyanna said, appearing quietly from the shadows. She turned to Toklo and added, "I said I would come."

Toklo ducked his head in acknowledgment.

Aiyanna was carrying a squirrel in her jaws and added it to the prey Toklo and Lusa had caught earlier that day: a young deer, which had been a real catch, and a couple of grouse.

"Okay," Toklo said. "Let's get this prey down into the ravine before the wolves come."

Together he and Aiyanna dragged the prey to the top of the rocks and pushed everything over the edge. By now the moon was shining brightly enough to show the carcasses as they bounced their way to the bottom; their scent hung on the air, tempting and warm.

"This had better work," Toklo muttered. "That's a lot of good prey."

Somewhere in the distance Lusa heard a howl. Her pelt started to prickle as the howl was answered by others from different directions. "They're coming," she whispered.

Lusa and Toklo had deliberately left strong scent trails through the forest as they dragged the prey to the ravine. Wherever the wolves were, they should be able to pick up one of the trails.

Makya and Maniitok were looking over the edge of the ravine, while Yakone explained the traps they had set. Both of them looked startled when they realized the amount of preparation that had taken place.

"I'm more used to straightforward fighting," Maniitok said dubiously.

"We've tried that. It will take more than fighting to beat these wolves," Toklo retorted.

The howls grew closer, though as Lusa peered up the slope toward the trees she still couldn't see anything. She shifted her paws impatiently. *Come on, wolves!*

Then she heard a rustling from the edge of the forest, and the pack broke out of the trees. They ran down the slope, as silent and swift as black water.

"Hide!" Toklo growled.

Lusa ducked down behind a boulder, making sure that

Makya was keeping the cubs safe. The wolves streamed past her and headed down the track, snouts to the ground, following the scent of fresh prey. Moments later she heard howls and yelps of pain. *They found my thorns!* she thought.

As the last of the wolves disappeared down the track, the bears came out of hiding.

"Move the tree!" Lusa called to Toklo.

He and Yakone began hauling the fallen tree to the cliff edge. When it was in position they heaved it over; it rolled faster and faster down to the bottom of the path, partly blocking the way out.

Toklo turned to the others. "Makya, Aiyanna, Maniitok," he began crisply. "You should leave now to take up your positions in the trees. We'll keep the wolves here for as long as we can, and then herd them right to you."

Makya paused only to tell her cubs to stay where they were, then headed around the top of the ravine to the hillside that led up to the ridge. The cubs looked disappointed.

"We want to chase wolves!" Fala protested.

Aiyanna shook her head. "But Toklo needs you here! You must help him and Yakone throw things over the cliff to frighten the wolves."

Fala and Flo looked wide-eyed with seriousness. "Okay," they barked. "Toklo, tell us what to do and we'll do it!"

Aiyanna turned and bounded after Makya.

"You're sure you don't want me to stay and help fight?" Maniitok asked, on his hindpaws again and batting at the air.

"No," said Toklo. "We need your speed instead."

The old bear puffed out his chest. "Okay."

To Lusa's surprise he took off like a hare, outpacing the two she-bears before they reached the hillside, and vanishing into the trees in a flash.

"Wow!" Lusa exclaimed. "He really is fast!"

"Lusa, you'd better go, too," Toklo told her. "Yakone and I can fight the wolves, and you can chase them when they're tired and scared."

Lusa nodded. "I'm on my way." She raced away but paused before the trees to look back.

Toklo was running downstream, to where the other tree cut off the wolves' escape that way. Yakone and the cubs had begun to hurl sticks and stones down into the ravine. Howls and snarling rose from the bottom as the wolves realized they were under attack. From her vantage point on the slope, Lusa could just see into the ravine. Several wolves were sprawled at the foot of the track, biting at their paws as they tried to get the thorns out. Another had blundered into one of Toklo's concealed bramble bundles and was rolling over in an attempt to untangle itself. A few of the wolves had limped far enough up the ravine to reach the prey, but they couldn't settle down to feed because of the hail of stones. One of them leaped aside to avoid a falling branch and landed on a stone at the edge of the stream. The stone gave way under its weight, plunging the wolf into the water. Lusa let out a snort of amusement as it clambered out, water streaming from its pelt.

The ravine echoed with yelping, squealing wolves, thrashing around like dark fish in a tiny pool. A few of them fled downstream, and at once a mighty bellow sounded from the darkness beyond the fallen tree.

Toklo sounds really fierce! Lusa thought.

The wolves hesitated; then, as a second bellow sounded, they turned back, too scared to go any farther that way.

Makya's cubs were bouncing up and down with excitement, letting out loud screeches every time they hurled a stone. Their aim was wild, but that didn't matter, since they weren't really trying to hit the wolves.

Lusa felt on fire with energy. *We're really doing it! We're taking back the forest for the brown bears!* She took a deep breath and began to scramble up the slope. She could just hear Aiyanna, Makya, and Maniitok far above her, plunging through the trees to their positions. As she pelted after them, Lusa heard Toklo begin attacking the first wolves to make it over the tree barrier. There was a bellow as Yakone joined him. She could hear blows being struck, snarling and whining and the sound of ripping fur, but when she cast a rapid glance over her shoulder, she had gone too far to see the ravine.

"Spirits help them!" Lusa panted as she ran.

Toklo and Yakone were desperately outnumbered. All Lusa's instincts were telling her to go back and help, but she knew that for the plan to work she had to be able to chase the wolves at the top of the hill. Even though she felt like she was abandoning her friends, she forced herself to keep going.

Hauling herself over a cluster of rocks, Lusa spotted Makya just ahead of her. She followed her, knowing that the brown bear knew the quickest ways through the forest. As she climbed up and up through the undergrowth, the noise of battle faded behind her, lost in rustling leaves and the sound of the wind.

The forest was dark, the branches overhead cutting out most of the moonlight, and soon Lusa was following Makya more by scent than sight. Struggling around a particularly dense patch of brambles, she collided with another bear, letting out a surprised yelp.

"Aiyanna?" she said, recognizing the scent that washed over her.

"Yes, it's me," the she-bear's voice came back. Lusa could just make out her shape in the gloom. "I'm taking the first post. Makya and Maniitok have gone farther up."

"Good luck, then," Lusa said.

"Good luck to you, too!"

Lusa bounded on. Makya's trail was taking her to parts of the forest she had never explored before. Sometimes she had to scramble up near-vertical banks and splash through hidden streams. Her legs started to ache, and she had scraped the skin off one of her pads. She felt as if she had been climbing all night, but the mountain still loomed above her, stretching black and forbidding into the dark-blue sky. Then all the hairs on Lusa's pelt rose as she heard howling break out behind her, faint at first but growing clearer with every pawstep.

The wolves are on the run!

Now Lusa knew that Toklo and Yakone had scared the wolves enough to send them fleeing. Soon they would be driving the pack straight up toward the ridge. The bears had to be in place before then! Lusa forced her tiring legs to run faster, and as she rounded an alder thicket, she spotted Makya just in front of her.

The brown bear glanced back. "Hi!" Lusa panted. "They're coming!"

The two bears ran on side by side until they came to a steep slope covered in scree, with only a few plants clinging on among the loose stones. Lusa's paws scrabbled frantically as she tried to push herself up. Makya gave her a boost from behind, and Lusa managed to haul herself upward, digging her claws in to find a grip.

"I'll wait here," Makya said when she joined Lusa at the top of the slope. "You keep going and find Maniitok."

"Right." Lusa bounded away. Exhaustion dragged at her limbs, and in the distance she could see the milky line of dawn just breaking over the horizon. She had been climbing all night! But she was nearly at the top; she wasn't going to give up now.

Bursting out of the trees at last, Lusa saw that she had emerged not far from the cliff; she could see the shaft leading up to the ridge right ahead of her, just like Kallik and Yakone had described.

A dark shape loomed up beside her. Lusa jumped, startled, then recognized Maniitok. "Oh, it's you!" she exclaimed. "For a moment I thought you were Old Grizzly!"

Maniitok snorted. "Don't talk to me about that bear." He was panting, but his eyes shone in the darkness. "This is the most fun I've had for suncircles," he went on. "I can't wait for the wolves to get up here. Just let me at 'em!"

"We're not supposed to fight them," Lusa reminded him.

"I know. We'll just wait here, and then chase the stupid mangepelts right up the shaft! It'll still be fun."

Lusa glanced behind her; she could hear the howling, but it was still a ways off down the mountain. "Stay here," she said to Maniitok, and took off across the open ground toward the shaft. Where was Kallik? Had she finished building the avalanche? If there was no snowfall waiting to block the shaft behind the wolves, their whole plan was ruined.

When she reached the bottom she peered upward, but she couldn't see any sign of the white bear. "Hello?" she called up the shaft. "Kallik? Izusa? Are you there? It's Lusa!"

Enormous relief washed over Lusa as she spotted a brown bear's head poking out from the top of the cliff. A faint voice replied, "Lusa? The black bear? Yes, I'm here. Send up the wolves!"

"Where's Kallik?" Lusa barked.

"Here," said a voice behind her.

Lusa spun around and saw the white she-bear, ruffled with dirt and sway-legged with exhaustion. "You made it!" Lusa squealed.

Kallik nodded. "The avalanche is ready. Izusa knows what to do. Come on, let's get into the trees."

At the same time, Lusa heard Maniitok calling to them. "They're coming! Get back here!"

Lusa and Kallik ran back across the rocky ground and reached Maniitok just as the wolves broke out of the undergrowth, only a couple of bearlengths from where they were waiting.

Maniitok took one look at Kallik and growled, "You stay right where you are. You're too weak to take on a moth in that state." He held Lusa back with one huge paw until all the wolves had fled past them. Most of them were limping, battered and bleeding from several injuries. Their tongues lolled with exhaustion as they staggered across the open ground toward the shaft.

Lusa and Maniitok sprang out of hiding and gave chase, not getting too close to the wolves, but keeping them moving with threatening roars. At first Lusa worried that the wolves would turn and fight, but she soon realized they were so hurt and worn out that they had nothing on their minds but escape.

It's going to work! Lusa thought triumphantly.

But before the wolves reached the shaft, a couple of them broke away from the pack and headed back toward the forest. Finding an extra burst of speed, they swerved around Lusa and Maniitok.

"I'll get them back!" Lusa gasped to Maniitok. "You keep the others on track!"

As she pelted after the wolves, Lusa saw that Aiyanna and Makya had emerged from the forest. Instantly they began bounding along the edge of the trees to intercept the runaway wolves, but Lusa could see how exhausted the bears were. She knew that the wolves would disappear into the cover of the undergrowth before the brown bears could reach them.

Worse still, as she glanced over her shoulder she saw that some of the other wolves had broken away, too, and were following their packmates.

Once they get into the forest, they'll scatter! Lusa thought, almost ready to give up in weariness and frustration. *And we'll never be able to do all this again!*

Lusa felt hot breath on her pelt and turned to see that a wolf was running along at her shoulder. Its eyes were fixed on her with a fierce yellow gleam. Before she could turn to defend herself, it charged into her, knocking her off her paws. Lusa rolled over and forced herself back up, her teeth bared for a fight.

But the wolf never sprang. The loud bellow of a brown bear came from the forest, and the leading wolves, which had almost reached the trees by now, doubled back as a huge bear erupted out of the undergrowth, his jaws parted in a fierce roar.

Chogan? Lusa thought disbelievingly.

A moment later she saw that she was wrong; this was a strong young bear, and Lusa thought she could detect a faint shimmer of stars in his fur. He charged at the wolves, and they fled back up the slope, passing Lusa without even glancing at her. The wolf that had run her over joined them, and the whole pack of them streamed across the open ground to where Maniitok was waiting to chase them up the shaft.

Lusa stood gazing down at the young bear, who stayed close to the trees. His brown eyes were warm and sparkling like the night sky. "Thanks, Ujurak!" Lusa called; then she spun around and raced back to the shaft to help Maniitok.

By the time she reached him, most of the wolves were scrabbling up the shaft in a panic, sending down a shower of small stones from their frantic paws. But three or four of them had turned around at the foot of the cliff, where they snarled and snapped at Maniitok as he tried to drive them upward.

"Filthy mangepelts!" he roared. "Take your tails out of here!"

Lusa leaped to his side and hurled herself at the nearest wolf, raking her claws over its shoulder. It tried to bite her, but she ducked to avoid the snapping jaws and rammed her head into its chest. That was enough for the wolf; it whirled around with a yelp and began clambering up the shaft.

Meanwhile Maniitok was driving another wolf backward with repeated battering from his forepaws. The wolf snarled defiance, but Maniitok kept coming. "Take that, you disgusting lump of fur!" he growled. "Carrion-breath! Buzzard-food!"

That wolf, too, fled for the shaft. As it vanished into the darkness, Lusa heard Izusa's voice coming from up above. "Are you ready?"

"No, wait!" Lusa called back. "There are two more wolves to come!" She knew they had to get the last two up there quickly, so that Izusa could start the avalanche and get to safety herself. She didn't want her to have to be up there with a pack of angry wolves any longer than needed.

The last two stragglers were growling around Maniitok, darting in to slash at him with their claws. Lusa could tell the old bear was growing tired. His courage never faltered, but he couldn't fight both of them at once. With a last desperate effort Lusa lunged at one of the wolves, gripping its shoulder in her jaws as she tried to throw it to the ground.

While they struggled together, Maniitok drove the other wolf up the shaft and turned to help Lusa. As if it realized it was the last of its pack, her wolf tore itself free from the fight. Lusa hurled herself after it as it leaped for the shaft.

"Now, Izusa!"

Above her head Lusa heard the rattle of sticks, then a rumble like thunder. The whole mountain seemed to shake, and Lusa lost her footing. Snow from the shaft poured down around her as she struggled to get to her paws.

"Lusa!" Maniitok roared.

Lusa felt teeth meet in her scruff. A moment later she was hauled out of the way as the rest of the avalanche plunged down the shaft, filling it from top to bottom. When the crashing had died down and the snow and debris pouring out of the shaft had slowed and then stopped, Lusa found herself standing beside Maniitok, with snow up to her chest. Aiyanna and Makya were trudging toward them.

"That was terrifying!" Makya said. "Are you okay?"

"Fine," Lusa replied, though her near miss with the avalanche had made her head spin and her ears buzz.

Maniitok pushed her from behind, while Aiyanna and Makya waded into the snow and cleared a path for her. Lusa staggered to the edge of the snowfall and flopped to the ground.

Kallik limped up, her eyes shining. "The wolves have gone!" she breathed.

From up above, Lusa could hear the sound of howling. A moment later Izusa looked down from the top of the cliff. "Did it work?" she called.

"It worked fine!" Lusa replied. "Are you and the cubs safe?"

Izusa snorted with amusement. "Perfectly. The wolves went right past us, limping off down the ridge as if all the bears in the forest were still after them."

"Great!" Lusa said. "Thanks for everything."

"Thank you, Izusa!" Kallik called hoarsely.

"Glad to help! Good luck on your journey!" With that, Izusa vanished.

Lusa turned back to the other bears. "We did it!" she cheered.

"We sure did," said Aiyanna. "The forest belongs to the bears again."

She and Makya both pressed close to Lusa, their eyes glowing. "Thank you," Makya said warmly, nodding to Kallik. "We could never have done it without you and your friends."

"We all did it," Lusa responded, and glanced back at the old bear. "You were great, Maniitok."

Maniitok ducked his head. "My pleasure," he mumbled.

"There's one thing that puzzles me," Aiyanna said. "Who was that brown bear who burst out of the trees when the wolves broke away? I've never seen him around here before, have you, Makya?"

Makya shook her head. "No, and I couldn't find him afterward."

Kallik met Lusa's gaze, an unspoken question in her eyes. Lusa gave her a tiny nod.

"Oh, he's another friend of ours," Lusa said. "He never stays long, but he's always around when we need him."

CHAPTER TWENTY-FIVE

Toklo

Toklo finished the last mouthful of grouse and stretched his jaws in a huge yawn. The sun was hot on his fur as he stretched out comfortably beside the den in the vines.

Two sunrises had passed since he and his friends had driven the wolves out of the forest. Since then they had done little except rest and take care of their wounds. Toklo knew they had been very lucky. Even he and Yakone, who had fought the wolves by the ravine, had nothing worse than strained muscles and a few scratches. Kallik had been exhausted but unhurt, so Toklo had told her to stay in the den and catch up on some sleep. Lusa had foraged for herbs and Toklo had hunted, but they had spent the rest of the time resting and sunning themselves.

Now the four bears were sitting under a redwood tree.

"Last time when I traveled to Great Bear Lake with Toklo and Ujurak," Lusa said, "we walked along the ridge. But I don't think we should go that way now."

"We can't, with the shaft blocked," Kallik pointed out.

"We'll have to travel lower down, among the trees."

"Yes," Yakone agreed. "At least until we're clear of angry wolves!"

As Toklo listened, he began to feel unsettled. He didn't want to hear his friends planning a journey that he wasn't going to take part in. He rose to his paws.

"There's something I have to do," he announced abruptly, and padded off through the trees.

Toklo headed toward Chogan's territory. His last encounter with his father had been inconclusive. Now he knew that he had to prove himself. *I have to make Chogan see that I'm not a whimpering cub anymore.*

The forest was quiet, and the scent of the wolves was already fading. Toklo's sense of achievement about what they'd done gave him new energy and focused his determination for what he was about to do. Passing Chogan's scent marks, Toklo headed several bearlengths into his father's territory. Then he halted, taking in a huge lungful of air.

"Chogan!" he bellowed. The echoes of his roar rolled through the trees.

Toklo was drawing breath to call again when the undergrowth in front of him parted and Chogan lumbered into the open.

"You again!" he hissed. "What do you want?"

"I've come to give you what *you* want," Toklo replied. "Or have you decided that you're afraid to fight me?"

"Afraid?" Chogan took a threatening pace forward. "No bear has ever called me afraid and lived to boast of it." He ran his gaze scornfully over Toklo. "At least you've come back to fight me like a real bear," he added, his tone grimly pleased. "Like my son."

"I'll never see you as my father," Toklo spat. "But I am ready to fight."

Chogan let out a snort. "Good. You might learn a few things."

Maybe you're the one who will learn something, Toklo thought. But he didn't waste breath taunting his father. Blows, not words, would decide this.

Chogan reared up on his hind legs and bore down on Toklo, who ducked to one side and raked his claws over Chogan's haunches. Chogan turned almost lazily and let out a roar as he dropped down on top of Toklo, as if he was going to squash him like a grub. Toklo wrapped both forelegs around his father, pulling him down and rolling over so that he was on top. But Chogan clamped his paw over Toklo's snout, pushing his head back until Toklo had to let go or risk having his neck broken.

Chogan clambered to his paws. "Had enough yet?" he snarled.

"We haven't even started!" Toklo replied through gritted teeth.

He scrambled up in time to dodge to the side as Chogan plunged toward him, his jaws snapping, and hit his father with a blow over the ear.

Chogan turned, a sneering look on his face. "You'll have to do better than that," he growled.

Toklo realized that his father wasn't taking the fight seriously. *Even though I beat him last time, he still thinks I'm a cub who he can just scare off. Well, we'll see about that!*

With a roar of rage Toklo hurled himself at his father. Meeting him head-on, he batted at Chogan with blow after blow, feeling his claws rake through fur to the flesh below. A sharp reek of blood caught him in the throat. Chogan let out a furious bellow. Thrusting Toklo back, he crashed into him and carried him off his paws. As Toklo writhed helplessly like a beetle on its back, Chogan raked Toklo's exposed belly over and over again. His head reeling from the pain, Toklo raised his hindpaws and slammed them into his father's chest. Chogan lurched upright, giving Toklo time to roll away and scramble to his paws.

Toklo's blood was turning the grass scarlet and slippery. With a jolt, he realized that he was fighting for his life. At last Chogan was putting out all his strength, and Toklo didn't know now if he could win.

As Chogan charged at him again, Toklo leaped up and pulled himself onto his father's back. Lashing out with one forepaw, he aimed for Chogan's eyes and ears. But Chogan reared up on his hind legs again, and Toklo couldn't keep his balance. He hit the ground with a thump that jarred every bone in his body. Before he could get up, Chogan was on top of him. Locked together, the two bears rolled over and over, crushing the undergrowth and sending a bird squawking into the trees.

Chogan was the first to break away, surging to his paws and

flinging himself back into the attack. But as he hurled himself at Toklo, he tripped over an oak root and crashed to the ground, his paws waving wildly.

Toklo knew that he could leap on top of his father while he was half-stunned and finish the fight. *But where's the satisfaction in that?* he thought. *That doesn't show either of us that I'm stronger.* He stepped back and waited for his father to get up.

Chogan staggered to his paws and faced Toklo. "Weakling!" he spat. "You'll never win if you give me a chance to recover!"

The taunt made Toklo seethe, but he still made himself wait until his father had regained his balance. Then he lunged forward again, rose to his hindpaws, and used his forepaws to pummel Chogan over and over, forcing him backward pawstep by pawstep. Chogan fought back viciously with snapping teeth and raking claws, but his strength was ebbing.

At last Toklo knocked him off his paws and landed on top of him, pinning him down. "You thought I couldn't win?" he snarled into Chogan's ear.

Chogan lay still, his chest heaving as he panted. Toklo knew that he could kill Chogan now and take his territory. Instead, after a moment, he stepped back. "Get up," he ordered.

It took effort for Chogan to rise to his paws. His head lowered, he gave Toklo a look full of the bitterness of defeat. "Aren't you going to kill me?" he hissed.

Toklo shook his head. "No. For now, you can stay on your territory," he said. The certainty of what he would do had only just occurred to him. "Remember, though, that I'm getting bigger and stronger, while you're only growing older and weaker. I'm going away for a while, but I'll be back before snow-sky, and when I return, I'll claim this territory as my own."

Chogan snorted. "If you try, I'll fight you again."

"Then I'll beat you again," Toklo replied.

With a last look at Chogan, Toklo turned and padded away. He had no fear that his father would attack him from behind. He was thoroughly beaten. *This will be my home one day,* Toklo told himself. *Chogan has had his time, and now it's my turn.*

When Toklo returned to the den, he found his three friends waiting anxiously for him.

"Where have you been?" Kallik demanded. "We were about to go looking for you."

"And look at the state you're in!" Lusa exclaimed. "There aren't still wolves around, are there?"

Toklo shook his head. "I've been fighting Chogan," he told them.

Yakone gave a reluctant nod of understanding. "I suppose you had to."

"He really hurt you!" Lusa said, still trying to understand that some kin-bears just weren't meant to get along.

Toklo huffed out a long breath and flopped down among the vines. "Yeah, well, I hurt him, too. And I won."

"Does that mean you'll be taking over his territory now?" Kallik asked.

Toklo shook his head. "Not yet."

"Why not?" Lusa asked as she bustled up with a mouthful of herbs for Toklo's wounds. "Isn't that what you wanted all along?"

"It's still what I want," Toklo agreed. "But I can wait. First, I want to come with you to Great Bear Lake." Raising his voice over their exclamations of delight, he went on, "Our journey isn't over. I'll stay with you until I know you have found black bears you can make a home with, and that Kallik and Yakone will make it back to the Endless Ice with other white bears."

"Oh, Toklo!" Lusa gazed into his eyes, blinking affectionately. "I'm so glad. I wanted to ask you to come, but I didn't think you would now that you've found your home."

"My home won't go away," Toklo told her. "One day I'll return for good. And I'll have you three to thank for getting me back here."

When Lusa had tended to his wounds, Toklo slid into a doze. The sound of pawsteps roused him, and he opened his eyes to see Aiyanna pushing her way through the vines.

Lusa bounced up to greet her. "Hi," she said.

"Hi, Lusa. I came to see Toklo," Aiyanna replied, looking over at him. "Great spirits, what attacked you?" she gasped, her eyes widening as she saw his injuries.

"Chogan," Toklo told her. "And I attacked *him*, actually. And won," he added defiantly.

Aiyanna nodded. "I'm not surprised. Anyway," she went on, "I came to ask you if you'd like to visit my territory. There's something I want to show you."

Toklo stared at her in surprise. Aiyanna had always been so

sensitive about any bear going near her borders. What was she up to now? *Could it be a trap?* He told himself he could beat her in a fight if it came to it, even after battling Chogan. "Uh . . . yes, thanks," he stammered.

"Come on, then."

Rising to his paws, Toklo followed Aiyanna out of their denning place and up the hill toward her territory. After a while she turned onto a narrow path that wound between the trees until it reached the dead pine that bore Aiyanna's scent marks.

Toklo's heart started to pound, and he halted. *I know where we're going.* Aiyanna turned and looked back at him. "Don't you want to come?"

Unable to speak, Toklo nodded. Aiyanna led him on, past the tree and around a jagged rock into a patch of mossy ground surrounded by berry bushes. An overhanging rock stretched above a small mound of earth and broken twigs. Aiyanna stood beside it and waited for Toklo to join her.

"How did you know?" he asked hoarsely as he padded up.

"Lusa told me," Aiyanna replied. "And she was right to do so. This may be my territory now, but Tobi's burial mound will always belong to you."

When she had finished speaking, Aiyanna slipped away into the bushes. Toklo stood for a long time in front of Tobi's mound, his head bowed. The pile looked so small and insignificant; his brother deserved a better resting place than that. Working steadily, ignoring the pain of his wounds, Toklo gathered earth and sticks and moss together and rebuilt the mound bigger and stronger than before.

"Sleep well, little brother," he whispered, patting the last pawful of earth into place. It felt warm under his pad.

By the time he had finished, the sun had set and the first stars were appearing in the sky. Aiyanna still hadn't returned, and Toklo was reluctant to leave. Sighing, he settled down on top of the mound, laid his snout on his paws, and drifted into sleep.

Light gradually strengthened around Toklo, and suddenly he was standing on the banks of a huge river. The fast-flowing current surged past him, and he caught glimpses of salmon forging upstream. On the far bank of the river was a lush forest; tantalizing scents of prey drifted to Toklo across the water. As he stood there, a small brown bear cub padded out from the trees on the far bank and stood at the edge of the water. His gaze met Toklo's.

"Tobi!" Toklo called. He was filled with a great yearning to leap into the water and swim across to his brother. But just then he heard the call of another bear in the distance.

"Tobi! Tobi!"

"That's Oka!" Toklo whispered.

Tobi turned toward the sound of his mother calling him, raised one paw to Toklo in farewell, then scampered off into the forest.

Toklo opened his eyes to find himself still lying on Tobi's burial mound. The sun was just rising; all around him dew glittered in the golden rays. Toklo's heart was full of fresh grief for his brother. Why hadn't Tobi crossed the river to speak to him? *He's still far away from me,* Toklo told himself. *But he and Oka are happy now. And one day, when it is time, I will join them.*

As he rose to his paws, shaking loose earth from his pelt, Aiyanna appeared through the bushes and padded up to him.

"Thank you," Toklo said, dipping his head to her.

"You're welcome," Aiyanna responded. "You can come back anytime you like. But don't even think of stealing my prey!"

"I won't," replied Toklo.

"What will you do now?" Aiyanna asked after a moment.

"I'm traveling with my friends to Great Bear Lake, for the Longest Day gathering," Toklo explained. "I promised Lusa I would help her find black bears to live with." He was surprised to see a shadow of disappointment on Aiyanna's face. "But after that, I'm coming back here," he went on. "Then I'll claim Chogan's territory as my own."

Aiyanna nodded; her disappointment faded, and she looked impressed. "That's quite a journey!" she said.

"I'm definitely coming back," Toklo assured her. "This is my home."

"Then I'll see you again," Aiyanna said. "And I promise to watch over Tobi until you return."

Toklo said good-bye to Aiyanna and padded back to the den to find Lusa, Kallik, and Yakone. All three of them leaped to their paws as he thrust his way through the vines.

"Are you ready to leave?" Kallik asked.

Lusa sounded more anxious. "Are you sure you're well enough to travel?"

"I could walk all the way to the Endless Ice and back!"

Energy was thrilling through Toklo, and his paws itched to be on the move. "Let's go!"

As Kallik led the way through the forest, Toklo took a last look around at his birthplace. He'd made it back once, after a much longer journey, and he knew that he would return again.

I'll be back before snow-sky. And Aiyanna will be waiting for me.

Lusa

Lusa swallowed her last mouthful of elk and swiped her tongue around her jaws. "That was great," she sighed. "We must be the best hunters in the whole wild."

"I'm stuffed," Toklo said, shuffling back from the carcass. "I feel as if I could sleep for a whole suncircle."

The four bears were sharing the prey near their temporary den, the hole underneath the pine tree. Sunlight glanced through the branches, and the air was full of warm scents. Lusa was struggling with drowsiness, too.

"It was a good idea to stay here an extra day and hunt, Toklo," she said. "We needed to build up our strength."

Toklo shrugged. "It just seemed sensible."

Lusa butted Toklo's shoulder gently with her head, knowing that he didn't want to act like he was in charge. "We all appreciated it."

But looking at her friends, Lusa was still worried. They all looked so tired, and their pelts seemed to be hanging from their bones, even though they had eaten well since they left the Sky Ridge. *Have we traveled too far?*

Still, it was good to see Kallik and Yakone contentedly sprawled out side by side, and the extra day's rest had helped Yakone's paw start to heal again.

"I know why you love the mountains so much," Kallik said to Toklo. "You hunt best among rocks and trees."

Toklo gave a pleased grunt. "True. But it's time to move on now."

He took the lead as they set out across the open grassland and then down a steep slope that led into denser forest. But as they plunged back into the shade of the trees, Lusa heard high-pitched yelping sounds, and the thump of heavy pawsteps, drifting up from somewhere below.

"Flat-faces!" Toklo exclaimed, halting.

He jerked his head, signaling to the others to scramble back to higher ground. Kallik and Yakone dove into the cover of a rocky outcrop, while Lusa joined Toklo behind a huge boulder a couple of bearlengths away.

The sounds of flat-face voices and the clump of their clumsy paws grew louder. Peering cautiously from behind the boulder, Lusa saw a ragged line of flat-faces heading diagonally across the slope. They all had huge black eyes that seemed to poke out of their faces, and brightly colored pelts. They moved slowly, looking around them, but Lusa didn't think they were hunting. They weren't concentrating enough for that.

"What are they doing?" Lusa whispered to Toklo. "They

didn't touch the berries on that bush, and they stomped right over those deer tracks. What do they want?"

The brown bear shrugged. "Who knows? We'll just wait here until they've gone, and then move on again."

But the flat-faces didn't pass by. Instead, they stopped, removed bundles tightly wrapped in pelts from their backs, and sat down. Yapping cheerfully to one another, they began pulling packages from their bundles. Even though she had eaten well, Lusa's belly began to rumble as she picked up the scent of food, and her jaws watered as the flat-faces opened the packages and began to pass the food around.

"Oh, spirits!" Toklo groaned. "If they're stopping to eat, they could be here for a while."

Looking around, Lusa spotted another path that curved upward, away from the slope where the flat-faces were sitting. She nudged Toklo to point it out to him. "There might be a way around the flat-faces," she murmured. "But we'll have to climb a little higher."

"It's taking us in the wrong direction," Toklo grumbled, then shrugged and grunted agreement, signaling to Kallik and Yakone. Lusa took the lead as they headed up the new path. It was wide enough for all of them to pass, but narrower than the paths they had used so far, and it wound around the hillside with a sheer drop on one side. Lusa began to worry that if it shrank any further, one of them might fall.

Yakone, just behind Lusa, slipped and dislodged a stone from the edge of the path. "Seal rot!" he muttered, but he managed to keep his balance. The stone bounced down the side of the mountain with a rattle.

The flat-faces had heard the noise. All of them looked up and pointed their paws, making chuffing noises. Lusa didn't think they were afraid; they seemed delighted to see the bears, their voices growing shrill with excitement as they raised small black boxes.

Lusa flinched, afraid the things might somehow hurt them. But she soon realized they were harmless. Still, her fur prickled at being exposed to the flat-faces' gaze.

It's like being back in the Bear Bowl.

A powerful vision of her first home flashed into Lusa's mind. The expanse of earth in the Bear Bowl seemed so small to her now, with a single tree and flat-face walls all around her. She remembered how the flat-faces had crowded around the edge of the Bear Bowl, gazing down at her and chattering. The first time she had ventured out from her BirthDen, she had been terrified.

Be brave and keep playing, her mother, Ashia, had said. *They won't hurt you, little one.*

For a moment the soothing sound of her mother's voice filled Lusa's head, blocking out everything else. Ashia had rolled over with her paws in the air and let Lusa scramble all over her; then she'd given her a piece of fruit to eat, and soon Lusa had almost forgotten the flat-faces. She felt safe, cared for, and so tired that she could sleep forever. . . .

Yakone stumbled against Lusa, jolting her back to the sun-scorched mountain and the stones sliding beneath her paws.

"Lusa!" Toklo hissed from behind her. "What's wrong with

you? We have to get moving!"

Lusa realized that they might have only moments before the flat-faces started to pursue them. *That was then; this is now,* she told herself, shaking off the memories like a troublesome fly. *I'm a wild bear now.*

DON'T MISS

DAWN OF THE CLANS

WARRIORS

BOOK 1:
THE SUN TRAIL

A mysterious vision leads a group of cats away from their
mountain home, in search of a land filled with prey and shelter. But great dangers await them, and competition within the
group grows fierce. In an unfamiliar world, faced with loners
and fierce rogues all vying for territory and power, the cats
must find a new way to live side by side—or risk tearing one
another apart.

JOIN THE ADVENTURE

SURVIVORS

BOOK 1:
THE EMPTY CITY

Lucky has always been a Lone Dog, but when the Big Growl strikes, his whole world changes. With enemies at every turn, Lucky knows he can't survive on his own, and he falls in with a Pack. He's not sure he's ready to rely on other dogs—or have them depend on him—but in a dangerous new world, he may not have a choice.

ERIN HUNTER

is inspired by a fascination with the ferocity of the natural world. As well as having great respect for nature in all its forms, Erin enjoys creating rich, mythical explanations for animal behavior. She is also the author of the bestselling Warriors and Survivors series.

Visit Erin Hunter online at
www.seekerbears.com!

For exclusive information on your favorite authors and artists, visit
www.authortracker.com.

Warrior Cats Come to Life in Manga!

SEEKERS

Three young bears…one destiny. Discover the fate that awaits them on their adventure.

Seekers: Return to the Wild
The stakes are higher than ever as the bears
search for a way home.

Available in Manga!

www.seekerbears.com

HARPER
An Imprint of HarperCollinsPublishers

SURVIVORS

The time has come for dogs to rule the wild.

Don't miss
the new
ebook
novella!